"There shall com⟨...⟩ ⟨...⟩all
shake, the sea ⟨...⟩ ars
become—"

"The last shall be first and the first last and the meek shall receive the Earth?" Eli stood as he spit the platitudes, but the preacher would not be put off.

"Nothing so simple. All shall be overthrown. The world we know shall be ruined, and only those who have prepared, those who have given proper worship to the Great Old Ones shall receive their favor." Eli walked behind Pomfret, but the preacher stared glassy-eyed at something Eli couldn't see. "All shall fall before them, whether strong, meek, black or white. Antiquated morality shall fail. Sinners and saints will share the same fate, all who are unprepared will be meat for the grinder."

Eli took a hammer from the wall. He stood over Pomfret, who was bug-eyed, staring at a private vision.

"Saints and sinners will share the same fate? That's a relief, brother." He smashed the hammer down.

The preacher's skull splintered from the force of the blow, making a dent the size of a teacup. Pomfret's hands flew up as his legs kicked at the table. A wordless gabble poured out of his mouth as his limbs spasmed. Eli brought the hammer up, but the body went limp. Eli caught the corpse's collar before it could slump forward and bleed on the table.

Dedication

For Matt Bechtel and Stephen Bissette
Excellent friends and excellent artists
without whom this book would be much less than it is

For Cat —
For a totally awesome friend,
with love and dark dreams

DARK DRAUGHTS

BY JOHN GOODRICH

[signature: John Goodrich]

MACABRE
INK

CONTENTS

ARKHAM RAIN

I am standing outside my brother's house, and the near-freezing November rain has already soaked through my denim jacket, but somehow the gun in my hand is colder still. It's like a chunk of ice, a frozen mass of hate; I don't know if my terrible intention is the lesser evil or not. The agony of my decision curls in my gut, and I uselessly ask a God I don't believe in why this is happening to me, why my grandfather had to die and take everything that I ever valued away from me.

I remember my grandfather Saltonstall was a gnarl-handed Yankee carpenter. In his small, dark, crowded house, he told my brother Ethan and I strange stories about the things that shared the world with us, lurking just out of sight. There was a certain light in his eyes as he told us of the mad doctor on Mount Moosilauke, Old Trickey the cursed sandman, the Devil and Jonathan Moulton, the invisible monster of Dunwich, and Indian tales of Old Slipperyskin, the bear that was smart like a man. It seemed that there wasn't a single corner of New England that didn't have some sort of haunt, monster, family curse, or strange religious sect lurking in it. And somehow our hometown of Arkham seemed to have more stories about it than anywhere else.

We watched him fade as we grew, my brother and I. As we got taller, and he seemed to shrink, arthritis twisted his hands until they resembled the branches of tortured trees rather than anything you might find on a human being. Despite this, he continued working as best he could, his tortured fingers fumbling with his carpenter's tools until, just over a month ago, he completely wore himself out.

What was there to say to the man who looked so small and

vulnerable on a white hospital bed, an IV and a breathing mask just prolonging the inevitable? How could a man who had been so full of life and stories be so helpless, unable to do anything but mark time until the end? I sat down next to his bed hand held his hand, and he squinted at me through his murky vision.

"Loved... you... the best... I... could..." he said with slow labor, taking a tortured breath after each word, clear despite the oxygen mask covering his face. "Even if... you... ain't... natural."

The phrase snapped my head around. What was he talking about? "Save your strength," I encouraged him. I didn't know for what, though. It was just something I was supposed to say, something to cover my own emptiness at watching my grandfather slip into darkness.

"You... got to... know..." he said, his eyes staring at me. "What... you... are...." He was very insistent, staring at me intently, his arthritic fingers gripping me with what little strength he had left.

"Innsmouth," he said, very distinctly. "The... look. The... change." His face twisted with a combination of anger and hatred I'd never seen in him before, and he gasped out the words as if they were dire maledictions. "Hell... take... that... sonofabitch... Ephriam... Babson...," he choked out, shocking me with the first profanity I'd ever heard pass his lips.

"What are you talking about?" I asked, genuinely frightened. He'd never said anything like this before, and his grip was insistent. It wasn't until then that I heard the high-pitched scream of the cardio-monitor on a stopped heart. I tried to pull away to notify the nurse, but he held me with all his dying strength.

He seemed about to say something more when the door erupted, and I was surrounded by fast-moving figures in white. One nurse rushed me out of the room as the others swarmed around my grandfather, but I knew what the outcome would be. He'd delivered his message, his final secret. I sat outside the room, trying not to listen to the talk and confusion spilling out of his room, and less than ten minutes later, a stony-faced doctor delivered the inevitable news.

The funeral was a simple but surprisingly well-attended affair, and his death left an emptiness that I had never known before. Grandfather Saltonstall had been the last piece of family I'd had outside of Ethan. We buried him in the Saltonstall plot in Christchurch Cemetery, next to his wife, near my parents, and I was the subject of a lot of condolences. All through the ceremony, though, his last words haunted me. What about me was unnatural? Had he secretly hated my father for marrying his only daughter all those years ago? Did he blame this Babson man for her death? Did he blame me? I had two pieces of information to work with; the name Ephriam Babson, and something about the mythical village of Innsmouth.

Innsmouth at least was familiar. Every schoolkid in Arkham knows that Innsmouthers were polluted mutant freaks, but nobody ever agreed on where it was. Some kids said there really was an Innsmouth, but belief in the mythical village as the source of all that was disgusting and unholy eventually fell away along with Santa Claus, cooties, honest politicians, and the guy with a hook for a hand. Certainly my grandfather had never said anything about it, and he knew more about Arkham's history than anyone else I'd ever heard of. Why suddenly bring the place up?

The name Ephraim Babson, however, meant nothing. There weren't any Babsons listed in the Arkham phone book, and after making some calls, I discovered that the Babsons living in Ipswich, Asbury Grove, East Parish, and Glouchester hadn't had an Ephriam in their genealogy for more than a hundred years. I considered hiring a private detective and having him find out all he could about this guy, but I decided to pursue my other, and probably cheaper, line of inquiry first.

A web search on Innsmouth turned up mostly rubbish— rehashed stories I'd heard in the schoolyard about degenerate weirdos living in a diseased town that was rotting into oblivion. A few had some authentic-sounding bits of history, but many of the websites contradicted each other only where they obviously hadn't cut and pasted text from each other. If anything has ever convinced me that any idiot can put up a website, it was my Innsmouth search.

Having gotten exactly nowhere with that, I decided to talk to one of my grandfather's old taleswapping buddies who I'd met at the funeral. Bill Thurber was an anciently creaky New Englander with rheumy eyes and only a few teeth, living alone in a small, yellowed apartment on Gendey Street. Despite his age, his greeting was friendly and his hospitality kind, if sparse. He was especially solicitous after my health, and invited me to share in his afternoon shot of whiskey. We talked for some time, as he smoked his foul pipe and he wove stories about Arkham, Kingsport and Dunwich.

"So," he said, laying his pipe aside after telling me a thoroughly disturbing story about the witch Keziah Mason and her rattish familiar. "What can I do for Jefferson Saltonstall's grandson? You don't look like you came here just to hear stories."

"I was wondering if you knew anything about Innsmouth?" I asked, figuring there wasn't much point to beating around the bush.

Instantly the charming demeanor faded, and the clear, storyteller's elocution degenerated into a distant mumble. "Nothing that concerns you," he said, not looking me in the eye.

"I'm just looking for some stories," I insisted gently, disturbed by his abruptly furtive manner.

"Innsmouth's got nothing to do with your family," he returned, a little more abruptly than he needed to. He was silent for a moment, then picked up his bottle of whiskey.

"I didn't ask about my family," I said, trying to keep the intensity out of my voice. "I just want to hear a thing or two about Innsmouth."

He poured a few fingers of the brownish alcohol into a shot glass, then downed it with a quick, almost guilty gesture.

"Stories like that aren't appropriate among friends," said the man who had told me about the horrible, child-murdering Brown Jenkin in disturbing detail. What about this topic disturbed him? What sort of family secret was he was keeping out of loyalty to the memory of my grandfather?

His evasions began to annoy me. What could possibly be so horrible about my heritage that I couldn't be told about? I was gearing up to give him a piece of my mind when he looked up, and I saw not anger or resentment, but a sad pity in his gaze which brought me up short.

"Look in the newspapers, if you want answers," he said in a haunted whisper, as if afraid someone was going to overhear. "Round about the time Lizzie Borden died, those two Eye-talian anarchists, Sack-o and Van-centi, got the chair, and they put that damn stupid fish on the license plates." His face contorted with some ill-defined emotion. "You better leave now. I expect you have things to do."

So abruptly dismissed, and without anything to say, I got up and left. Glancing back as I left, I saw Thurber hunched over, his whiskey bottle still clutched in a claw-like hand, watching me go. There might have been tears in his eyes.

The *Arkham Advertiser's* newspaper morgue was old-school, which is to say that an enormous volume of papers had been heaped more or less into decades in the little building's surprisingly-dry basement. And there, in the dry, dusty air of the newspaper's basement, I started to unravel the mystery of my grandfather's last words.

Lizzie Borden had died in 1927; that piece of information was pretty easy to find, and I discovered that Italians anarchists Nicola Sacco and Bartolomeo Vanzetti had been executed in 1927 to tremendous public outcry. But there was little in the *Advertiser* about Innsmouth in 1927.

However, when I started looking through the 1928 papers, I found what I was looking for. Innsmouth, it turned out, had been a real town, but one that had died or been abandoned. Apparently, in 1928, the government had staged a major military operation on the town, citing rampant bootlegger activity. But the more I read about it, and delved into the history of this mysterious little village, the more I was inclined to take a different view. Innsmouth, the *Advertiser* reported, had been the site of a mysterious disease outbreak in 1846, one that was never particularly well explained. Reading about the dynamiting that was done around the town in 1928, I was reminded of the treatment the federal government gave to the Arms Textile Mill in Manchester, New Hampshire after some anthrax deaths in 1957. It was odd that they'd be so secretive about it, but it was only ten years after the 1918 influenza pandemic, and maybe the feds hadn't wanted to create panic.

The more I thought about it, the more my little theory made sense. Arkham kids considered Innsmouthers polluted mutant freaks, which could easily have grown from handed-down tales of sick or diseased people out of Innsmouth, passing on parents' admonitions to avoid Innsmouth folk for fear of some unnamed infection. This did not, however, make any sort of connection back to me. If my hypothetical Innsmouth Plague was real, how could I have possibly contracted it, and anyhow, how could my grandfather know about it?

I never found out anything about the license plate fishes.

Not the least bit mollified, and becoming frustrated with my lack of answers, I walked through the streets, and Arkham enfolded me. After crossing the dark waters of the Miskatonic on the West Street bridge, I walked through the old merchant district until the gambrel roofs and Federalist facades of the University reared up, dark and aged, their brooding matching my own mood. It was here, with the dark, tottering houses broken only by the small-paned windows, that I could think the best. What should I do? I had little to go on but supposition, and a few tiny threads that my grandfather had gasped out just before he'd died. I couldn't just ignore this. What could possibly have been so terrible that he had waited until the last possible moment to tell me? Something for which he did not want to live to see the consequences. My mind rebelled at the thought; Grandfather Saltonstall hadn't ducked responsibility for a single thing in his life.

I walked past the black iron fence that delineated the old campus, each section holding with a plaque green with verdigris marking it as a gift from successive classes, beginning in 1898. My grandfather's condemnation of Ephriam Babson had been unprecedentedly stern. Who was he, and what was his crime that my grandfather had used his last breath to spit out the first and last epithet I'd ever heard him use? For this, I had no precedent, and no leads, except for his assertion that I was unnatural.

It was the fact that the condemnation has been so completely out of character for him that really bothered me. He'd loved me, and Ethan for that matter, and never had any difficulty expressing it. The sudden about-face was not just a mystery to me, it was a slap in the face, an abrogation of everything he had ever said to me. What could possibly have prompted those words?

I was unable to stop obsessing about my grandfather's last words, they echoed in my mind. I wondered what I should do. Babson had turned out to be a stone wall, and I was out of ideas. So, if I wanted to move forward with this, I was going to have to work some more on Innsmouth. I'd gathered a lot of information, but there was still a large gap between the town and myself. I wondered if there was anything left of the seaside village. There was enough talk about the cursed town, both by the local kids and the post-*Blair Witch* crowd, that I should be able to find out something about its location. Looked at the Neo-Gothic university buildings silhouetted black against the darkening sky, I decided I was going to take a trip to Innsmouth.

The following day, armed with what seemed like the least-unreliable map I could find off the internet, as well as a detailed map of the Massachusetts coastline provided by my local gas station, I set out in search of a myth. With European civilization settling and expanding over Massachusetts for over five hundred years, people seem to assume that there aren't any more out-of-the-way locations in this or any New England state. But you can still get lost on ridiculously isolated locations less than forty miles of Faneuil Hall, and find the strangest things on unnamed New England back roads. Going to a vacation spot in Maine, I once got turned around and drove through an active Shaker enclave. A friend in college said she'd been to Connecticut's lost village of Dudleytown. A surprising amount hides from winding New England back roads with the trees crowding close.

After two hours of driving back and forth on little-used roads, I had found nothing to indicate the reality of Innsmouth. The rutted and potholed road I was proceeding down couldn't have been paved less than forty years ago, and was littered with slippery October leaves. To my left, the East, lay a nameless and fetid swamp, the decomposing remains of long-abandoned tobacco barns passed by on my right. My internet map had proven worse than useless, and I was cursing the idiot who had made it when a small gap in the forested swamp slid past me.

I made an illegal U-turn, grateful for the near-complete isolation of the pitted road, and slowly proceeded back to examine the gap. This path, since calling it a road was to pay it far too much compliment, wound its way through puddles, around unexpected boulders that lay half-submerged in stagnant water, and vanished into the swamp. It might have been an old fire break, although I didn't think that particularly likely, as wet as the ground was.

In the middle of the road, engine idling, I hesitated. How badly did I want to follow this tenuous link to my grandfather's dying words? Enough to get my decidedly not-off-road car stuck in a swamp in the middle of nowhere? Down the path were sickly trees whose trunks stuck out of the water like naked bones from a shallow grave.

I pulled onto the muddy track, but only far enough to be off the paved road. Getting out, I locked my car, and walked down the old track on foot. No sense in getting my car stuck.

Walking a little way, I realized that I'd left my sense of time behind with the car. With it out of sight, I had few landmarks to mark my progress; all of the sickly trees looked the same. Like most people born in a town, I didn't have much of an idea how quickly I could walk, either, and my progress towards I knew not what was slow and torturous. This forgotten and overgrown swamp seemed a pocket of time that all civilization had neglected. I trudged forward, with the uncanny feeling that this was how the colonists had felt, lost amongst the tall trees and dark paths of a foreign continent, the world they had known inconceivably far away.

The scraggly, gnarled shapes of swamp maple and oak crowded close to the track, and mucky dirt sucked at my shoes. Little gurgling noises stalked me as my footprints slowly filled with dirty water. Where the track wasn't waterlogged, brambles and other scrub reached for my feet, and once nearly succeeded in removing one of my shoes. The further I went, the more the swamp filled my senses; the croaking dirge of large frogs I could at least identify, but mysterious splashes and odd cries filtered from in from across the stagnant water reinforced my feelings of loneliness and isolation in the face of so much nature.

The long-legged marsh-birds observed my passing like silent guardians standing in the fetid pools. I stopped and watched one back, some sort of greyish heron, as it stood motionless in the water. Abruptly, the long neck swooped, and came up with a struggling frog. A few short, jerky movements, and the frog was gone, and the bird was still again. For whatever reason, I felt an unexpected surge of pity for the frog.

Lost in more than thought, I was in Innsmouth before I noticed it. The trees had thinned out a little, allowing more sun to get through, and I left the dark, fetid water of the marsh behind. I could barely make out the susurrus of the ocean, and wet leaves lay in mounds and drifts underfoot. The tottering remains of an abandoned house were close to surrendering to the combined assault of scrub, rot, and tree told me that I had finally arrived. There could be little doubt that this was the legendary Innsmouth.

Further exploration told me that what was left of the abandoned town was little more than a rotting, forgotten heap that had mostly been reclaimed by nature. All that was really left were some cellar-holes, with the occasional chimney or larger part of a house protruding through the smothering carpet of wet leaves. Clearing some of them away, I could see that I was now walking on what had been a cobblestone street, but many of the cobbles had been pushed aside or enveloped by roots. In this abandoned place, the air was surprisingly still, the only sound the soft rush-rush of small Atlantic waves.

If people had lived in Innsmouth, trees inhabited it now. What had been homes were now collapsed shacks, cellar-holes, and single walls leaning against trees for support. A few rusted remains stuck out of the leaves here and there, but most of the household items had returned to nature, or deliquesced into foul-smelling sludge after decades of New England weather. I thought I saw the Bakelite handle to an umbrella underfoot, but I was in no mood to pick through Innsmouth's trash.

I wandered, trying to discern the layout of the empty

village. Even at its height, it couldn't have been much of a place.
I thought I could see a few roads meandering through the ruins;
I doubted it had ever been home to more than five hundred
people. Neglected remains of a few stone buildings remained,
huddled together in what had probably once been the center of
town. One was the broken husk of what had been a white-marble
building, and the shattered remains of columns out in front of
it confirmed that it had been a "fraternal order" building, of
the sort so popular in New England at the beginning of the last
century. Others looked like large, brick structures that had to
have been mills or other places of work, each in a different state
of destruction and decomposition. One remained somewhat
intact, while others were barely-distinguishable heaps of brick
rubble. I wondered at the lack of graffiti. For a place as famous as
Innsmouth was among Arkham children, I wondered that this
wasn't a stoner hangout with heavy metal emblems sprayed on
every available upright surface.

After some time in the quiet desolation, I remembered my
original purpose. What answers had I thought I was going to find
here? I had gone to this decayed wreck of a town, and for what?
The secrets to why I wasn't 'natural'? My frustration mounted.
What could this dilapidated, long-abandoned ruin of a town
have told me? I wanted to be home, doing some work, grieving,
finding a girlfriend, or just about anything else but wandering
around in stupid, forgotten towns that kids told ghost stories
about. There had been nothing for me in Innsmouth, and I still
didn't know what the hell my grandfather had been thinking
in his last moments. I must have been desperate for some sort
of answers to have thought that going there would answer any
sort of question.

I screamed out my wordless frustration and anger across the
decaying town, and threw some sticks in random directions. It
helped a little, and my rage quickly faded into a dull sort of
despair. Mildly interesting as this forgotten dump was, it held
no answers.

I thought that perhaps I could pick up enough impressions
to do a soft-news piece for the *Arkham Advertiser,* maybe
make some money on the side selling reprints to those hokey

ghost-hunting magazines, and I cursed my stupidity at not bringing a camera. My anger resurfaced, this time at myself for being unprepared, I nevertheless had a pen and paper handy. So, I walked towards the shore, where I could hear the sigh of breakers, scribbling down occasional phrases to build an article on.

There was a movement off to my left, and the unmistakable sound of something being dragged across the ground.

"Who's there?" I shouted, brandishing my pen in front of me like a knife. There had been a bear sighting in Northborough just last year; this place would be ideal for a bear. But it was quickly clear that whatever was crawling towards me in the dark shadow under a free-standing stone wall was no bear.

I stood, not wanting to run, yet not knowing what was coming towards me. It made a harsh, rasping sound as it came, reminiscent of my grandfather's agonized breathing at the hospital. I steeled myself, not wanting to succumb to the superstitious terror that was licking up and down my limbs.

The... thing crawled half way into the light, and I saw that it had a face, and limbs—a person! But there was something terribly wrong with the features, the bulging eyes, and the too-wide mouth, and the curious, yellow-pale hue to the thing's scabrous skin. Where before, I had steeled myself not to run, now I was rooted to the ground, staring at this twisted creature before me.

"Please," it begged in breathless, asthmatic gasps, its eyes protuberant under a rough and scabby forehead.

"Wh—who are you?" was all I managed to stammer out.

It broke down and wept, huddled under its tattered woolen coat. I was torn as to what to do. On the one hand, this was a human being that needed comfort not two feet away from me, and at the same time, I didn't want to touch it—him. What if this was the face of my Innsmouth Plague? If I already had it, then there wasn't much point in avoiding this person, but I still pulled away from the searching hand with the instinct of anyone avoiding the detestable.

"What happened to you?" I eventually asked, unable to take my eyes off the repulsive spectacle before me.

"The… change," he rasped, and a ripple of fear surged down my spine. The same words my grandfather had used. Here, in Innsmouth, I was about to find an answer, coming from the pitiful figure huddled figure at my feet. He looked up at me, and I was reminded of an abandoned puppy, desperately hungry for attention, yet at the same time terrified that the stranger would kick it.

"The change," I echoed back to him, some part of my mind struggling to make sense of what I see. "How did it happen? What started it?"

"Father… found me. Said I was… special. Said… I'd know… when go to… to Innsmouth." My mind reeled. Special? What sort of twisted individual would consider this… condition to be special?

"Are you all alone?"

"Used to be… others," the terrible gasps are coming faster. "They've all… gone to… the ocean."

"They drowned themselves?" By this point, I was numb with the overwhelming horror that was unfolding in my mind.

"Call of… the sea. Getting stronger. Dreams of… Him… in His… watery grave. Calling to… *all* of us." Great, desperate eyes sought mine, and I saw the unfathomable fear and untold horror of this tortured individual's existence.

"I can… *feel*… myself… fading… away," he clutched at its head, rocking back and forth slightly. "Drowning… in darkness…." He reached out suddenly, drawing me close despite my reflexive and ineffectual attempt to pull away. He pulled me close with a hideous strength. "He… calls."

A cold prickle worked its way down my spine; the utter conviction and desperation with which he spoke would not allow me to disbelieve him.

"Your father," I rasped with a terrible premonition. "What was his name?"

He let go of me and turned away, so I only heard the gasping voice,

"Ephriam… Babson…."

I couldn't speak; my shock and revulsion were too great.

"Boasted of… spreading his seed." Diseased and deformed

as he was, there was still someone this pitiable creature could look down on and hate. "Said he'd... fathered... a lot of us...."

He turned to me again, and for the first time, I saw his pale hands with moist webbing that came up between the knuckles, and the small claws that looked like no human nails.

"Come back... soon," he whispered. "With a *pistol*."

I'm not ashamed to say that I fled then, overcome with the horror of what I'd seen. Only the marsh-birds saw me running from that terrible, decrepit village. Once back in my car, a solid piece of the sane, rational twenty-first century, I sat behind the wheel and wept, overwhelmed with the horror I had experienced. I had come looking for answers, and now I couldn't face them. The childhood legends of Arkham were right; the Innsmouth Plague wasn't something you caught, it was genetic. Would that be my fate, to return to Innsmouth, transformed, hideous, and insane, only to drown myself?

Returning to Arkham did nothing to dispel the cloud of despair hanging over me. I had seen my doom; I was a walking dead man, like someone diagnosed with terminal cancer. Even after I bought a pistol, I couldn't bring myself to suicide quite yet. But I ended the misery of the pathetic thing that thanked me in a wheezing voice, and then the marsh-birds rose, startled at the sudden retort. I sat for hours, staring at the sad corpse of the person who had broken my life, and I never knew his name.

Numbly, not knowing what else to do, I continued my investigation. If I looked hard enough, maybe I could find a loophole and this wouldn't have happened. Even with all the secrets of Innsmouth that I cared to know, I still didn't know anything about Ephriam Babson.

I thought of the pathetic thing's gasping voice, and about Ephriam Babson spreading his taint, and realized that I hadn't been thinking large enough. It took me two hours to drive to Boston, and the *Boston Globe's* newspaper morgue. I looked for articles on serial rapists, starting a year before my birth. It was a tricky search; the police don't want to talk about them, and the newspapers really don't want to make a report until the bastard is caught.

Hours passed, and I picked up the trail. Here and there,

now and then, in between the constant articles on safety and not going out in Boston after dark, I saw a pattern that I could trace back at least as far back as seventy-six. One 'crime-beat' article confirmed my fears, discussing a number of common descriptors for a string of sexual assaults in areas surrounding Boston. Women described their assailant as 'fishy'-smelling and wide-mouthed, which had the police scouring a couple of the Oriental open-air fish markets for suspects, only to come up empty. Among others, one Ephriam Babson, address unknown, was wanted for questioning in relation to at least one of the linked assaults perpetrated in the Arkham area in nineteen eighty—a couple of months after I was born. Which would make it about eight months before Ethan had been born.

Simultaneously, I was dizzy with relief and yet my guts yawned with dread. Dying, his eyesight nearly gone, my grandfather had mistaken me for Ethan. I hated, still hate, the never-jangled relief that sat in my gut; my doom had passed onto another. To Ethan. How could I be happy knowing that my brother is going to mutate horribly into something like the pathetic thing in Innsmouth?

I haven't been able to sleep for the last three days; whenever I close my eyes I see Ethan, bloated, distorted, drowning in murky water, reaching out to me, and I would wake in a cold sweat. I have stopped going to my job, I stopped going out of my apartment at all. Ethan was doomed, and I wondered if I could even tell him. How could I burden my younger brother with the knowledge of what he is—of what I think he might be? And yet, would it be fair to not tell him?

The thoughts scrabbled incessantly around my head, and I knew the lack of sleep was making it harder for me to focus. I could see no good way to end this, unless I was greatly mistaken, and this was all some sort of psychotic episode, or maybe I'd looked at all the evidence wrong, but the question burned hot in my head, scratching at all my thoughts with tiny claws. What could I do? Babson was presumably long gone, and each of my trips to Innsmouth had been worse than the other. Where can I go now, what could I possibly do? My hands shook with exhaustion, and I prayed for sleep, thinking that if I could just close my eyes for an hour or two without seeing Ethan's distorted, terrified face superimposed on that horror from Innsmouth that maybe I'd be able to think straight enough to solve this mess. The only solution I could find, the one my mind always came back to, was the pistol.

An hour ago, I decided to go see my brother.

The Arkham rain is freezing, and I am standing outside of Ethan's small house, shivering with the cold, and I still don't know if this is the right thing, or if I even have the strength to do it if I have to. A memory flashes through me, of Ethan and me hiding out on summer days in a fort made of construction leftovers we'd found in the trees beyond Meadow Hill. Another one hits me, of being old enough to bike all the way to Kingsport, and the two of us, full of energy and youth, staying so long at the rock beaches that we develop terrible cases of sun poisoning. My frenetic thoughts pass through by me, and I think about how much I love my brother, and the bittersweet memories of all the things we have done do not strengthen my resolve. I press the doorbell with numb fingers, my knuckles aching from clutching the gun in the relentless, endless, Arkham rain. I think of my grandfather Saltonstall's gnarled fingers, I know how he must have felt at the end, unable to use his tools. Useless. Helpless. Hopeless.

Ethan opens the door. His expression immediately becomes concern when he sees me, soaking wet and shivering in the rain. I look at his familiar expression, and I remember the twinkle in his eyes when he said we should to go the abandoned island, and the way we fought off the three Wheeler brothers once. He is my brother, and I love him almost more than I can bear. I step into the house, and he closes the door behind me.

"Are you all right? Jesus, you look like shit," he says. My brother, always honest with me. He and moves to take my denim jacket, and if he does, I won't have recourse to my gun. I almost let him take it, but at the last moment I shake him off.

"It's been a tough couple of weeks," I croak at him, and he knows I'll tell him when I'm ready, and backs off. Instead, he moves to one of the windows and pushes the curtain back, and looks out into the hammering rain.

"When it's raining like this," Ethan said in a distant, dreamy voice. "I think this is what it must be like to live under the sea. Everything so wet and cold, and I keep thinking I'll see something swim by."

"Do you think about the sea a lot?" My voice is raw, but I think it conceals the emotions that battle each other like angry cats in my brain. How can I do this, and simultaneously, how can I not? How can I possibly let him slowly turn into that tormented thing from Innsmouth? And yet, how can I possibly use the pistol on the brother I love? I feel like my chest is going to rip itself apart.

He gives me an odd look, then turns back to looking at the rain streaming down the window. "Not really, but you know, I've got this urge to go down to the coast. Take a look at the stormy sea, or maybe a late vacation in a lighthouse in Maine or something."

A stillness descends on me, and there is no contradiction. Convulsively, my hand clenches around the pistol. There are no marsh-birds to startle with the sudden noise this time, and I am left numbly looking at the corpse that was my half-brother. At least now he won't have to hear the siren call of the ocean, and feel his mind slip slowly into darkness.

PHARAOH COMES TO LONELY MILE

Jeremiah Noakes burst into the Lonely Mile sheriff's office out of breath and reeking of horse.

"Sheriff Anders!" Naokes brayed as soon was he'd caught his breath enough to shout. Silence answered him. Seeing as the Sheriff wasn't in, Noakes trundled up to Deputy Wilson, who was carving a matchstick with the tip of his Bowie knife.

"Deputy Wilson, there's a wagon approaching town!"

"I can see why this is cause for some concern, Mr. Noakes. Do you think this is a matter for the law?" Bill Wilson didn't even look up.

"But it's a traveling medicine show!"

The deputy let out a small sigh of exasperation and stood.

"Right then, Mr. Noakes. We've got ourselves a shyster to deal with."

Noakes wanted to gallop all the way to the slowly-approaching wagon, but Wilson held them both to a walk. Let the wagon come to them, he said. Not like there was anywhere for the wagon to hide. Nearly an hour passed before Noakes spied the wagon trundling along the winding, rutted road. Once it was in sight, Deputy Wilson was quite content to sit on his horse and let the wagon approach.

It was painted in gaudy, eye-catching colors. With a little difficulty, Jeremiah read: *Hieronymous Jehosephat Ogrelfinger's Patent Medicines and Unique Collection of Astonishing Oddities.* Below the main sign, smaller letters said, "Witness the Healing Power of Barnham's Beneficent Balm, Observe the Amazing Traveling Stones of Pahranagat, Behold the Hide of the Apache's Sacred White Buffalo, See the Crystal Skull of the Ancients, Experience the Mystical and Miraculous Gan Kurna Ceremony, and Gaze in Wonder at the Genuine and Ancient Mummy of Pharaoh All the Way From Egypt!" Apparently, Ogrelfinger had never met a long word he didn't like, but a picture of each wonder was thoughtfully painted above the words. For a patent medicine show, it didn't look half-bad. Jeremiah had never seen a mummy before, and the Traveling Stones sounded interesting.

The driver was a small, neat man, dark like a Negro, but his features looked wrong. He didn't look much like an Indian either. Dressed in a teamster's outfit and coated with a thick layer of trail dust, he appeared to be in good health, even though Jeremiah pegging his age past fifty.

"Do I have the pleasure of addressing *the* Hieronymous Jehosephat Ogrelfinger?" Deputy Wilson asked once the brightly-painted wagon had rumbled to a stop.

"Certainly not. I am Ali Khan, and I have the honor to be the Indian servant of the illustrious Mr. Ogrelfinger." The small, dark man's accent was curious but somehow refined.

"You don't look or talk like any Indian I've ever met. What are you, a Blackfoot from Canada?"

"I am from the country of India, which is in Asia, and a subject of Her Majesty Queen Victoria, you understand." Jeremiah was somewhat puzzled by the way the words poured so easily out of the small man's mouth.

"It's my guess, Ali Khan, that you got a Quaker and two German doctors in the back of that wagon, is that right?" Wilson wasn't the sort to be impressed with accents.

"Allow me to introduce mahself," cried out a voice, and around from the side of the wagon stepped the most foppishly dandified-looking man Jeremiah had ever seen. His pants were a brilliant, stainless white, his black knee-high boots so well polished that it seemed the dust of the road would never sully them. He wore a red jacket with tails, and a green-and-gold waistcoat. His black stovepipe hat was black and shiny as midnight sin. He was a little round, but Jeremiah reckoned that if you were the sort who could come up with patent medicines, you hadn't grown up as a farmer in the first place.

"I am *Hier*onymous Je*hose*phat *Ogrel*finger!" The newcomer emphasized his syllables like a preacher. "I *bring* to this *esti*mable *town* the patent *mirrracle* medicine that is *absolutely* and one hundred percent *guaranteed—*"

"Save your chiseling for someone who might buy," Wilson snapped. "I assume you haven't heard what happened to the last tripes and keister man that came to Lonely Mile?"

"Can't say that I have, good sir, can't say that I have. Would you be so kind as to enlighten me?" Ogrelfinger doffed his hat and polished it with an immaculate cuff.

"Doctor Thaddeus Pickman's Mysterious Cabinet of Miraculous Wonders burned down to the axles when it got struck by lightning."

The huckster shrugged, then replaced the hat on his head.

"Such things happen in this world of pestilence and misfortune that surrounds us."

"But seldom on days when there ain't a cloud in the sky." Wilson's horse nickered and shifted a little.

"Some men are born unfortunate. Perhaps it was an excess of those lightning pills that Doctor Pickman sold." Ogrelfinger again removed his hat and made a sorrowful show for Pickman's misfortune. "I certainly hope that no one was seriously injured."

"Not directly, no. However, before you enter our little town, you may wish to hear about the sad fate that befell Professor Felix McWirter's Elixirs, Potions and Balms, which visited here not two months ago. There occurred an unfortunate incident when the good people of Lonely Mile found that his McWirter's Medicinal Compounds to Cure Women's Complaints tasted almost *precisely* like the Taos Dynamite that our Miz Luella serves." Wilson leaned forward on his horse, looming over Ogrelfinger. "Only at three times the price. The ill-starred professor was ridden out of town on a rail after his wagon and everything it contained was tipped into the river. The Sheriff and I were sadly helpless to stop them."

Jeremiah started to object, seeing as Wilson had supplied the rail, but a sharp look from the deputy made him shut his mouth.

"As a precaution against such misfortune, I'll take a look in your wagon." The leather of the deputy's saddle creaked as he settled back into it.

"You wish to be the first in your town to experience the wonders of Ogrelfinger's Unique Collection of Astonishing Oddities, and I can't say that I blame you, sir. Why, there are things contained in this wagon that, though a man look upon it only once, that memory will become a cherished recollection around the hearth of his old age, and an oft-repeated story that grandchildren will ask for again and again, even as they do not believe."

"You aren't the first bunko artist to show up with a load of five-dollar words and a couple a' knicknacks for to gawk at. And I don't care a Continental about your continued health, if you catch my meaning. I'm making certain that you carry nothing hazardous."

"Easily done, sir." Ogrelfinger's smile was benevolent and disarming.

"And a bottle of your medicine—" the deputy started.

"Certainly, certainly. Many a man of the law has benefitted from the bounty of Barnham's Balm, which is good for both body and soul—"

"Which you will drink right here and right now."

The medicine man turned a bit pale and blinked rather rapidly, but he might just have gotten some sand in his eye.

"A whole bottle?"

"Yep." The deputy's smile turned nasty. "And one that I choose."

"S-surely you would want to ingest some of this miraculous substance for yourself."

"I am in fine fettle and high spirits, myself." Wilson patted his paunch. "Why I even had a bath less than a week ago."

Ogrelfinger was quiet for a moment, as if taking the measure of the deputy, and perhaps weighing his future as well. Certainly, his eyes rested on Deputy Wilson's pistol and tin badge for some time.

"Ali Khan, show these gentlemen our supply of Barnham's Beneficent."

The dark man walked over to the wagon and, with a small flourish, opened a cleverly hidden drawer. Wilson dismounted, and examined the rows and rows of identically-labeled bottles.

Reaching in, he picked out one that seemed to take his interest. He wrenched the cork off, gave the bottle a sniff, then thrust it at Ogrelfinger.

"Go right ahead."

"Although it is the most beneficial of all patent medicines, the rich reserves of healing that it represents were not meant to be taken by the entire bottle. Do not be surprised if I act in an overly-energetic fashion, such as turning hand springs, kicking my heels up, or whooping like a Comanche chief on the warpath."

"I consider myself duly warned." The deputy seemed bored. Ogrelfinger looked at the bottle and then back to the deputy. Ali Khan was watching the scene with great interest.

With a despairing look at the implacable deputy, Ogrelfinger took a deep breath, placed the bottle between his lips, and threw his head back. The desert held its breath as the miraculous brownish liquid gurgled down the man's throat. When the dregs were drained, Hieronymous Jehosephat Ogrelfinger threw the bottle away and whooped it up a bit, but he didn't sound much like a Comanche, truth be told.

In less than a minute, the effects of the Balm faded, after which Ogrelfinger resumed his more dignified mode of speech.

"Who is your companion, if I may inquire?"

"This is Jeremiah Noakes, who runs the best smokehouse in Lonely Mile." Jeremiah felt the blood rush to his face and looked at his saddle-horn. "Now, Mr. Ogrelfinger, we'll be taking a look at your Astonishing Oddities."

Inside the medicine wagon, it was dim and stuffy after the blinding desert sun, with an odd smell that was somewhere between the Taos Dynamite and Jeremiah's own smokehouse. The open door let in enough light so that all of Ogrelfinger's Mysterious Oddities could be seen.

He was disappointed by the Traveling Stones of Pahranagat, but Ogrelfinger explained that they were 'going through a quiescent period.' Bill Wilson snorted and moved on, leaving Jeremiah to tap the screen enclosure in an attempt to awaken the stones.

The Sacred White Buffalo hide was indeed white, but

rather moth-eaten. It didn't even smell like buffalo anymore. Jeremiah touched it while Ogrelfinger was introducing Wilson to the Crystal Skull of the Ancients, but the patchy buffalo hide gave off no surge of healing power that Jeremiah could tell. He started when he saw Ali Khan watching him from a dim corner. Jeremiah thought he was going to get thrown out, but a wink from the small Indian seemed to indicate that his indiscretion would be overlooked.

The Crystal Skull of the Ancients looked like a skull made of glass, although Ogrelfinger assured Wilson that the Ashtec Indians hadn't been able to make glass, and that the skull was made of the purest crystal. After that Jeremiah had a lot more respect for it, as well as the marvelous ingenuity of the Ashtec Indians, whoever they were.

Wilson seemed to take a real interest in an odd brass statue of a woman, some two feet tall, with four arms, frozen in some sort of odd dance.

"What's that?"

"Bhowani, the wife of Shiva." Ali Khan made a small, heathen obeisance to the idol.

The deputy put his hand on his hip and snorted. "Well that's a new one on me."

"The world is wide, Mister Wilson," Ogrelfinger shouldered his way into the conversation. "Who among us has seen all it has to offer?"

"So, she's involved in that Gan Kurna ceremony you perform, Mr. Khan?"

"Very perceptive." Ali Khan smiled and tilted his head. "A little exotic incense and a few invocations are all that this poor servant can achieve so far away from home, but it serves to give the curious American a taste of something from half a world away. And how can that be bad?"

Deputy Wilson grunted and rubbed at his chest a little. Jeremiah had heard that Wilson had some scars there, but he'd never seen them. The Deputy turned away from the idol and started to open a tall cabinet that stood in the front of the wagon. Ogrelfinger stopped him.

"Normally, I charge an extra two bits to see Pharaoh, he

being the pride and greatest treasure of my collection."

"Undoubtedly, Mr. Noakes will tell the rest of the townsfolk how impressed he is by ol' Pharaoh and his good word will increase your business."

Jeremiah wasn't so sure. The thought of seeing someone so long dead frightened him. Ogrelfinger, by now used to being at Wilson's mercy, produced a key and opened the cabinet.

Jeremiah would gladly have paid two bits to see Pharaoh again. He lay upright in an ornate, fitted coffin covered with incomprehensible symbols that Jeremiah sensed were somehow mystical. Within, Pharaoh was covered from shoulders to feet in dark brown wrappings, but they had been peeled away from his head, leaving his ancient, sunken face exposed. He exuded an aura of terrible, unimaginable age, and Jeremiah thought there was something menacing, even unholy about the motionless face, as if the curse of God had stuck to him through these thousands of years. Behind him, Deputy Wilson sighed.

"I don't suppose you know which pharaoh you've got hold of, do you?"

"Why *the* Pharaoh, Pharaoh hisself. The ill-starred and hardhearted ruler of the Kingdom of Egypt who tried to chase Moses down and was drownded in the Red Sea by the will of Our Lord God."

"Which would certainly explain the excellent state of preservation." Wilson started for the exit.

As the two argued, Jeremiah snaked a hand under the protective wire mesh and touched the preserved body. The linen strips that wrapped the mummy were stiff. He moved his hand up to Pharaoh's face, which was pliant and unpleasantly sticky. His fingers came away with an odd brown stain. Frightened, Jeremiah tried to wipe it off on his dungarees, but the stain clung to him like a sin. He shoved his hand into a pocket, and looked around for Ali Khan, but Ogrelfinger's servant had slipped away. Jeremiah wondered how long it had been since anyone had touched Pharaoh. He hoped no evil would come of the brief contact.

Back outside and remounted, Deputy Wilson had one more surprise for Ogrelfinger.

"Of course, you still haven't turned a handspring, like you said you might."

"I don't recall saying that I *necessarily* would turn hand springs." Far from being energetic, Ogrelfinger seemed so full of goodness that he was having difficulty walking straight.

"You said it was a distinct possibility,"

"I gave you a war whoop, wasn't that quite enough?"

Wilson considered for a moment.

"Nope."

Ogrelfinger gave the deputy the dirtiest look Jeremiah had ever seen. No one had ever given the law in Lonely Mile such a look; this was indeed something Jeremiah could tell his grandchildren. Slowly, with the air of a martyr, Ogrelfinger doffed his hat and handed it to his servant. The medicine man then shot up his shirt cuffs. With slow showmanship, he raised his hands. He started off in a forward cartwheel, somehow managing to land on both feet simultaneously, then leapt abruptly backwards, feet going straight up in the air, hands touching the ground, and then was on his feet again, breathing hard and swaying slightly.

"Welcome to Lonely Mile, Mr. Ogrelfinger," Wilson broke the ensuing silence. "Keep peaceable with her citizens, and we shall part company as friends."

"Easily done, sir." Ogrelfinger received his hat from his servant. "Easily done."

Wilson seemed inordinately pleased with himself as he and Jeremiah rode back to town. When Jeremiah asked what made him so happy, the deputy just chuckled.

"Never seen a man work so hard to get into Lonely Mile."

The town developed a sort of carnival atmosphere as the news spread that a medicine show was in town. Farmers and ranch hands came from miles away; even the O'Dells came, and Blacky even ponied up for the missus to see Pharaoh. Miz Luella's place was full of drinkers talking about the wonders they'd seen, more than a few of them with pockets that clinked with bottles of Barhnam's Beneficent. Jeremiah discovered that the story of Deputy Wilson and Mr. Ogrelfinger was such good currency that he didn't have to buy himself a drink the entire night. He always left out the part about touching Pharaoh's face, though.

Something rich was in the air, because when the big clock in Miz Luella's struck ten, Ogrelfinger announced that he was going to have to retire for the night, but that by popular demand, Hieronymous Jehosephat Ogrelfinger's Patent Medicines and Unique Collection of Astonishing Oddities would remain in town until the very final person who wanted to see the Astonishing Oddities could. Jeremiah thought that was awfully nice of him.

Rather than go home for the night, Jeremiah decided to stay in town, and he even went so far as to pay for Doreen. Some people didn't like Doreen because she closed her eyes and called you 'Jack,' but it didn't make much, nevermind to Jeremiah. His pigs would be in a nasty mood in the morning, since they'd missed their evening feed, but they'd be all right if he got an early start.

Jeremiah was awakened by a fierce pounding at his door. At first, he thought it might be his momma, angry at him sinning with Doreen. As the cobwebs of sleep melted away, it became clear that his door was not being assaulted. He pulled on his overalls and went out to see what the racket was.

The first of the early morning light was seeping into the upper floor of Miz Luella's, and Jeremiah could see Deputy Wilson hammering at the door next to Jeremiah's own with his big fist. And just as he was poking his head out, the next door swung open, and Ali Khan appeared, dressed in a flowing white garment such as Jeremiah had never seen.

"Get Ogrelfinger. Now." Anyone who knew Deputy Wilson knew that his tone meant trouble.

"I shall have to dress him," Ali Khan said.

"I said now." The deputy's voice was hard and dangerous. Ali Khan ducked back into the room, and Ogrelfinger himself appeared, clad in an elaborately ruffled and beribboned nightshirt.

"What could you possibly—" the huckster started.

"There's been a murder. You are hereby warned not to leave town."

"You have no evidence that I or any of my—" Ogrelfinger swallowed and continued. "Nothing I carry is in any way dangerous. You yourself inspected my wagon."

The law man struck a match on the door jamb close to the medicine seller's face, then lit one of his foul cheroots.

"Nobody's been killed in this town since that Whateley feller came through, eight months back." He punctuated the statement with a precise puff of smoke. "Now the very first night you stay, someone turns up dead. I say that's not bad evidence, but Sheriff Anders insists we keep an open mind. You run, and you'll never see the inside of a courthouse, you understand?" Ogrelfinger was about to object when Wilson grasped the salesman's neck and pulled the huckster's face close his burning cigar. "Is there an understanding between us?"

The salesman, turning red, managed to nod, and Wilson released him.

"I don't give a coyote's dingus how many fancy words you know. You murder someone in my town, and the price will be paid." With that pronouncement, the deputy turned on his heel, and stalked down the hallway.

Jeremiah hustled after him.

"Great Jehosephat, Deputy Wilson, what's happened? Who got shot?"

Wilson chewed his cigar, and gave the pig farmer a hard look as they moved down the stairs.

"Go home, Jeremiah. It's a nasty business, and you don't want to get mixed up in it."

"How come we didn't hear no shots, Deputy?"

"Listen to me, Jeremiah. You don't want to be involved." Wilson straight-armed the saloon's front door hard enough to jar the hinges.

Lonely Mile was still as death in the morning light. The only motion in the town came from a collection of vultures sunning themselves on the gnarled tree behind Miz Luella's.

"He wasn't shot, was he? There's something strange 'bout the way he was done, ain't there?" Jeremiah whispered to keep the vultures from overhearing.

"Dammit to Hell, Jeremiah, why can't you be dumb all the time?" Wilson rounding on the hog farmer, and Jeremiah felt his face tighten with embarrassment. After a moment, Wilson let out a big sigh.

"Look, I didn't mean it like that. You caught me off-guard, and you're right, Enos wasn't shot, and that's the last we're going to talk about it. Now I got to go and talk to Becky, and I'm not looking—" Wilson stopped, realizing that he'd put his foot in it again.

A secret thrill ran from Jeremiah's head to his groin, and it wasn't the pleasant kind. Enos Thurston was dead? Jeremiah couldn't imagine it. He'd known Enos for years. Enos usually stood at the other end of the bar when they both were in town on a Saturday. His corn was nothing to crow about, and he smelled a lot like his chickens. A couple of years ago, he'd let Jeremiah dance with his pretty wife Becky at a social, and that was the kind of thing a bachelor didn't forget. He was the proud father of two boys, and even if he came from Virginia, he seemed all right. How could he be dead?

"Go home, Jeremiah. This isn't like the medicine wagon; I can't have you tagging along."

"Yes sir," Jeremiah mumbled. Satisfied, Deputy Wilson gave him a small shove and walked off. In less than a minute, Jeremiah was alone in the morning quiet. He glanced up toward the buzzards, and shuddered to see that they were all looking his way. Had those same buzzards and crows had been at Enos the way they did with most things that died in the desert? He shuddered at the thought, clenching his fists, and felt the vague, leftover stickiness on the fingers on his right hand. Like a thunderbolt, Jeremiah knew why Enos Thurston was dead without a shot.

Once the terrifying revelation had sunk in, Jeremiah realized that he had a bigger problem. Who could he tell? Was it possible that he had awakened the ancient and dried-up Pharaoh with just a touch? He fought the panic that rose in him. He didn't know for sure that Enos had been killed by Pharaoh. There were a lot of ways for a man to die without being shot, but Jeremiah couldn't shake the haunting feeling that he was responsible for Enos's death.

He was crossing the street to get his horse when he saw a light on in Doc Smith's office. That light must have something to do with poor Enos, and Jeremiah's feet were taking him toward that window.

Doc Smith was a smart feller who had gone to college and everything, while Jeremiah barely had his letters. Whatever lie Jeremiah thought up had to be pretty good. It wasn't long before he struck on something. Squaring his shoulders and settling the butterflies in his stomach, he tapped on the doctor's door.

The door was opened almost immediately by the doctor's old Negro. Tiny, wrinkled, and evil-smelling, nobody knew her name, or how the doctor had come to employ her. Her steady, unsettling gaze cut through Jeremiah.

"I need to talk to the doctor."

A harsh cackle boomed out of her and echoed across Lonely Mile, sending the buzzards flying off in different directions. As suddenly as she had started, she stopped.

"I get him." And she vanished into the doorway.

No more than a minute later, Doc Smith was at the door. He was dressed neatly, right down to having his hair slicked and his shoes shiny. His eyes were a little bloodshot, but that was probably from being up early.

"What can I help you with, Jeremiah?" Before he could even open his mouth, Jeremiah's insides were all turned to jelly.

"I—Doc, Deputy Wilson said I should look at Enos's body, just in case I seen anything." The doctor's gaze brushed aside his lies. Only Jeremiah's loyalty toward Enos and Mrs. Thurston gave him the determination to see this through.

"Wilson really think the medicine show's got something to do with it?" The doc used a finger to smooth out his moustache.

"I—well—he don't know. Uh, that's why he asked me to look."

Doc Smith looked at Jeremiah. They taught people strange things in medical school; showed them what was under your skin, the way Jeremiah knew with hogs. The thought made Jeremiah very uncomfortable.

"He said it might be important."

The doctor considered Jeremiah in a moment of terrible silence.

"You better come in," Doc Smith allowed, and moved back so Jeremiah could enter. He then turned to a cabinet, and for a moment, Jeremiah was sure he was going to get a gun to shoot him dead for lying. Instead, he pulled out a bottle and two glasses and placed them on the counter. Uncorking the bottle with some solemnity, he filled both glasses.

"You're going to need one or both of these before you look at Enos."

Jeremiah never drank before noon; his momma had always told him no good ever came of it. But his momma wasn't here, and Doc Smith was, after all, a doctor. Jeremiah picked up a glass and drank.

The whiskey was unlike anything from Miz Luella's. This was like swallowing velvet. It burned on the way down, but this was a warm, lingering smoulder rather than a wildfire. There was a smoky taste, too. How they'd managed to spit-roast a bottle of liquor, Jeremiah had no idea.

"Need t'other?"

"N—no sir." Jeremiah's mouth was still wondering exactly what he'd put in it. There were little tastes like fleeting notes of a far-off fiddler.

"I'll let it sit in case you need it after. You sure you're ready for this, Jeremiah?"

"I think I am, yes sir."

Doc Smith led Jeremiah into the surgery, which he remembered from the time a pig bite had turned bad on him. Lying on the surgical table was a white-sheeted form that had to be Enos. Some early-rising flies buzzed around the still form, and there was a stink like a hog run. He didn't want to look. He would much rather think of Enos happy and playing with his sons, or holding hands with his missus. And even as he shrank back from what he didn't want to see, a greater, almost mortal dread spurred him on.

Doc Smith lifted the white sheet so Jeremiah could see Enos's face, even as the doctor averted his own eyes. Jeremiah took a step back, fear screaming through him. Enos had been strangled—his neck had a long bruise on it like he'd been hanged, and his waxy face was a horrible black, his tongue sticking out, his dead eyes open and bulging.

"Oh dear Lord, oh my Savior." Jeremiah wasn't a praying man, but now seemed like a good time to start. The world lurched around him as the truth smote him. Enos Thurston had been strangled by Pharaoh, and it was Jeremiah's fault. And he didn't know what he could do. Would Pharaoh be satisfied with just one murder, or was he going to pursue his hatred from beyond the grave on every man, woman and child in Lonely Mile? Who would be able to stop him? Blind panic erupted in him, and he ran from the room.

He was out of Doc Smith's in a flash, mind screaming over and over that he had to find some protection, that Pharaoh was coming for them all. Running blindly, he found himself at the Sheriff's office.

He burst through the front door, into an arguing throng.

"Oh Lord God help me, Sheriff. It's my fault. I killed Enos, it's all my fault!"

There was an instant silence, and in the aftermath of his confession, Jeremiah found himself somewhat calmer. And then he noticed everyone's eyes were fixed on him. He also saw that many of them were carrying guns, because most everyone had a hand resting on one. Jeremiah knew that he had to say something, fast, or he was going to get shot, but his tongue was suddenly too big for his mouth.

"Everybody out of here but Jeremiah," Sheriff Anders thundered. All eyes turned from Jeremiah to the sheriff. "Get. I won't say it again. And nobody says anything to anyone until I've had a talk with Jeremiah."

"We hear him confess." Uter Gundersson was taller than anyone else in the room, and was rumored to have killed men in Kansas. But Sheriff Anders was not one to be intimidated by size or reputation.

"Any one of you sons-a-whores touches a hair on Jeremiah's head without my say-so and you'll get what that Laboda fella got, you all hear me?" The crowd went abruptly pale, and shrank back. "Now get out so I can hear what Jeremiah's got to say."

Cowed, the men filed silently out the door, although there were dark looks in Jeremiah's direction. Anders slammed the door after them, and Jeremiah stood stunned by the sudden silence. He hadn't considered that other people would blame him for Enos Thurston's murder. And Gundersson was one of Jeremiah's best customers. How could he turn like that?

Jeremiah was pulled from his stupor by Sheriff Anders's hard grip on his arm. He led the dazed Jeremiah to a chair and made him sit.

"I advise you to make this both good and quick. Most people don't know you like I do."

"It's my fault, I touched him, and probably that was what woke him up, and he was probably huntin' around for me in the dark and thought Enos was me from behind. I swear I didn't mean no harm, I just wanted to see what he was like under that—"

"Slow down. Who woke up?"

"Pharaoh! I touched him, and I still got his mark on me!" He thrust his right hand with the brown stains at Sheriff Anders, who grabbed it, and studied the fingers. "Pharaoh's come back to life and it's all my fault, he's going to come after me, and I don't know what I'm going to do! You got to do something or he's going to kill us all—"

"Jeremiah." The Sheriff said it with such authority that Jeremiah stopped. "You're telling me that you touched that mummy Ogrelfinger is pushing as a genuine Pharaoh, and it came to life to hunt you down?"

Jeremiah nodded, too overcome to speak.

"Well you didn't do yourself any favors coming in and sayin' what you did. I better give Gundersson and his cronies some time to cool off before I let you go. So, I'm going to put you in the pokey for a coupl'a hours, and then we'll see what's what."

Jeremiah burned with shame as the iron bars of the cell closed behind him. He'd never been in jail—he'd never broken the law. But he considered that it wasn't any less than what he deserved, and he couldn't help thinking of poor Enos Thurton's blackened face, his tongue sticking out, the livid bruise around his neck. That was Jeremiah's fault, as surely as if he'd done it himself. Pharaoh had come back to life because of him. He'd brought the curse of God down on Lonely Mile. The thoughts and the guilt ran furiously through his head. His momma had always said that the Devil would find work for his hands.

Jeremiah sat miserably on the edge of the prison cot as time crawled by. There was nothing to do but sit and think, and he wasn't good at that. He wondered if the prison bars would hold Pharaoh back, or if he'd snap them like kindling and kill Jeremiah like a cornered rat. He tried not to picture himself dead with a blackened, fear-filled face.

After some time, the door to the office opened. Sheriff Anders rose quickly, hand on his gun, only to realize that the figure in the door was Deputy Wilson.

"How'd she take it?"

"Not so good. And Amos Finkelstein thought this was a good time to sell me some books."

"What did Mr. Finkelstein have to sell, Bill?"

In response, Wilson dropped two heavy volumes onto the sheriff's desk.

The men held a hushed discussion over the two books, with lots of finger pointing as they called the other's attention to one passage or another. The only words Jeremiah could make out from their conversation was something about fancy seegars. What was Deputy Wilson doing buying books on fancy seegars when poor Enos Thurston had been murdered? As far as Jeremiah knew, they didn't make cigars in Egypt.

A long time later, their conversation finished, Sheriff Anders left with the books, and Deputy Wilson was alone with Jeremiah.

"All right Jeremiah, you're free to go. But there's a couple of things you should know about what's going on here..."

Less than ten minutes later, Jeremiah was enjoying a sarsaparilla at Uter Gundersson's expense in Miz Luella's. He liked the way people would ply him with drink when he knew something they wanted.

"Sheriff Anders said that everyone, even a ruler, got to have eyewitnesses to the crime, so we can't burn Pharaoh until we're sure it's him. We got to catch him in the act."

"We may have to get ourselves a new Sheriff, come election time." Brett Friend gave a sidelong glance toward Gundersson. "We ought to just burn that cursed wagon down, Pharaoh, bunkum medicine and all."

"Deputy Wilson is on the boardwalk, watchin' the medicine wagon," Quent Meinder reported from the window.

This led to a general deflation among the conspirators. No one was going to come near the wagon while Wilson was on guard duty. Jeremiah had once seen the deputy shoot a hole in a silver dollar thrown into the air. The group shifted restlessly as they wracked their brains trying to come up with a new plan.

All eyes were then drawn to the figure of Ali Khan, who had furtively entered the saloon. The room went quiet, as everyone watched Ogrelfinger's Indian servant walk up to Miz Luella, pay for a bottle of her best whiskey, tip his hat politely, and walk back out. A whispered suggestion was floated that they ought to make Ogrelfinger pay for bringing the murderous Pharaoh to town.

"I better be off. My pigs ain't been fed for a day, and I expect they'll be more than a little put out about it." While he was not as smart as Deputy Wilson, Jeremiah knew to get while the getting was good. He could feel their eyes on this back as he walked out of the saloon and into the bright afternoon sun.

The pigs were in a nasty mood when he got back. He spent a few hours doing chores around the farm, but every time he saw the brown stain on his fingers, his conscience ate at him. As the sun was lowering toward late afternoon, Jeremiah took his gun belt down from its peg, and buckled it on. He trusted Sheriff Anders and Deputy Wilson to do the right thing, but he had started this. He had a duty to help set it right.

The ride back to town was long and Jeremiah had plenty of time to reconsider. He nearly turned Buttercup back a couple of times, but he forced himself grimly on. An icy thrill of fear traced its way down his back when he caught sight of Lonely

Mile. The setting sun painted the town a disconcerting, hellish red, and there didn't seem to be much argument that God had set His curse upon the town. Lonely Mile's streets were empty, and a brooding watchfulness had settled in. Jeremiah saw a furtive movement behind closed curtains as he rode past. The abandoned medicine wagon now sat in front of the sheriff's office. Uter Gundersson, a rifle across his lap and a deputy's badge on his chest, had a clear view of anyone who approached. Gundersson started in surprise, his rifle halfway up before he recognized Jeremiah.

"You get on and see Wilson, right swift." Gundersson wasn't at all pleased to see Jeremiah.

Jeremiah tied Buttercup to the hitch outside the sheriff's office, and checked the bullets in his revolver. Then, mindful of how he'd run through the sheriff's door the last two times, tapped politely before walking in.

"Jeremiah. I should'a known." Deputy Wilson, looking a bit haggard, opened the door and greeted him with a lopsided grin. "Are you sure you want to do this?"

"I owe it to Enos Thurston to try and kill that terrible pile of bandages that did for him." Jeremiah said it with all the bravado he could muster. He couldn't stop imagining those hard, bandaged hands locked around his throat, and that terrible, eyeless face as the last thing he would ever see. Jeremiah shuddered. He shouldn't have come back.

"It's going to be dangerous, all right, but you stay with me. You do exactly what I tell you, Mr. Noakes, you understand me?"

"What you say, Deputy Wilson. On my honor."

The two of them fell into a watchful silence as the last of the sun's light disappeared, and darkness swallowed the town. The occasional light peeped out of a window or two in the gathering gloom, but the darkness went largely unchallenged. Wilson meticulously disassembled one gun after another, cleaning them thoroughly with a wire brush, then reassembling them.

"Why is Gundersson a deputy?" The clock on the office wall stood at ten past ten, and Jeremiah wanted to shriek into the brooding quiet.

"So he didn't cause no trouble. He likes to feel important, so we gave him something to do before he did something stupid."

The silence returned, as oppressive as ever, measured only by Jeremiah's restlessness and the slow, measured ticking of the clock.

Jeremiah must have fallen into a doze, because he jumped when Deputy Wilson grunted, "Listen." And Jeremiah could hear it—a clanking, like a ghost rattling its chains in the distance. He shrank in fear, but Wilson was up on his feet, quick as a cat.

"Stay close behind me."

Wilson drew his gun and ghosted out of the office door. After a moment of hesitation, Jeremiah followed, hand tight on his holstered pistol, trying not to think about grasping hands, or brown faces with empty eyes.

The clatter drew them forward, and it wasn't long before even Jeremiah could identify it as the sound of a cowbell being vigorously shaken. He followed the surprisingly-quiet Wilson past the muted lights of Miz Luella's and the dark windows of the General Lee boarding house. Wilson broke into a trot, forcing Jeremiah to move quickly to keep up with him. Just before they got to the Ross's store, across from blacksmith's, the bell was loud enough to wake the dead. Jeremiah's hands were trembling with fear. Ghost or Pharaoh, he didn't want to meet anyone that Death hadn't seen fit to keep.

In the moonlight, Jeremiah saw Uter Gundersson clawing at his neck and bucking like a bronco, a big cowbell on his belt clanging like a stampede all by itself. To Jeremiah's surprise, the small, dark-clad figure of Ali Khan was hanging from a length of cloth looped around the big man's neck, as if trying to break him.

Jeremiah's gun was in his hand, but he just didn't know what to do with it.

"Get off him now!" Deputy Wilson's command rolled across the darkened town like sudden thunder.

Ali Khan must have heard, because his grim slash of a mouth set itself a little harder, and he tightened the knotted cloth around Gundersson's neck. Uter was already weakening, his attempts to dislodge the little man becoming clumsier.

Wilson fired, and the bullet tore through Ali Khan's right shoulder. The little man shuddered, and blood darkened his suit. But he did not let go. The big Swede fell to his knees, eyes bulging, face darkening, his mouth desperately gasping for air that wouldn't come. Wilson fired again, striking Ali Khan again in the shoulder, and Ali Khan let go of one end of the cloth. Gundersson flopped down on his face, and lay still.

Ali Khan still stood, though his right arm hung uselessly at his side, blood soaking down the right side of his jacket. With a murderous gleam in his eyes, he charged straight toward the two of them, swinging a weighted and knotted cloth over his head left-handed. Wilson fired again, striking the small Indian in the center of the chest, but even this did nothing to slow Ali Khan. Racing toward them as if he had nothing to fear, he whipped the weighted end of cloth over his head, catching the deputy around the neck.

Jeremiah stood frozen as Wilson dropped his gun, hands going to his throat. Ali Khan jerked the cloth savagely, pulling Wilson off-balance. Noakes was paralyzed with fear. Ali Khan was more terrifying than the bandaged, shambling creature he had been expecting. Soaked in his own blood, Ali Khan seemed only inconvenienced by the three bullet-holes Deputy Wilson had put in him. What could anyone do against a will that terrible? Deputy Wilson struggled in the dirt, eyes bulging, mouth working but nothing coming out, and Jeremiah could only watch as Wilson died.

The thunderclap of a pistol-shot rolled over the scene and a bullet tore through Ali Khan's neck. Hate in his eyes, the murderous Indian turned, and Jeremiah saw Sheriff Anders, smoking pistol ready to fire again. Ali Khan took a few stumbling steps toward the sheriff, blood spurting from between his fingers. He took three steps, then lurched to his knees. The murderous light in his eyes changed to a glow of holy reverence.

"I didn't—" Ali Khan choked out, a pink foam dribbling from his mouth and nose, his eyes fixed on Sheriff Anders. "I didn't recognize you." With those last words, he crumpled to the ground and stopped breathing, his blood soaking in the dust and grit of Lonely Mile.

Freed from his trance, Jeremiah leaned over the still-choking deputy and loosened the knotted cloth that was around his neck. Soon the deputy was taking great, rasping gulps of air. He looked toward Uter, who was rubbing the livid bruise on his neck, and then to the Sheriff, who stood, pistol still in his hand, gazing at the corpse of Ali Khan.

"Do you have any idea what he was talking about?" Jeremiah asked the sheriff.

"No." But even Jeremiah knew he wasn't telling the truth. He also knew that Ali Khan's last words were the sort of thing he should keep to himself, no matter how many beers or whiskeys he was plied with.

Deputy Wilson helped Uter to Doc Smith's, and Sheriff Anders threw the body of Ogrelfinger's murderous servant over his shoulder. He didn't walk proud, like the sheriff who'd just shot a murderer. He seemed kind of sad. While they walked, people came out of the woodwork, until it seemed that half the town was following Anders as he kicked open Miz Luella's doors. He ignored Miz Luella, he headed straight up to Ogrelfinger's room.

With the hand that wasn't keeping Ali Khan's body steady, he pounded on the door, not letting up until it opened. Ogrelfinger was trying to look fierce, holding a tiny derringer at the ready, but he wilted at the sight of Sheriff Anders carrying Ali Khan. With a grimace, Anders let go, and Ali Khan's bloody corpse collapsed in a heap between the two men.

"It seems that your servant was a member of a fraternity of assassins called Phansigars, also known as the Thuggee. They strangled people in India for a coupl'a hundred years, until Sir Henry Sleeman rooted them out some thirty years ago. I'm guessing your Mr. Ali Khan fled, and decided to take his trade abroad."

Deputy Wilson shouldered his way through the crowd and shoved the two volumes Jeremiah had seen earlier that day into Ogrelfinger's arms.

"The Thugs or Phansigars of India: Comprising a History of the Rise and Progress of That Extraordinary Fraternity of

Assassins; and a Description of the System Which It Pursues, and of the Measures Which Have Been Adopted by the Supreme Government of India for Its Suppression," Wilson recited for the benefit of the crowd. "You may want to read it before you hire yourself another Indian. And out of concern for your safety, Mr. Ogrelfinger, I think it might be best if you left town tonight."

Ogrelfinger had no reply. He stood, clutching the books to him. He just stared down at the bloody body of the man he had called Ali Khan, his face a mixture of sadness and horror. The people of Lonely Mile stared with him.

THE PATRIOT

"Contact!"

My brawny mechanic muscles my propeller around, and it finally catches on the fourth rotation. Clouds of smoke rise from my sputtering engine. He steps back from the whirring propeller of my SPAD VII and scurries, quick for a man of his bulk, to remove the chocks. I can barely contain my nervous excitement. The date is 12 July, 1917, and I am about to fly my first combat mission. We four are on patrol looking for Boche; Lieutenant DePout, Sous Lieutenant Alibert, and myself, with Capitaine Lefeure himself as the flight leader.

The engines roar as we race them, and on the Capitaine's signal, our formation moves towards the end of the airfield. We lift more or less simultaneously, clearing the trees at the end of the field, and climb into the sky over France. We soar for some time, continuing to gain altitude. Once the uncertainty of take-off is over, my nervousness turns into a pleasant sort of sloth. Flying is a pleasure, despite the hundred things I have to remember in order to keep my fragile SPAD in the air and flying in formation. On the ground, the air is hot and still, but up in the sky, it rushes past, making the flight pleasantly cool. The green fields of France stretch below me, verdant despite the war. I cannot imagine a more pleasant day, or a better way to fight for my country.

Ahead is the great scar of churned-up Earth that marks the trenches. I can see fast-evaporating puffs of smoke that mark artillery emplacements, so far below that they look like balls of cotton. Surely nothing so far away can possibly affect me, safe in my plane, five thousand feet above the endless slaughter on the ground. I've done my time as a member of the infantry—more

than any man should have to. I remind myself that I am not
a tourist, and I look around as I was taught in flight school; I
see no black specks, but only peaceful, empty clouds like those
from a Monet painting.

After thirty minutes of pleasant flight, Capitaine Lefeure
dips his wings, indicating that he has seen Boche aircraft. I
search the sky, but see nothing until the Albatrosses are among
us. The flight scatters like children let out of school, each going
our own way. By some miracle we do not smash into each other.

The fight is an abrupt and terrifying whirlwind of planes
and open sky. I twist and turn, listening to my ailerons protest.
I cannot count the black Albatrosses, but their color and birdlike wing-extensions distinguish them from our brown SPADs.
Working myself around to a position behind where one black
planes should be, and I see nothing but open sky. The fight is
behind me, and I kick the rudder pedals and wrench the stick
around.

Bullets hammer into my plane; an Albatross is coming down
on me from above my right fore-wing, tiny flames spitting from
its guns. Despite everything I have been taught, I freeze like
a rabbit confronted by a poisonous snake as I hear the bullets
tearing into the fabric of my plane. A shadow passes over me,
and a plane—Captaine Lefeure's—flies through the rapidly-
narrowing space between me and the onrushing Albatross. The
moment's relief I feel gives way to horror as his engine blooms
flame, and he passes so close to me that I choke on the smoke and
heat from his burning craft. The Albatross zooms past us, but
all I can do is watch as Capitaine Lefeure, Fernand, I remember
his name is, leaps from his aircraft, choosing a quick death by
impact rather the prolonged agony of burning. In seconds, he is
little but a tumbling speck quickly lost against the brown scar
that is No Man's Land.

His death jars me from my unresponsive dream-state, and
I am filled with the desire for bloody revenge. Kicking the
rudder pedals as hard as I can, and nearly standing my plane
on a wingtip, I whip my SPAD around and drop in behind the
murderous Albatross. He twists and turns as I cling to his tail;
he cannot get rid of me, and yet I cannot get a good shot at him.

I wait for my opportunity, rather than waste bullets on air, and it comes when he pauses to look behind him. Just as he sees me, my bullets slam into his fuselage, and the murderer slumps down in his cockpit, his black plane winging over to dive for the ground.

I have done it! My first victory!

My exultation at this bloody deed is cut short by the *spack spack spack* of bullets hammering at the fragile wooden frame of my machine. I wasn't watching my tail! I wrench my plane around, and with a heart-stopping *crack*, my right, lower wing snaps off. My plane begins to follow my erstwhile opponent's in a terrifying, spinning dive for the ground.

I have no time to worry if my opponent is still on my tail or not, I am too busy fighting to stop my plane's disastrous descent that will certainly kill me. The stick tries to wrench itself out of my hands, and I pull on it as hard as I dare, knowing that I could snap off the remaining wings if I'm too violent. Somehow, I manage to stop the whirling dive once, less than two thousand feet above the ground, only to resume it. I again wrestle desperately with my plane, which seems determined to meet the ground with as much force as possible, and I curse gravity, wind, aerodynamics, and my instructors as the ground spins wildly and looms in my vision, inescapable.

"Sorry, there. I didn't see that you were still alive."

I open my eyes and see an overwhelming dark, punctuated only by the occasional flash of artillery. The reek of death is all around me. I must be in No Man's Land, pinioned somewhere between friendly trenches and the Germans.

My leg is an agonizing ball of fire. Even without the intermittent light of exploding shells, I can see the white gleam of bone jutting from my shin amidst a fast-growing black stain that I know is my blood. I wonder how I managed to drag myself from my plane, which I cannot see in the darkness. Everything is cold, although it's July.

I try to slip my belt off, but my fingers are too clumsy and too weak to pull the belt from under me, and more pain grinds my torso when I try to lift myself.

"Help," I say, but I am desperately weak, and the word is

absorbed into the torn and bloody mud.

"Is anyone there?" I have a vague recollection of being woken by words, and look around. I am unimaginably alone in the midst of the greatest of all wars.

A dark shape in the lesser darkness of the ground shifts near me, and I can see that his head is tilted sideways in curiosity. He is bareheaded, and I cannot tell if he is German or not, although I seem to recall him speaking French.

"My belt," I gasp. "Help me make a tourniquet for my leg."

He is strong, and I clench my teeth against many pains scattered throughout my body as he rolls me to one side and pulls my belt from under me.

"Now what?" His speech is odd, he must be some sort of provincial, or perhaps British.

"Fasten it around my leg, as tightly as possible, to stop the blood."

It is torture, as sure as any a medieval man suffered, but it will keep me from bleeding to death. His strong hands are not gentle as the belt becomes a throbbing noose just above my knee, and what little strength I have left goes into throat-shredding screams of agony, and then oblivion claims me.

I awake, I do not know how much later, a waning quarter moon is up—it must be past midnight. I can distinguish only the few things that are close to me, but the thick, choking reek of opened graves assailing my nostrils tells me that I am still in No Man's Land. The shelling continues, the stuttering light revealing that I am in a wasteland of corpses. Sticking up out of the mud are hands, legs, heads, coats, helmets, rifles, arms, and other, less identifiable parts. Some are whole, many have been torn asunder. Where the exposed flesh is not coated with mud it has been blackened from days of exposure to the sun. They surround me as far as I can see in the wan moonlight. My hands are resting on them, and surely I am lying on them. These must be the remains of some poor infantry platoon sent over the top, now left to rot, forgotten amidst the mud and stench. My leg is on fire, but the agony is not what it was. I risk a glance at my leg—it is a barely-visible dark shadow, caked with dried blood and mud. I won't be walking anywhere, and I won't make much progress by crawling, either. Staring at the black sky, I wonder which direction the French lines are, and which way are the German. If I choose wrongly, a sniper will get me. If I choose correctly, there's still a good chance a frightened and inexperienced sentry will think I'm German.

I try to crawl into a shell hole, because I don't want to be exposed when the sun comes up, but there is no strength in me. I am weaker than I remember feeling when I nearly died of mumps as a child. The simple act of lifting my arms is an effort, and even attempting to drag my heavily inert body triggers a grinding pain in my chest that leaves me gasping. I giggle, then begin to laugh at the mordant irony. I had transferred out of the infantry just to avoid a death like this, lying helpless in the loathsome, sucking mud of No Man's Land. What foolishness, what a stupid, useless waste of time to learn how to fly an aircraft just to end up back in the mud, weak and dying.

In the abrupt flash of a shell burst, I see a crouching silhouette that hasn't been there before. My mouth is dry, and when I try to call out to him, all I can manage is a weak croak. If he hears me, he makes no indication. He is somewhat closer in the next flash, bent down to examine something. In the next burst of light, I see he has picked something up—an arm! He is a robber, one of those horrible people that live out in No Man's Land, stripping the dead of their possessions. I flounder briefly, but just the attempt to sit up sets my heart pounding. I have no weapon; there is no way I can stop this defiler of corpses.

The next flash of artillery burns an image forever onto my brain. The shape has brought the arm to his mouth. Horror and revulsion send a hot shock through me, and I find my voice.

"*Cannibal!*" I scream, outrage lending me strength, and I again flail around to find a gun. The muzzle of a rifle comes to my hand, but I am too weak to free it from the mud. Nothing else comes to hand, and I am too weak to drag myself away. I cannot kill this horror, cannot catch him and break his spine even if I were able to reach him. A sense of my own weakened helplessness overwhelms me, and he shuffles over to me with a curious slouching movement

It is only when he is close to me that a shell flashes brightly enough to confirm that I am in some sort of Hieronymous Bosch nightmare. Something is wrong with the cannibal's face, as if it were more wolfish than human, with powerful, prognathous jaws so exaggerated they suggest a muzzle. He is caked in mud, and I am unable to tell if he is even wearing clothes. In one claw-like hand, he carries a forearm, and I can see where he has taken bites from it. He shuffles towards me, and I scrabble for something—anything—with which to defend myself. My hands encounter other, colder hands, open mouths, boots, coats, and mud, but nothing with which to fend this monster off.

It squats down to pluck the eyes from a helpless, dead face. I close my own eyes, but the sound, like that of someone enjoying a juicy olive, repulses me even as it reminds me how hungry I am. It swallows loudly.

"Not a cannibal," it says in a curious but perfectly understandable French. "In Arabia, the word for us is *ghula*, and that satisfies me well enough."

The words and civilized accent are utterly at odds with the hideous, distorted appearance. Somehow this thing should drool when it speaks, and slur his words in a vile fashion that lets me know he is purely evil. How much of a monster can this creature be if it can speak French? And yet, for his inhuman and vile diet, he had saved my life by tightening my tourniquet.

War makes all men mad. I am lying on a bed of unknown corpses, staring at the infinitely distant and uncaring stars. Soon I will join the dead men, unless I am found by a night patrol or a rescue party. I watched my Capitaine step from his plane and plummet to his death rather than burn, and the madness of this war rolls on like an unstoppable juggernaut, crushing and mangling the lives of all in its path. Is it any wonder that someone has turned to cannibalism? The only thing this war has in plenty is dead victims, and somehow, it doesn't surprise me that something—someone—has learned or been driven to take advantage of that. Certainly, the rats and lice live better than kings, with all the food they could possibly want, enduring only the occasional enmity of the living soldiers who resent them only briefly.

"Tell me you are not Boche," I say.

"I am loyal to France, if that is what you are worried about," he replies.

I turn my head away, only to hear him shuffling towards me. I am helpless. My heart thunders; he will kill me to preserve his secret, and I can do nothing. I grasp the rifle muzzle I had found before, but the mud's grip is too sure.

I look back to see his dark shape standing over me, just far enough away that I cannot touch him, and he can't touch me. He is holding something out, and it takes me a moment to realize that it is a canteen. Staring at it, I can feel how dry my mouth is. I don't dare scoop water out of the stagnant pools in the large craters; the water in No Man's Land is scummed over with a layer of trapped poison gas. But what is it that this … person has in store for me? Is it poisoned?

If he wants fresh meat, he can easily overcome me. I would lose a wrestling match with a six-year-old in my current state, but he might not know that. I have no gun, no knife, and no means of defending myself. But my mind comes back to the fact that he applied the tourniquet to my leg. Why preserve my life only to poison me now?

I grasp the canteen, my hands shaking with weakness. It is full and heavy, and I almost drop it, but I am so parched that I drain it completely. I feel some energy return to me, but also a renewed insistence of the throbbing pain in my leg.

"Thank you," I say, lowering the canteen, gasping for breath. I pray that he does not offer me food. With my thirst slaked, I am hungry enough that I might accept.

"I am Gaspard, by the way," he says, crouching on his haunches like a bush man.

"Michel," I respond automatically.

"How came you here, Michel?" he asks. "Your uniform is not like theirs." He uses a sweeping gesture to indicate the legion of bodies that surrounds us, half-swallowed in the mud. "My airplane crashed," I say, and wonder what I am doing. I am talking with a ghoul, an eater of corpses. Something that will see me as food as soon as I am dead, and perhaps is only waiting for a moment of obvious weakness to pounce on and devour me. And yet, the fundamental human need for companionship makes me desperate. I do not want to be alone, more than that, I don't want to die alone, even if I am speaking with one who will feast on me after I am gone.

"Air-plane?" He is testing out the unfamiliar word. "What is an *air*-plane?"

"A heavier-than-air craft with wings that flies."

"You're mocking me," Gaspard's voice is offended.

"I swear it's true," I insist, amazed that I care what this corpse-eater thinks of my conversation. But talk—any sort of communication—is better than sitting and waiting for a rescue that will never come. "You must be very isolated."

"True enough," Gaspard replies, and looks away. I regret striking the nerve, because he does not elaborate. The silence is interrupted only by the bursting of a distant shell.

"Must you feast on soldiers, like a rat?" The question bursts out of me, the only thing I can think of. Somehow, I imagine he could be some sort of vastly overgrown rat. The rats in the trenches are so enormous that I would not have believed it without seeing them. "Is there nothing else that you can eat?"

"Our earliest stories are told of Sumer and Babylon, where city-states rose and made war on each other, and we feasted on the dead." Gaspard says it in a dreamy and reverent voice that no longer sounds offended. "Other lands have been greater sources of provender for short periods of time, but few countries have ever been so truly generous or so consistent as my beloved France."

The 'we' sends a wave of horripilation across my skin. There is more than one of him—and they have stories that go back as far as recorded history? A *ghula*, he called himself, a ghoul. One of my fellow history students, one with a more morbid bent than myself, had once related a repellant story of a race of underground creatures that lived among the catacombs and sewers of Paris, degenerate remnants of people who fled there during the Terror, living and breeding in the reeking dark, coming up only to steal the unloved and unwanted for their unhallowed feasts. I had dismissed it as a gothic fairytale. Did sanity permit a race of creatures that dwelt below France, gnawing away at her dead?

"You aren't just waiting for me to die, are you?" I ask.

A long, daemonically howling cachinnation that might be a laugh erupts from him, and it chills me to the bone.

"Young men seem so eager to fight and to die for whatever cause, and yet you come over all squeamish if it turns out that you might get eaten," he says when he regains his breath. His eyes glow weirdly in the stuttering light of the bombardment.

"Why does it bother you? To know that after you are dead, one of us will creep up on you and chew your flesh and suck the marrow from your bones? You'll be dead, and so far as we can tell, you won't feel it. How can anything that happens to your unfeeling corpse be worse than dying? If you ask me, it's the killing that's the real crime." Those uncanny eyes fix on me.

"Wouldn't you rather have lived a full life with a wife to make love to, and then some fat children to coo over? Wouldn't it be better to spend cool autumn afternoons at a café sipping coffee, rather than lying at the bottom of a crater, covered in mud, waiting to die? Don't you deserve friends to love and argue with, books to read, wine to drink, and a fire to warm your bones when you get old? Some warm and happy memories to comfort you before that final black oblivion sucks you down, down, down into nothing? Are your lying leaders and their war-profiteering friends worth sacrificing all that for?"

These things I have thought myself; I remember similar sentiments as I waited to go over the top with the 146th at Verdun, while politicians whose incompetence had started it, the generals whose indifference prolonged it, and the profiteers who gained from it, risked nothing. No one who had ever been at the front lines could refer to the massacre of thousands as "the usual wastage" or talk about the loss of half a million men as "quite acceptable." General Sir Douglas Haig had been talking about enough men to fill the city of Lille twice, and he had done so from the quiet drawing-room of some appropriated chateau, I am certain. What makes my life worth so much less than Pétain's, de Castelnau's, Joffre's, or Nivelle's? At least I have never sent a thousand, ten thousand, or a million men into a blind, pointless slaughter. Before I had arrived at the front, I would have said that his was a right war, that defending French soil from the Germans was worth my life. Watching the war as it was conducted had thoroughly eradicated that noble fiction.

"At least it's better for us; it won't be a complete waste," Gaspard says. I should be horrified by his monstrous indifference, but I ask myself if he is any more atrocious or ghastly than the old men who had lead us into this war. "What's this one about, anyway?"

"Curbing rampant German imperialism," I say automatically, then feel the need to explain in more concrete terms. "They invaded France."

"What will happen after they've been expelled?" he asks. "Will you destroy all the Germans? Murder their children, burn their homes, kill their women, taking some home to be your slaves, or maybe a war bride, to make sure that they never invade again?"

"We don't enslave people anymore." I am about to say something about slavery being uncivilized, but I don't want to hear that horrible howl of a laugh again. As it is, he snorts his cynical indifference.

"We'll stop Germany, and then… ." I trail off. What will we do then? "Then the world will be safe." I know how hollow the words sound.

"I dare say so, with so many men dead," he says with casual misanthropy. "And you will trust the same butchers who have turned France into an enormous garden of corpses to create and govern a lasting peace when all is done?"

"What do you know of war?"

"A great deal." He is unruffled by my outburst. "I do consider myself a patriot, Michel. France has long been kind to us, and where you tell your history by the wars you fight, we tell it by the times of plenty. Caesar's forces were unlike anything anyone above or below had ever seen, and they left mounds of corpses wherever they went. After they conquered old Gaul, there was good fighting over who exactly got to be the Emperor of the Gauls, and Roman executions were always enough to keep us in provender without having to hunt it for ourselves. Imagine thirty, eighty, or a hundred sides of beef left hanging by the roadside. We were mad for choice; the Romans were our best friends for hundreds of years. It was a lovely time, I am told. And when Rome crumbled, there were barbarian invasions; the Rhenan Franks, the Burgonds, Visigoths and Salic Franks, all laying waste to the countryside, all leaving us meat."

He looks up at the stars, and then down at the darkness of the lines.

"We remember Atilla as a great friend to us and ours." His tone is reverent. "He killed anyone he could catch, leaving them in great heaps, and we gorged ourselves until we couldn't even crawl. Sometime later, Clovis unified himself a kingdom, mostly by killing anyone who resisted him, and for two centuries his successors followed in his footsteps. Those were days of easy plenty, and then Charlemagne got it into his head to have a bigger kingdom than anyone else, and we dined regularly on Bretonian and Aquitanian.

"At the same time, there was always something happening with the Emirates near the Pyrenees, and we used to say, 'if you're still hungry, go South.' After the internal struggles settled down somewhat, the Vikings invaded from the sea, and the Hungarians attacked in the East. Again, we were spoilt for choice. Charlemagne's grandchildren and later descendants never really got along, and they fought each other to claim this or that bit of empire, always leaving a fresh provender lying in the fields. The Capetians were no different, and we gnawed the bones of many a Norman duke, thanks to their lust for power.

"We glutted ourselves on Albigensian heretics. The War of Lord and Vassal provided us with nearly a century of fine dining, although we could never tell who was on whose side. A bounty of Plantagenêts and Capetians ended up dead on the ground, with no one but us to look after them. It was difficult to go from a century of such plentitude to nearly as long of relative peace, but we adjusted. We moved into the great cities, and wormed our way into graveyards and catacombs, living on such scraps as we could scrounge.

"We were saved from that ignoble state by the British, bless their ambitious hearts. For more than a hundred years, we stuffed ourselves on the best the British had to offer. And once they were finally driven out, the South began to be interesting again, with another extended conflict with Hispania. When that was done, the French started fighting themselves as the Wars of Religion started up, which we found blessedly filling. But nothing that good could possibly last, and what followed was the longest famine we have ever experienced. Nearly two hundred years, and not a single war on France's soil. And while the good times don't go on forever, neither do the bad ones. The Prussians and the Austrians invaded, and we gorged again. But these were merely appetizers for what was to come.

"The Revolution was a glorious time for us." He sighs like an old woman remembering her younger, wilder days. "The food was so rich, so plentiful, and so very tender. I remember a group of us passing around scraps of royalty, because it was too important not to share. Later, when the Terror was in full swing, some of us were bold enough to walk openly among the surface dwellers. Few noticed, and I discovered then that people above really aren't that different from us below.

"After that, there was the little Corsican, who did little for us until he was driven back into France. Still, we get a great laugh out of all those monuments he put up to himself, since all he accomplished was feeding ghouls in other lands. His grandiose Arch of Triumph should be called 'The Feast of Foreign Ghouls.'

"We were afraid that there would be another two-hundred-year dearth after that, but the Prussian invasion whet our appetite for this great and glorious feast." His sweeping gesture includes all the corpse-filled darkness. "Truly, it is more than we deserve."

I have no answer. I am tired, my spirit drained, and sick to my soul of Gaspard's horribly twisted version of history. The sky above me is black and uncaring, filled with a million infinitely remote pinpoints of light. No matter what happens, no matter the course of human history, it won't matter at all to the brilliant, eternally distant stars. I can feel myself drifting towards that final blackness, like a final rest from which there is no waking. I, too, will feed the ghouls as I lay in No Man's Land. My mother and sister will weep for me. It is hard to keep my eyes open, although something nags at me.

"Gaspard," I whisper, but there is no answer.

"Gaspard," I repeat.

"Yes," he replies.

"Promise me you will make sure I am dead before you eat."

A hand with thick claws instead of nails comes down on my shoulder, and I look up into the disturbingly wolfish face. "I promise," he says. Although I can sense some dark and still-unfathomed amusement behind his eyes, I believe him, and am in some small way comforted.

"Thank you." Consciousness is slipping away from me. I fight it; I don't want to die, I don't want Gaspard to crack my bones and suck their marrow. Pleasant thoughts drift through my mind, of not lying in this field of death and stench, but of family, and the simple, homey comforts that I miss. I miss the clean feel of getting into a freshly-made bed, the cool touch of a hardwood floor in the morning, the thousand variated greens of a forest, the careless laugh of children, and the company of family. But these longed-for pleasures slip away, and as I close my eyes for the last time, my thoughts are not of my mother, but of the lovely Francine, who I seduced before I went off to war. Her skin was wonderfully soft and warm, her breasts ripe and full, her lips always in a knowing smile.

I wake again, and I am under a white ceiling. The reek of death and decay has been replaced with the sharp stench of ether and gangrenous rot. Around me are numerous white-sheeted beds, filled with the shapes of the wounded. Somewhere near me, someone is coughing so hard that I cannot see how he will live through it, and everywhere I hear the moans of the dying. It takes a moment for the reality of my survival to sink in, and my head swims with the memories of No Man's Land. Did I imagine the entire grotesque encounter with the inhuman Gaspard? No, it was far too vivid to have been anything but reality. I shudder.

A nun, seeing that I am awake, appears at my bedside.

"You are lucky to be alive." Her matter-of-fact tone carries over the calls of the dying and the coughing which I know will not end while the damned soul lives. "We weren't sure you would survive the amputation."

Shock runs through me as I look down at my … foot. I stare incredulously. I would swear that I am wiggling my toes, but there is nothing below the sheets past my knee. Whipping the sheets off, sure that it's some sort of cruel joke, and I am confronted with the heavily-bandaged stump of my right knee. My foot is gone.

"They say that you may think you have a leg for some days," the sister says soothingly, a hand on my shoulder gently urging me to lie down again. "You may even forget that you have lost it and try to stand up. These things are normal, and will fade in time."

I am mutilated, a cripple, but all I can think is that I am saved, saved from that hell of No Man's Land, saved from becoming a living sacrifice presented by my country's generals for the ghouls' colossal feast. I weep with relief. The nun pats my shoulder in a comforting way, and it occurs to me that she thinks I am weeping for my lost leg. I do not correct her. I will not be devoured. I will go home, where there are no corpse-eaters, and when I die, my body will lie undisturbed, my bones ungnawed.

So weak am I that even weeping exhausts me. The sister fluffs my pillow and sets it behind my head, and despite the cries and moans of the unfortunate souls around me, oblivion comes quickly.

In the dark I am jarred awake. The pain that woke me strikes again, even worse than before. I scrabble with the bed dressing, and where the pain strikes I find nothing but stained sheets. It is my leg—my missing leg. When I realize what I am feeling, an inarticulate shriek tears itself from my throat. Two nuns hurry up to my bedside, even as another wave of agony, so like and yet unlike being stabbed with a knife, runs up my right leg.

"*My leg*," I scream in desperate agony at their calm, disbelieving faces. "*I can feel that son of a bitch Gaspard eating my leg!*"

DEATH ON THE AMERICAN FAMILY FARM

George Orne was drinking his morning cup of coffee and listening to his father's old AM radio when he got the first inkling of what was coming. The radio was a worn, maroon Bakelite monstrosity nearly as old as George. Like everything on the farm, it was a bit run down, but hadn't given up the ghost yet. The radio newsman reported that a New York City gang, high on some cocktail of drugs, was rampaging through the city. Chaos, panic, and blood were streaming through the city streets, and nobody knew what was going on.

George shook his head.

Damn city people weren't good for anything, he thought and shut the radio off.

"I was listening to that." Martha held a cup of steaming tea to warm her hands. She'd given up coffee nine years ago on account of her stomach. George suspected that she snuck a bit when he left to do the morning chores. He wasn't about to say anything. They were both in their sixties, and had precious few pleasures left. What harm in a little coffee?

"Just wait until I've gone out before you turn it back on. I want a little peace this morning." It wasn't long before George went out into the chill October morning to milk the cows.

George forgot about the news over the day. Most news didn't much affect him. East Harrow was too small for even a traffic light, a small, dying farm community in the remote hills of Vermont. Whatever happened in New York City or Boston was their problem. His taxes were killing him, the state dairy subsidy had expired last year, and some developer was pressuring him to sell his best field to build McMansions on. George had enough troubles without borrowing New York's.

The next morning their usual radio station was out. George cranked the needle up and down the dial, and found nothing but a few automated beep stations. He turned the power off in disgust. Clearly, the ancient vacuum tubes had finally packed it in. Well, that was just great.

That afternoon, he took a moment to talk with Bob Ford, who kept the farm next to him. At seventy, Bob was no longer the thick trunk of a man he had been. Neither of them was getting any younger, and farming wasn't getting any easier.

"You have a problem with your radio this morning?"

Bob flipped off his battered John Deere baseball cap, rubbed a calloused hand over his brown, hairless pate, then pulled the cap back into place.

"You should watch more television, George."

"There hasn't been a newsman worth watching since Cronkite went off the air." George felt his lips compress in distaste. Bob ran a thick hand under his cap again.

"Boston's a big mess, and New York is, too. People are just going crazy." Bob brought his weathered, moon-round face conspiratorially close. "They say they're eating each other in dark alleys, George."

Bob Ford was a good man. He was steady, and didn't spread gossip. If Bob Ford said it, you could rely on it. And either he had lost his marbles, or the rest of the world had.

"Damn city people. What the hell's wrong with them?"

"Dunno." Bob's face was set in a perturbed scowl. "The TV announcer looked pretty scared. Then there wasn't anyone on the air this morning."

"Probably some Halloween prank. Television people got too much time on their hands."

Bob peered at him. "You think so, George?"

There was an uncomfortable silence, and George looked back over his fields.

"I really hope so."

Above them, a swift-moving line of geese stretched from horizon to horizon. It took a moment for George to realize they were flying north, the wrong way for migration. He wondered what they were fleeing.

That afternoon, the phone came up dead, and George decided not to share Bob's fears with Martha. He saw no sense in upsetting her. But the thought of cannibalism in the cities kept him awake long into the night. What was going on? He didn't realize he'd fallen asleep until the frightened lowing of cows woke him.

In the dark, he pulled his winter coat and muck boots over his flannel pajamas. Probably some damn fox had come in from the cold. On his way out, George picked up his old shotgun, loading it with deer slugs.

The cows were in a frenzy, now he could hear them kicking at their stalls. George broke into a trot when he smelled blood. The stars were remote pinpoints, the moon not yet up, the barn dark as a coal cellar.

The door opened easily.

Shotgun at the ready, face set in a grim frown, George flicked on the light.

A stick-skinny girl in a torn and filthy evening dress was crouched over the prone form of his best milch cow, who'd collapsed in her stall. The air stank of blood and the urine-drenched panic of cows. The woman didn't react to the lights. Instead, she wrenched a mouthful of red, bloody muscle out of Daisy's neck and bolted it down like a starving dog. Most things didn't rattle George like they used to but this sent a shock of electricity from his groin to his neck. He stared at the skinny girl, trying to figure out what she thought she was doing. She swallowed the raw gobbet she'd been chewing, the blood running down her chin, and dove in for another bite.

"Get your damn self out of that stall right now, missy!" George bellowed.

She turned her head toward him. The cow's blood was smeared from her neck up into her hair. Below the fresh crimson layer her face was painted with a cracked black that might have been week-old blood. Dark clotted chunks matted her hair and dress.

Goddamn kid was playing at being a zombie. What the hell was wrong with people? And why did she have to come here?

She moaned something unintelligible, and started toward

him. If she'd run, he would have just shot her right then. Instead, she stumbled towards him, as if she needed leg braces, or her knees didn't work right.

"I'm not kidding here." His voice came out shrill.

She was out of Daisy's stall now, less than ten feet away, twitching fingers reaching for him. She was almost close enough to touch the shotgun's barrel when he let her have it in the gut. The discharge was deafening in the enclosed barn, and the slug smashed through her abdomen. She didn't fall. She didn't even hesitate. George fell back, eyeing the thumb-sized hole he'd blasted clear through her torso.

Only someone hopped up on serious drugs could ignore that. George fired again, this time in her chest. Black, gooey blood and chunks of bone spattered over the stalls, and girl went down in the scattered hay on the floor of the barn.

She wasn't done yet. She couldn't move her legs, but her arms scrabbled around until they found purchase. Then she crawled painfully toward him.

The barn door slammed open, and Martha stood in the doorframe, her shotgun at the ready.

"Stay back," he warned her.

"What the hell, George?" came Martha's voice from the door.

The dead woman's head whipped around at the voice, the jaw snapping hungrily.

Martha moved up next to George. Together, they watched the determined torso drag itself across the packed dirt of the barn.

"What's going on?" Martha demanded again, but he still had no answer. He'd only just noticed that the front of the intruder's dress had come open, and her pale and rubbery breasts were in full view. He stared at them for a moment before he figured out what was wrong.

"She's not breathing."

Martha didn't contradict him. She bent down for a look, and realized her foolishness when a hand clawed at her.

George fired again, the deer slug slamming a fist-sized chunk of putrescent brain out of the crawling thing's skull. That seemed to do the trick. The woman collapsed, her arms twitching without purpose. After a moment, she lay entirely still.

"I think she was dead," he said. George felt stupid, but what could he say?

Martha rested her shotgun's buttstock on her hip.

"That's pretty certain. You took off most of her head, George."

"No, I mean before. She was dead before." His voice softened. "And I think we should have gone to church a little more."

There wasn't any more sleep for them that night. Between deciding what to do with the dead girl, dragging Daisy's dead bulk out of the barn, and hosing the sticky mess out of Daisy's stall, it was dawn before they were done. The shattered, bird-boned corpse of the woman didn't have any sort of pocketbook or identification and they couldn't call the sheriff with the phones out. Martha took some pictures of the girl in her tattered dress, as well as the mess she'd made in Daisy's stall in case someone came inquiring. They buried her in an unmarked grave in an unused corner of the property.

Martha read a few words from the Bible about her sending her soul to peace.

Since they wouldn't be getting any milk from the cows that morning, George and Martha sat down at the dinner table and had a discussion. Both were of the opinion that the dead girl and the general disaster in the city were related, and that it might take a couple of months before everything was back to normal. The first thing they needed to do, Martha argued, was to get to town and be with other people. See what was going on; see what other people were doing. George said they should sit tight. Going into town would leave the farm unprotected. What if more dead people wandered onto their land? Who knew how much livestock those *things* could eat, and how quickly? While he allowed it was unlikely that they'd be able to catch chickens, he worried about the cows. It hadn't taken the skinny woman much time to do in poor old Daisy. They agreed not to head off in different directions. They were going to stay together, whatever decision they made.

Eventually, George wore Martha down, the way he usually

did, by being more stubborn than her. They'd stay on the farm, keep within earshot of each other, shotguns close at hand.

He was glad he'd replaced Martha's old double-barreled shotgun, which she'd inherited from her mother, with a newer pump-action model. He'd bought it for her just after they'd seen *Terminator 2*.

"Just like an action hero," he'd said. And while she'd flushed with a mix of embarrassment and frustration at his absurdity, she never told him to take it back.

The next few days were quiet.

George was figuring out how to work the farm without electricity or gas, planning for the worst-case scenario. It wouldn't be easy, stepping back a hundred years; not at their age. They had a wood stove, but how much chopping would they be able to do? On the positive side, George figured he could safely skip this quarter's tax bill.

Three days after they'd buried the zombie and Daisy, Bob Ford pulled into their driveway. Martha had her shotgun at the ready, even though George argued that zombies couldn't drive cars.

"George, Martha? You there?" Bob called out in his querulous voice from next to the suburban, ready to jump back in at any sign of trouble.

"We're here, Bob," George replied.

"We were afraid they'd gotten you," Martha added.

"Nope, I'm fine. I thought the same about you two," Bob said as he stepped towards the house.

"Not yet, at least. Come on in," George said.

The electricity was still on, so they treated Bob to a hot cup of tea.

"They got the Wolfes in their beds, near as I can tell. Tore them apart," Bob told them.

George's heart sank. Howard and Judy Wolfe made the best pies in East Harrow. Not the politest of neighbors, but who deserved to get eaten?

"That's a real shame. Anyone else?" George asked.

"We think they got Annie Harwood. Nobody's seen her for two days," Bob said and took a sip of his tea.

Annie had been just sixteen. She was a smart kid, well-behaved, got good grades, and spent a lot of nights with a telescope. She usually won a prize for her astronomy notes at the County Fair. Probably, that was how they'd gotten her, when she was out alone at night, gazing up at the stars.

"Anybody selling ammunition or anything?" Martha wanted to know.

"There was a bit of a run on it a couple of days ago," Bob said, "but there's still some left. Andy Tritter's got five AK-47s that he's brought out of his barn, and he's charging people an arm and a leg for bullets and guns."

"Andy's been twitchy since he got back from Iraq. He's not causing trouble, is he?" Martha asked. There was motherly concern in her eyes.

"He might, once he figures out he can't eat his guns. Bob Keeler's keeping an eye on him."

Martha nodded.

"Do we have any idea how many of those things are out there?" George asked.

Bob just shook his head. "There's a lot. And we don't know how many more are coming. You'd be safer if you came into town."

George looked at Martha, then back at Bob.

"We're not leaving the farm."

Bob nodded. "There's a couple of people that're stubborn like you two. The gas station's dry, so you'd better hang on to what fuel you've got left."

Bob got up.

"Thanks for the tea."

"We going to see you again, Bob?" George asked.

"Don't know. I'm seeing who's still around."

George nodded.

"Well, thanks for coming out."

"You sure you won't reconsider coming into town?" Bob pleaded. "We could use your help."

"I'm not going to leave my cows," George said firmly.

Bob turned to Martha.

"You staying with this stubborn old fool?"

Martha's smile was sad.

"I won't leave George, no matter how pig-headed he's being."

George put his hand over hers and smiled.

"All right then." There was something in Bob's voice that sounded frightened, and that got to George. Bob had served in Korea. He never talked about it, but nothing seemed to shake him after he came back.

George stood and shook Bob's rough, honest hand.

"You two take care, then," Bob said as he turned to leave.

"You too, Bob."

Bob climbed back into his Suburban. It wasn't long before the sound of the car was lost in the distance. George felt alone, then. He went back to the porch and put his arm around Martha, and the two of them watched the vast empty expanse of sky above them.

The army of the dead came for them the next day.

The first one showed up around the middle of the afternoon. George noticed it shuffling along in the dead, stripped corn stalks, heading for the barn. He wondered if it was the heat or the lowing of the cows that attracted the dead things. He retrieved his shotgun, and warned Martha. Side by side, they headed for the stranger.

From a distance, he could have been anybody, but the jerky, unnatural walk made it clear he was dead. He'd been a businessman. Now his expensive suit was torn, and only one loafer remained on his shuffling feet. Like the skinny girl, his face was caked with a black, flaky layer of blood where he'd buried his head in something.

He smelled pretty bad, too.

George slammed a deer slug through his face, shattering it like an overripe pumpkin. The black, tarry substance was like nothing George had ever seen in a body before. Martha tugged at his sleeve. George turned, and saw more than a dozen dark figures shuffling out of the corn. One was a big guy in a leather jacket, another a middle-aged woman in mourning black, her torn and ruined face filled with metal piercings. He could see a naked couple with terrible wounds on their bodies, who looked like they'd been in the shower. Many wore business suits; others dragged the straggling remains of what they'd been wearing. None of them looked like Annie Harwood, and for that George thanked God.

He missed the head-shot on the guy in the leather jacket, but his follow-up took the lid right off the man's skull, showering the woman in black with a filthy goo that smelled worse than a chicken coop on a hot day.

After the first five went down, their bodies lying in pools of tarry black glop, George stopped thinking of them as people. The jerky walk and the putrescent liquid they had instead of organs made it clear these were no longer human beings.

It was easier to do the work after that.

They all walked with an eerie, jerky gait that made him think of a half-squashed spider. And they were deceptively fast, like a toddler when you weren't watching. While he was reloading, one popped up close to him. He should have seen it, but the zombie had been quiet, and his peripheral vision wasn't so good. He froze, shells dropping from his nerveless fingers.

The zombie's head vanished in a geyser of black, sticky tar that landed on his face. The bitter taste overwhelmed the metallic fear that was flooding his mouth. Martha just looked at him, nodded, then swiveled to take out another shambling, reaching form. He spat, trying not to retch, and wiped at his face. There was an itchy tingle where the evil-smelling fluid had landed on his skin. He hoped nothing bad would come of it.

Martha fired twice more, and then the yard was silent.

George fumbled a couple more shells into his shotgun, noting the way little red tubes were scattered over the yard, small satellites of the ugly pools of black sludge the dead left behind. Martha stood, strong like an oak tree, and racked another shell into the chamber.

More forms emerged from the corn. Six, then a dozen, then more. A flood of the shaking, twitching zombies attracted by the sound of gunfire.

"Back to the house." Martha said it low, but insistent.

They headed for the house as best they could, the dead too slow to follow closely. After slamming the solid oak door closed, he fumbled with the box of shells on the dining room table. After they had reloaded, he took the luxury of a moment to gaze at her. She was, and always had been, his rock. He took her hand and squeezed it. She squeezed his back. No words were necessary.

He took a deep breath and opened the front door. Jerky, slow-moving forms were pouring out of the tall, dead corn.

"We don't have enough ammunition." Martha let it out as a breath rather than words.

What would they do now? They could board up the house, and that might keep them off for a little while. The hundred and fifty-year-old farmhouse had solid, sturdy doors, but what were they going to do about the cows? He turned toward Martha, about to ask her a question, when she came up with one herself.

"Is there diesel in the combine?" she asked.

George felt a smile spread over his face.

"Fill your pocket with shells. We'll have to run for it," he said.

The longer they delayed, the harder it would be to get to the barn. Martha dumped shells into her coat pocket, spilling most of them on the floor. She knelt to pick them up, but he took her by the arm.

"We'll clean up *when* we get back." He didn't say *if.*

More than a hundred forms had emerged from the corn, making their slow way towards the barn. A couple of the leaders had come across their fallen companions, and nausea roiled up in his gut when he realized they were worrying the rotting corpses like dogs at a bone.

Still, it slowed them down enough that George and Martha made it to the barn, stopping only once to blow a hole in a blubbery man with a squashed face. Then Martha was watching his back as he opened the wide doors.

The combine still had the corn head on—eight long, wide prongs designed to channel the cornstalk and pop the ears off. Chains pushed the stripped ears into the feed throat. George didn't know if it would work on zombies, but it was sure as hell going to be a mess.

The combine roared to life like God clearing His throat.

George sat in the enclosed cabin, and Martha took up a station outside the protective glass. He didn't like her being exposed like that, but there wasn't anywhere for a passenger to sit in the tiny cabin.

The combine groaned and lurched into gear. Once clear of the barn, he swung it toward the corn field and the mass of the shuffling dead. From the cabin's height, he could see hundreds of forms moving through the ragged cornstalks. He raised the corn head to about five feet, and pushed down on the accelerator.

The smooth, round prongs neatly channeled the zombies like cornstalks waiting for harvest, and the chains ripped through rotten necks like they were made of wheat. A quick glance behind showed the combine vomiting chunky, black slurry onto the ground.

He imagined this was how guys in tanks felt, on top of the world, nearly invincible. He turned toward another cluster of the jerky forms, aiming straight for one that looked like a banker. Beside him, above the roar of the combine, he heard the explosion of Martha's shotgun going off. He'd missed a dead man in jeans and a black t-shirt over to the right, and she'd taken care of him.

The combine ground away, greedily stuffing more heads into the feed throat. George was sure he'd never want to eat food harvested by the machine again.

Over the racket, he heard Martha swear. He turned and saw a clawed hand tearing at the cuff of Martha's pants. One of them had gotten on the combine, and was climbing up the large farm machine, its snapping teeth ready to rend and tear. He stared at the struggle helplessly. The zombie was about to dig its teeth into Martha's leg when she wrenched away. A solid smash with the butt of the shotgun snapped the wrist at an unnatural angle. With a smooth efficiency, she reversed the shotgun, laying the muzzle directly on the thing's forehead. It looked up the barrel, apparently curious in the moment before the deer slug turned its head into sludge and bone shard soup.

The combine scythed through the massed dead. Heads snapped off, bodies were crushed under its wheels, and reeking sludge poured out the back. The ride and George's heady sense of invulnerability lasted almost until sunset, when the combine choked, and expired. By that time there wasn't anything else moving in the dim sunset.

They walked back to the house together, hand in hand, each cradling a shotgun in the other arm.

In the spring, East Harrow mourned their dead, burning them out of fear. Toby Monroe brought a pair of oxen to the Orne's farm and ploughed five acres on the promise of part of the yield.

As the green corn came up, George noticed a strange, crazily wandering trail where the crops didn't grow. He stared at it for a couple of minutes before realizing it ended at the dead hulk of the combine. The zombies' fetid bodies must have poisoned the ground where the black sludge had soaked in.

"Damn city-folk," he groused to Martha over dinner. "Not even good for fertilizer."

QUEEN ANNE'S LACE AND JUNIPER

George Orne and Harry Whitfield were chopping up a stump when George glimpsed movement out of the corner of his eye. Like everyone who'd survived the attack, George paid close attention to movement from unexpected quarters. A cluster of motorcycles crested the hill about a mile distant, on the only road that came to East Harrow. They were too far away to hear, but they were coming in fast.

"Harry, take your axe and get to the house. Tell Donna and Martha to get their shotguns."

"You're sixty-two, George. You going to fight them off yourself?"

"Do it, Harry."

Harry ran to the farmhouse.

George jammed his shovel into the dirt and leaned on it, watching the motorcycles approach. The summer sun beat on his back, and he was sweating freely. Even Vermont got hot in the summer. The job would have been a lot easier with a chainsaw and a pickup, but George didn't believe in worrying over what couldn't be changed.

Maybe the strangers were indicators of the resuscitation of civilization.

The throng vanished as the road dipped, then roared back into view. Eight or ten of them rounded the curve near the big oak tree. They were clad in black leather. He didn't see any with guns out. The apprehension that made his shoulders tight loosened just a hitch.

They cut their engines and coasted to a stop in front of him. Five had zombies in steel collars and restraining chains secured in their sidecars. Even so, the creatures strained to bite the booted legs of their drivers.

George didn't see any vehicles following, or anywhere they could hide a gas can. East Harrow wasn't near anywhere, and he wondered if the bikers would have enough gas to get back to home. Some of them might have been as old as forty. A couple, maybe three, were women. They shared a hard, quiet look, and who could blame them. A little less than two years ago, the world had gone insane. Nobody was as innocent as they had been.

"Holy fuck, it's Mister Greenjeans!" This from the youngest of the gang, a lean kid no older than eighteen.

Another, a woman, got off her bike and strode forward, the leather of her chaps and jacket creaking.

"Is Benny right, old man? You a farmer?"

"Yep."

She ran a hand through her close-cropped hair, a gesture that reminded him of his neighbor, Bob Ford. The thought of his departed friend made George scowl.

"They have trouble biting through leather." She seemed ill at ease.

"Sensible."

"And they can catch long hair."

"What's it like out there? We haven't heard much."

Several of them were off their bikes now, walking aimlessly along the cracked pavement. George kept an eye out and didn't let any get behind him. The spokeswoman shook her head.

"It's still a mess, nowhere is safe."

"You see anyone in Harrow when you came through?"

She shook her head again, and looked away.

George set his jaw and counted bikers, who were now off their hogs and stretching their legs. He came up with nine, then counted ten motorcycles. A fist closed in George's hair, and a gun muzzle was shoved under his jaw. The woman who'd spoken before strode forward.

"You really growing food?"

If they were trying to scare him, they'd failed. Too much had happened since an army of the dead had come through his cornfield. George wasn't going to panic just because someone had a gun on him. He glared at the woman.

"If you shoot me, you'll have no one to bring the crop in. You'll starve this winter."

"How fucking hard is it to farm?" This from the foul-mouthed teenager.

"The man's got a point, Hannah. We don't know shit about farming. Do you want to try to bring in his corn?" The voice came from behind George.

"Shut it, Oliver." And yet he could see the pensive look on her face. "Let's go to your house, Farmer Bob."

"I live alone."

"Then we'll have some privacy."

The rest of the bikers produced pistols. With Oliver's gun still stuck under his jaw, George led them back to the farmhouse. If he got his head blown off, they'd still get to the farmhouse and the women. He tried not to think about a Bonnie and Clyde massacre, or of the men taking turns raping Donna and Martha. They'd have to kill him before that happened.

Harry stood, back to the front door, shotgun in hand. George tried not to react to the man's stupidity.

"Let him go, get back on your bikes, and get out of here."

The gun was away from George's chin, and went off with a terrifying bang. The world was wrapped in cotton as the shotgun fell from Harry's nerveless fingers, and he fumbled for the spreading stain on his chest. He stumbled a few steps, then fell.

"You goddamn butchers!" George's voice was muffled after the gunshot.

Three pistols turned on him, and he knocked the closest one away.

"He's a useful farm hand. Who's going to do the work if he dies?" He glared at the teenager. "You? How about Hannah? If you want to eat, put your guns away and help me."

He felt the dangerous moment. These people were used to guns as an answer.

"Let him go." At Hannah's word, the pistols were back in their holsters.

George hustled up to Harry, who lay in a pool of blood. He

felt the pulse in Harry's neck, and heard a whistling whenever he made a spasmodic breath. He looked up to see Donna Whitfield and his wife Martha timidly opening the front door.

"Martha, get your sewing kit and some tweezers. And some matches."

For a moment, no one moved. Then Hannah nodded, and Martha vanished indoors. Harry squeezed George's hand. The strength was going out of him. What was taking Martha so long?

"Hold his hand, Donna." Harry's wife Donna was useless in a crisis, but someone should hold the man's hand. She surprised him. She pulled out a small paring knife, and knelt next to Harry. He tried to smile. Martha was suddenly at his side with her sewing kit, the three of them leaning over Harry on the big front porch. George lit a match with hands that trembled, held the tweezers over the flame. There was so much blood. Donna put the knife-handle between Harry's teeth, and gripped his hand.

"Sorry, Harry."

George stuck the tweezers into the bullet hole and felt around. It felt like ages before he felt the contact of metal on metal. Even then the thing was slippery. Blood covered everything, and Harry jerked and moaned through the knife every time George moved the tweezers. After an eternity, the bullet was out, and he dropped it to the floor. Martha shouldered him aside, the needle in her hand trailing thick quilting thread. She made quick work of sewing the wound closed. Then she made him dry-swallow some aspirin.

The bikers had been silent, watching this. Their expressions were sullen.

"Can we get him to his own bed?"

"Yeah."

George, Martha, and Donna managed to half-carry, half-walk Harry to his bed. A towel staunched the bleeding, and they laid him down. When he was as comfortable as they could make him, George and Martha left Donna to care for him.

Back downstairs, George wasn't surprised to see the bikers pigging down everything they found in Martha's kitchen.

Carrots, uncooked potatoes, unwashed spinach, even the raw eggs collected that morning. Desperate and hungry people did stupid things. If Harry recovered, George might find it in his heart to forgive them. Just because the world had gone mad was no reason to act like animals.

"Come on, Mr. Greenjeans. You and the missus are going to take us to meet your neighbors." Hannah wiped fragments of eggshell off her chin.

"George. You can call me George Orne, and my wife is Martha."

"All right, George. Time to tell your shit-kicking neighbors there's a new boss in town."

"We'll need to get a few things straight, first."

"I'm the one with the gun." She patted her midnight-black pistol for emphasis. The rest of her gang made similar gestures.

"And I'm the one who can grow food."

"I could shoot you right now."

"And you'd starve. There's no gas in town, and there wasn't a lot of food last winter. Kill me, and I guarantee that you'll all starve."

"I don't need this shit." Hannah's gun was out, and pointed dead at his left eye. George's heart raced, but he didn't move. He stared straight back at her.

Oliver walked up beside her.

"Listen to him, Hannah. We're in the middle of nowhere. No towns, so no zombies. He's growing his own food. If he's got neighbors, we could take charge and eat regularly again. Come on Hannah, let's not fuck up a good opportunity."

Her gun went down, up, then down again. George didn't move. She holstered her pistol.

"Sorry about your guy. You can't make an omelet without breaking some stuff."

"Be careful about which eggs you break. Go through too many and there won't be enough to do the farm work."

She grunted, and bit into a carrot.

Donna tended to Harry, but infection set in. Without any medical help there was little anyone could do besides listen to him scream himself hoarse. The screams turned to moans as his strength faded, and then to apologetic whispers. Finally, there was only Donna's weeping.

They burned Harry on a bier out in one of the fallow fields. Nobody knew what woke the hungry dead, but it didn't happen if the body was reduced to ash. Martha said a few words out of the Bible, and the small group that had gathered sang a few hymns as the fire lit up the evening. When it was all done, Donna scooped the ashes and bits of bone into an old plastic yogurt container.

The new bosses of East Harrow established themselves in four days. They took over the Titcombs' house, since it was large and empty. They staked a trio of zombies outside, and kept the others securely chained in the house with them. Fear tactics, George knew, to keep East Harrow cowed. The bikers swaggered around town, and often went into the woods to hunt. They liked their meat.

East Harrow had eight functional farms left. Only the Hendersons trained oxen, but they'd loaned teams out so everyone got their couple of acres ploughed, in exchange for a portion of their yield. They'd been damned lucky to find three old but usable ploughs lying forgotten in barns. The New Englanders' compulsive packratting had saved them. What they were going to do when those rusty old ploughs broke or wore out, George had no idea.

Two weeks later, Martha sat George down at the dinner table for a talk.

"We're not going to make it through the winter if they keep eating like this. And I mean if we all pull in most of our crops. If there's a black frost or a hail storm, those parasites are going to starve us all."

"They are hunting. Deer meat's pretty plentiful, even in the winter."

"The deer won't run out, but what about bullets? And have we seen any of the meat they've brought in, George Orne? They're ruining the Armstrongs' crop by making them cut and dress everything they shoot. They don't have time to tend to their fields the way they need to. If we're short food, do you think they'll go hungry?"

George had no reply.

"And what do you think about Benny? That boy's going to start looking for a pliable woman. And what happens if he doesn't find one that's interested?"

"All right. Yes, Martha, something needs to be done about them. And before you ask, no, I don't think talking will get us anywhere. I can only assume you have an idea."

"Nothing I'd ask you to do alone, and we can't tell anyone but Donna."

George looked at her closely.

"You want to poison them." He said it low, his voice nearly a whisper.

"Yes."

"Then we won't be any better than them. The world has changed, and the dead are walking, but that doesn't mean we turn on people just because we don't like them. There's got to be some way to get along with them. Something other than murder."

"You think on that, George Orne. You think about how much work it is to raise the food we have, and how much work they've done. You think about Harry Whitfield, and how much though they put into killing him.

"It's still murder, Martha."

"We'd need something fast and sure. If they realize what's happening, they'll kill us all. Cowbane should do it."

"*If* we can find some. And *if* we can get them all to eat it at the same time. We could serve it as parsnips and they wouldn't know the difference, but they're pretty picky about what they eat. If we serve them cowbane, how are we going to make sure they all eat it? It's too risky."

"Then how do we do it, George?"

He was about to retort that it was suicidal, that there was no way to get all of the bikers to eat a something poisonous at the same time, when an idea struck him. Frowning because he didn't like it, he tried to poke holes in it. He could find a few, but it was better than cowbane.

"You remember the week after we dragged all the zombies out of the corn field?"

Her eyes lit in recognition. "The circle of crows."

"None of them more than ten feet away from the pile."

"We don't know how many of them it didn't kill, but it's fast."

"We have to be certain." George realized he'd been talked around to Martha's side, yet again. All things considered, he was glad he'd married her.

"Then it's a good thing we've got some captive zombies to hand."

George had little to do but think as he and Martha made the walk to the old Titcomb place where the bikers kept house. The full buck moon was bright enough to cast shadows. Even so, the woods were dark but alive with the sounds of insects and the flicker of fireflies. Despite, or maybe because of the ugly work ahead, George wanted to take Martha's hand, but he couldn't push a wheelbarrow one-handed. It wore him more than he liked, and it would only be worse on the way back. George had shirked duty once in his life, but he'd never been afraid of hard work.

The moon's silver light gleamed off the mass of bikes parked on the lawn in front of the ghostly white house. They slowed down. They hadn't seen the house since the new tenants had moved in. It looked like a fraternity house. Shutters hung askew, and a few bottles littered the weedy front lawn. A chain rattled, and something scampered past them in the dark.

In the pale light, George could make out three chained zombies standing in the tall grass, silent and immobile as statues. They tried a quiet approach, but the things sensed them, and reaching fingers turned in their direction. George stopped to look at one of the dead things. At the very end of its lead, the zombie's clawed hands reached and bear-trap jaws snapped, ready to rend and tear. The lower half of this one's face was black and flaked with dried blood. It smelled awful, like a woodchuck corpse that had been left in the hot sun for a week. Its cataract-white eyes were empty, all consciousness, all individuality burned away by unfillable hunger. George had watched a zombie tear twenty pounds of meat off a blue-ribbon Guernsey. And yet, there was something sad in this one's slack-skinned expression, as if she missed her mother.

It strained at its metal collar. George wondered if he left it long enough, would it pop its own head off? Or would the stake work its way loose? The bikers were idiots for thinking they could keep something this dangerous as a watch dog.

"Martha, hand me the axe."

The axe was no longer than the dead woman's reach. George swung in a horizontal arc, the axe-head thunked into the dead neck just above the collar. She staggered, the axe stuck in its neck, wrenching handle slipped out of George's numbed fingers. The dead woman caught George's forearm. Muscles in its neck strained with the desire to tear into fresh meat. He pulled back, but the grip was too strong. Sharp fingernails dug into his flesh. George pulled with everything he had, but the grip would not budge. Panic rose in him. He would tire, and quickly. The dead flesh would not.

The macabre tug-of-war for his arm lasted until Martha stepped behind the thing, and swung for its neck with the edge of the shovel. With a metallic clank, the axe fell into the grass, the head lolling on a few strands of tough muscle and now-visible vertebrae. The grip weakened, and George jerked his arm free.

The zombie fell to the ground, arms flailing like a half-squashed spider. George stepped on its face with a heavy boot, and swung that axe clean through the neck. At last, the body lay quiet. Rank sludge oozed from the neck stump.

The two of them listened. There was no movement from the house. No motion on the outside either, except for chains that swayed as the zombies fought against them.

When he'd gotten his breath back, George grabbed the dead woman and half-dragged, half-slung the corpse into the wheelbarrow. Martha picked up the shovel and the axe, then threw the head into the wheelbarrow. It was a long five miles home, and they took turns pushing the body.

The next morning, George cut the meanest butcher hog away from the other pigs, and got it into its own pen. He wasn't as sure as he had been. A two-hundred-pound hog was a lot of food in the winter, as well as fat for soap. What if this didn't work?

He was going to say something, but Martha had already appeared by the sty's fence. She put the head in the feeding trough, and pulled her arm out of harms' way. The hog wandered over, and snuffled at the rotting face. After a moment, it started in on the face with a sound like a sloppy man gobbling down greasy ribs. George turned away, repulsed. Back in the fifties his cousin had been eaten by a farrow of pigs. He had no doubt it had sounded like this.

The pig screamed, the nerve-rending, human-like sound tearing the air like a siren. George turned to see the hog thrashing in the mud, letting out an endless squeal of agony. His guts churned. The pig's big red face was turning dark, its tongue protruding. Its eyes bulged, it choked and convulsed. And then it was still.

Martha stood, grim-faced, looking from the carcass to the half-eaten head. Long, quiet moments passed before she said anything.

"That wasn't much more than four mouthfuls." Her voice quavered.

George nodded his agreement, not yet trusting himself to speak. He loathed this business. But it was this or everyone would starve.

Two days later, George came back from his fields to find Oliver lounging at the dinner table.

"George."

"Oliver. We've got lettuce, chard, collards, summer squash, zucchini, cucumbers, and snow peas."

"Some of the boys are grumbling that there isn't any corn or onions yet."

"If they know of a way to alter time and speed up the harvest, let me know."

Oliver shrugged.

"Someone made off with one of our guardians. Know anything about it?"

"What do you mean 'made off with'?"

"We woke up and one of the chains was slack. Went out to find that black zombie stuff killing a hole in the yard."

George considered for a moment.

"I hope it wasn't a bear."

Oliver looked at him, the question unasked.

"I don't want to see what happens if one of those damn things bites a bear," George said.

"Hadn't thought of that. We'll move them into the house."

"Don't know if I could sleep with one of those things under the same roof as me."

"I've done a lot of things in the last two years I never thought I would." Oliver's distant tone said he wasn't proud of all of them. "Would you believe I used to be a dentist?"

"I wouldn't have thought you were a medical man."

Oliver looked at the floor.

"I got lucky and was out on the road when everything happened."

"So, you used this catastrophe to run around playing *Mad Max*?"

"I did what I had to survive. Hannah's a good leader, but she needs someone to show her the big picture. Without me, you'd be dead in your field, and we'd all starve this winter, so you may want to remember that."

George closed his eyes, imagining it. The world might have changed, but people hadn't. He opened his eyes to find Oliver glaring at him. George let him. After a few moments, Oliver's anger subsided.

"How are Martha and Donna?"

"As well as can be expected."

"I wanted to say hi."

"I wouldn't suggest it. Donna's still grieving for Harry."

"Right."

Oliver tilted his head, his neck making a series of disconcerting pops. With one hand, he rubbed at a white scar that peeked out from under his ratty shirt.

"What's that?"

Oliver's smile was lopsided and rueful.

"That's what convinced me I couldn't survive by myself."

"A zombie bite?"

Oliver eased the collar of his shirt open, and over his shoulder. A divot of flesh had been ripped from the base of his neck, and was now healed over with a gummy white scar.

"I didn't think anyone survived a bite from one of those things."

Oliver grimaced and covered his shoulder again.

"Sometimes it doesn't take. Don't know if that means I'm immune, or if I just got lucky, but I don't intend to risk it again."

Silence settled heavy between them, interrupted only by a tiny summer breeze. Oliver sniffed, turned his head, and sniffed again.

"Something smells good."

"Martha's cooking some herbs to put into sausages. Her special recipe."

Oliver's expression turned to a glower.

"You didn't mention sausages when I asked about food."

"They aren't done. And besides, you lot have plenty of venison." George folded thick arms across his chest.

"You holding out on us, George?"

George's impassive face could have been carved in stone. Oliver's glare had no more effect than if he'd tried to stare a hole in a granite cliff. He pulled an ugly snub revolver and aimed it at George's face.

"You know better than anyone that you'll starve if you do anything so damn stupid as pull that trigger," George said.

Behind Oliver, George caught movement. Oliver saw the glance and spun, pointing the revolver at Donna. She froze.

"How much work does she do?"

"Jesus, Oliver."

Donna's eyes were glued to the blunt muzzle of the gun. Oliver reached up with his thumb up and cocked the hammer back.

"Stop it," George said.

"Shut *up*. The only way this is going to work is if you are honest with us. You tell us all of the food you've got, and everybody gets enough."

George's heart thundered, his hands clenched with a rage he'd thought he was long past. Tears streamed down Donna's face, and her breath came in ragged sobs.

"We run this town, you got that, George?"

"Yes, Oliver. You run this town."

"Who's going to protect Donna if something happens to you? Who protects you from the zombies?"

"You and Hannah." George kept his voice low so Oliver wouldn't hear his simmering fury.

Oliver pointed the pistol at the ceiling and eased the hammer down.

"You're damn right we do." He turned to glare at George who did not meet his gaze. Donna ran to him, and he cradled her as she wept. His chest was tight. George stroked her hair, keeping his breathing slow and regular.

"We'll be expecting those sausages."

"Yes, of course."

"On a platter. Two days from now."

"Martha and I will serve them up if you like."

Oliver's smile was hard.

"That's more like it."

And then he was out the door, vegetables forgotten. George stood, holding Donna to him, waiting for the tightness in his chest to ease. After some time, he could breathe again. He stroked Donna's hair, calming her as best he could.

Martha's plan was working. Please, George whispered a prayer. Let it all work.

George, Donna, and Martha had a council of war over vegetable soup that night.

"Oliver was a dentist. I think he would be a great asset."

"He's been with that Hannah woman too long," Martha said.

"We're none of us the same as we were two years ago. But that doesn't mean he can't change. We need someone who hasn't just read medicine out of a book. The Landry girls are going to grow up and what then? What happens if we get Lyme disease, or eat pork that's gone bad? What if Donna remarries and has kids?"

"And you want a dentist to deliver her children?"

"You got any better ideas? Reach in, tie a rope around the kid's legs and pull her out like she's a calf?"

Martha subsided, chewing her stewed vegetables with a vengeance.

"He shot Harry." Donna said it quietly, but George had no argument.

"Donna, I don't think you should be with us when we go to serve them. There's too many men who haven't known a woman for some time. Some of them might get ideas."

"I'm part of this household. And Oliver was right, how much work do I do around the farm?"

"We didn't want to intrude on your grief." Martha said it with gentle sympathy, laying a knotted hand on Donna's.

"I'm through with mourning what can't be changed. I want to be part of this."

"You want revenge," George said.

Martha pursed her lips, and Donna gave him a hard look.

"Is there anything wrong with that, George Orne?" Martha wasn't asking a question, she was issuing a challenge.

"Plenty."

"Are you going to tell me you're in this for better reasons than us?"

"What if they want us to taste-test the sausages?" George asked.

"Are you saying you have courage that Donna doesn't? You dodged the Viet-Nam draft. Are you so sure of yourself now?"

George pursed his lips and put his fork down.

"This is different. They're a threat to us."

"Yes. To all of us," Donna said. She tapped a small paring knife on the table. George could see Harry's teeth-marks in the wooden handle.

He couldn't remember the last time he'd talked Martha out of something she'd set her mind to. He didn't want to admit that he wanted her with him. But Donna... . He didn't want to put her at risk. Harry was dead. Revenge wouldn't bring him back. He didn't want her to live with the memory of the bikers choking, their mouths gaping as they convulsed on the floor, the way the pig had. And that was if they succeeded. If it went wrong, East Harrow would need Donna more than a pair of old and worn-down farmers.

"It's my idea. If anyone says who can participate, it's me." Martha was at her most imperious now. "The more of us there, the better."

"I don't want her to be there if there's a problem."

George and Martha turned to Donna. She said nothing, thinking it over. George started to say something, but Martha laid her hand on his.

"I want to go." Donna's voice was small, but there was steel in it. "Three is better than two if it goes wrong."

George nodded in defeat.

The bikers' house was a rookery. They'd carved their names through the pleasant, flowery wallpaper, and into the plaster underneath. Pieces of metal junk, as well as shattered bits of undesired furniture littered the entrance hall. The carpet on the stairs was torn, and tracked with mud. It pained George to see it this way. The Titcombs had been good people. A little stuffy like city transplants could be, and they'd sometimes complained about farm smells. George put those memories aside. He didn't want to think unkindly of anyone who had been eaten.

He nearly dropped what he was carrying when he saw the zombies in the living room. Attached neck and arm to the walls by chains with no play, they snapped as he went past.

Most of the bikers lounged around the house, waiting for their meal, but Oliver offered whatever help he could. Martha shooed him away from the stove, afraid he'd try to snitch a sausage. Unwilling to have him work with Donna, George got him to setting the table. The dishes were dirty and greasy, but the bikers didn't seem to mind.

"What's the point of keeping the zombies? I don't know if I could even eat with them in the next room."

"You never know. Some of you lot might get it into your

heads that we aren't doing our jobs, and come for us. We've rigged up a spring-release, so we can set them free if necessary." Oliver didn't need to complete the threat.

Soon the smell of the bitter sausage meat layered with sharp pine permeated the cooking area.

"What's in them?"

"That's Queen Anne's lace and juniper. It overpowers any rank taste in the meat. I'm sure you understand." George flushed. It wasn't a lie, but the question alarmed him. Was Oliver on to them?

"Sounds about right."

Donna was having some trouble cutting up the squash with her trembling hands. Martha stoked the stove with a long iron poker, and turned her attention back to grilling the fatal sausages. With a hot flash, George realized they didn't know if the zombie meat killed after it had been cooked. He closed his eyes, then opened them again. Nothing he could do about it now.

In no time, the places were set, and the bikers sat at the table. George brought out a steaming bowl of hot squash, but it was ignored. He returned to the kitchen just as Martha finished placing the last sausage on the platter.

They looked at each other across the platter, the pile of deadly sausages between them. She gave him a brief, grim smile, and he turned to go to the dining room.

Oliver met him at the door between the dining room and the kitchen. He blocked George's way, and took the platter from his hands.

"Don't eat them." George breathed it.

Oliver started at him for a moment, face blank in surprise. He glanced down at the zombie-meat sausages. George's heart thundered. Had he just betrayed and killed the entire town? Oliver started to ask something, but his eyes went to his comrades, waiting at the table. George silently begged him not to betray them.

"Come on you fucking dickhead, you going to hog all those sausages or what?" Benny's voice cut across the silence like the snarl of a motorcycle.

With a last, unreadable look, Oliver turned away, the platter of poisoned meat in his hands. He approached the table slowly, then put the steaming pile of meat in front of Hannah. Even as he set it down, hands grabbed the sausages, and they were being gobbled down.

One tension merely gave way to another as George waited for an eternity, watching the bikers stuff themselves with zombie meat. Each of them carried a gun at shoulder or hip. Would they try to shoot? Would the convulsions come on fast enough? Were the sausages even poisonous?

Hannah looked up at him, her eyes bulging, her mouth no longer chewing. She knew. George went rigid. Hannah continued to stare at him, wide-eyed, her jaw slack as a wad of meat fell out of her mouth. She made a choking sound, more animal than human.

The other bikers were choking. Some of them tried to spit out what they had just wolfed down. And then there was a chaos as they thrashed convulsively. They fell out of chairs, spasming and contorting, their limbs twisting into unnatural and frightening configurations. Oliver stood in front of them, his back rigid.

Hannah's hands twitched and shook so much that her attempt to reach a gun left her fumbling. They were all gasping for breath. Lips and then faces turned a cyanotic blue and then a terrible black. George stared at his appalling work, his guts in knots. What had he become?

Quiet as a shadow, Donna darted around George. He reached for her, but she had already buried the knife up to its wooden handle in Oliver's neck. George could see Harry's bite-mark in the handle for an instant before it was covered with a red welter of blood.

Oliver's hands were on his neck, blood spurting rhythmically from between his fingers. George had Donna by the arm and was pulling her away. Oliver did not go for his gun. He staggered to a wall, and turned. George saw the betrayal in his eyes. The floor was slick with blood.

Oliver found a switch on the wall, and slammed his palm into it with the last of his strength.

George turned as he heard the rattle of chains. The zombies

were free. Denied their hunger for so long, they reached for George and Donna.

Shoving Donna behind him, George grabbed a plate and smashed it into the face of the closest zombie. It didn't react. He fell back, scrabbling to find a weapon.

Martha emerged from the kitchen, the tip of the poker she carried a dull red. A large zombie dressed in the remains of a police uniform turned toward her. Without hesitation, she drove the hot poker through its eye. The thing fell.

Fingers scrabbled at George's ankle. Benny wasn't dead yet, but his agonized contortions kept him from getting a grip on George's ankle. George lost his balance and fell. Cold fingers seized his arm, and this time there was no restraining collar. Dull teeth driven by hideous strength dug into his forearm.

With a sound like a smashed cantaloupe, the zombie's head exploded in a welter of black disgusting filth. Donna stood over him like an avenging angel, a baseball bat clutched in her white-knuckled hands.

Two dead men remained. Donna charged, shrieking as she ran. A swing shattered the forearms of one zombie. It tried to grasp at her anyway, but a swing worthy of Henry Aaron smashed its eggshell skull. As it fell, Donna whirled to face the next one. She swung low, and the bat broke the shambling creature's knee with a crisp snap like a green branch. It fell, and Donna was on it, stepping on its hands, great overhead hits smashing its torso. Black muck seeped from fissures in its skin. Donna screamed with every strike now. She beat its shoulders into shapeless lumps. When its rib cage was a leaking and liquid ruin, she hammered the skull. Bone shards and black tar exploded onto the wall, leaving a splash pattern like a shotgun suicide.

At last done, she straightened, breathing hard, and looked back at George. Without a word, he held up his bloody, bitten forearm.

Oliver hadn't been turned by his bite. Maybe this one wouldn't take, either. He stared at his arm where the teeth had penetrated his skin. It throbbed as if he'd burned it. Tears leaked from his closed eyes. He couldn't bear to look at Martha.

"Someone get a gun." His voice was hoarse. "Just to be safe."

Fcky borfy stmy!
have fun!

CHAMPAGNE

It started, for me anyway, with organic milk. Most people seem to find it better-tasting. I find it bland. Dull. I'm naturally curious, so I tried to figure out what made non-organic milk, the stuff that's not supposed to be good for you, taste better.

I found out that cows that are treated with rBGH have a high incidence of mastitis, or udder inflammation, which causes open sores in the udders. So, the difference I was missing was cow pus. I'd call the taste sweet, but it's not. It's just very appealing, rich-tasting. And don't give me that look—you probably drink that bitter muck you call coffee.

Once I got over myself, and I will admit to a bit of self-loathing at the beginning, I sat back and wondered—well, where do I go from here? And then I started looking on the Internet. It turns out there's a small but quite dynamic group of pus aficionados. They encouraged me to accept my particular quirk, told me how to be careful and not get caught licking some random guy's pustule on a bus.

That group—no I'm not going to tell you where to find them. If you really want to find us, you will. Anyway, our little circle of like-minded people is a delight, and a real help to someone with my particular dietary interest. I no longer felt like I was alone. Turns out there have been pus-drinkers for a very long time. You know how some people rave about a hundred-year-old port, or that coffee they make from beans picked out of Civet shit? Well, the pus from different sources tastes different. Some of it is sharper, others more mellow. Occasionally, it has a sort of nutty flavor to it. It's a fascinating mix of species and body chemistry, and also what the neutrophils have been attacking. Each disease or infection has a slightly different taste, almost like the ethereal waft of a wine cork.

I stay with humans. They're easier to access than most forms of livestock, since I live in a city. I once fellated a homeless man for the walnut-sized pocket of smegma that had accumulated under his foreskin. What a thrill—the gooey and slightly chunky yellowish fluid filling my mouth. I still don't know what cocktail of diseases the guy had, but what it produced was just so right.

Of course, you can only go so long on the regular stuff, right? Like a lot of people, I got bored with what I could get, and went out looking for the exotic. *P. aeruginosa* infections cause blue discharge, which doesn't taste different, but there are just some things you have to experience for yourself.

The brown pus you get when someone has liver flukes is a bit more gamey than the usual infection seepage. The best analogy I can think of is the difference between actual cheddar cheese and Velveeta. One has a more complex character to it. But my palette is sensitive; you probably wouldn't be able to tell the difference.

Everyone has a yen for what they cannot have. Plunk them down in a Garden of Eden and tell them they can have anything but the apple, and you know damn well that apple's going to turn up missing one day.

Of course, the Internet group talked about what they'd had, and their best finds. Everyone over fifty agreed that the best vintage was something that hadn't been around for thirty years.

Variola. Smallpox. Champagne, they called it.

I'm sure that there was an element of nostalgia involved—you don't have a drink for thirty years, and it either fades from memory, or becomes the best thing you can remember tasting. I tried to put it out of my mind. Some things are best left undone.

And yet, I couldn't stop thinking about it. I'd be doing something, like drinking a McDonald's milkshake, and the desire for *Variola* pus would leap on me like an angry cat. What was it like? Smooth and creamy, they said, with an exotic flavor unlike anything else. My other activities seemed bland. I kept waiting for this notion to go away, but it didn't. Eventually, I had to act.

I'm not going to tell you how I managed to get my sample.

Let's say that while money can't buy everything, it can make life easier. It took time and patience and planning, but in the end, I got my sample.

Nor is it difficult to find and secure someone that no one will miss. It's depressingly easy.

I didn't think of them as people, they were the dregs of humanity, the most repulsive individuals I could find. The sort who make the world a brighter place with their absence.

I spent a few weeks in an isolated room watching, once the pustules appeared on the palms and soles of her feet, I knew I'd gotten my hands on the real deal. You can't imagine my excitement. I was watching someone develop a disease that hadn't been seen since 1978.

I was almost giddy as the pustules rose on my victim's skin, as I realized why they called it champagne. Blisters rose on every conceivable surface, until the body looked like it had been boiled. It would be a lot of work to get all the pus from each of these little containers. And yet, as I watched, my ambition grew. Now that I had the means within my grasp, I would not be satisfied with just champagne. I wanted the Dom Perignon.

I disposed of the body carefully and thoroughly. No sense in causing a smallpox outbreak just because I've got a little twitch in my palate. So, I procured another victim. The same result—the raised welts, discreet pustules. Medical articles do not tell you how to produce a specific effect or infection. It was going to be a case of trial and error. And so went my third, with familiar and ordinary pustules. My thirst was quiet now, and I was focused. Nothing would stop me, all I needed was time.

My patience was rewarded on my fourth try; a confluent infection. I'm not ashamed to admit that I did a little dance when I saw the small red rings on the woman's skin did not rise into pustules. Instead of forming discreet, individual blisters on the surface of the skin, confluent smallpox pustules erupt inward. They would grow thickly, and eventually burst, forming a layer of pus just below the skin. Given time, entire sections of skin would slough off, followed by a draining rush of glorious pus. Confluent smallpox pus was abundant and easy to get to. I just had to pick a time.

I touched her skin. It was unnaturally, velvety soft. She was ready.

I had considered drilling a hole in her belly and just sucking the delightful liquor out through a straw like she was a giant milkshake. But the taste of the plastic straw would interfere with a unique and refined experience.

I ran a scalpel down the taut skin in her back, and the skin ruptured, dumping more than a quart of viscid, yellowish fluid into the trough I had prepared. From there, it dribbled, heightening my sense of anticipation, into a glass pitcher.

I held myself back until it was all in the pitcher, but the smell was driving me mad. The bouquet was powerful, and unique. I poured myself some, admiring the thick liquid. It was primarily dead neutrophils, rather than the oily suspension fluid, and surprisingly pure. I swirled it, took in its texture. Without chunks or inclusions swished easily in the pitcher, and I trembled with anticipation.

It was the moment of my life to put the glass to my lips. The first taste confirmed what the old-timers had said. It was utterly unique, with a heavenly taste. I did not gorge myself, but rather made a day of it, sipping my treasure when the last aftertaste of the previous sip was gone. Some pus is meant to be savored.

CAPTAINS OF INDUSTRY

Boston, Massachusetts, United States, 1921

The strikebreakers formed a grim skirmish line opposite the strikers. Whatever the color of their greatcoats, they looked grey against the gently-falling Boston snow. Among the union men, an uneasy current of conversation sprang up, muffled by fear and snow. They held the bottleneck, the defensive ground just inside the black, wrought-iron gates of Emerson's washing machine factory. To break the line, or even get to the factory, the strikebreakers would have to smash their way through the striking workers.

"Come away." Dimitri's insistent hands plucked ineffectually at the threadbare cuffs of János's woolen overcoat. "The strike is over."

János looked down at the narrow shape at his elbow. Dimitri's mouth was full of rotten teeth, and his small, delicate hands would not be much use in the battle with the strikebreakers. The pipestem Russian read books aloud on the factory floor, to keep the workers somewhat entertained. He had been a good friend to János, even if their countries had fought in the last war. There was something somehow refined about the small Russian, but János couldn't say how the impression had wormed its way into his brain. While Dimitri had been a great supporter of the union and the strike, the fight with the strikebreakers was not going to be something he should be involved in. János placed a powerful, calloused hand on the Russian's smaller one in a gesture meant to reassure his fellow striker.

"I owe it to the union. But you should go."

"Little brother, they are the Pinkertons. They had coal miners hanged in Pennsylvania, and burned women and children who were hiding from their machine gun bullets in Colorado." His clutch on János's coat was hard with desperate strength. János watched the easy, familiar way that the strikebreakers held their long truncheons.

"It is 1921. Emerson cannot simply hire a gang of thugs to beat us into submission in the streets." János knew how hollow his words sounded.

"You will get your head knocked in." Dimitri's voice was hard and angry, but it did not make him any less right. The Agency men weren't here just to break the strike, they were here to break heads. Where anger had failed, Dimitri began to wheedle. "Who will look after your wife and beautiful baby?"

János's face clouded, and he gave the little man a hard shove.

"Run while you can, Dimitri. This will get bad."

The small Russian gave János a hard glare, and stalked into the crowd. He was lost to sight almost instantly. János hoped that he would find some way to escape the fight that was about to break out.

Looking looked around for a weapon, he found only a stick of wood. There were too many other men around him who were unarmed, so he passed even this impromptu weapon on to Josef Berger, who was young enough not to have been in the war. János would get a Pinkerton thug's truncheon, and then they would see what was what. He had built hard muscles and broad shoulders working on his farm before coming to America to labor in Emerson's washing machine factory. And he had been a soldier in the Imperial army during the war. Now he would put that strength to a use other than building Edward Emerson's fortune.

The strikers milled around in nervous contrast to the Agency's calm, hard line. János knew what was going to happen—he'd seen enough green troops in the Great War to know that the experienced thugs were going to smash the disorganized workers.

The union leader, Antonio Petricelli, had not been in the war. He was young and well spoken, a born organizer and good with people, despite being Italian. It was strange, János reflected, the way the sides had drawn up. János had fought the Italians in the Isonzo valley, and had been their prisoner. And now here he was, thousands of miles away in America, fighting under an Italian union leader alongside Poles, Irishmen, Russians, and even other Hungarians, against Americans.

Out of the corner of his eye, János saw Antonio remove his glasses and place them in his breast pocket, a gesture that meant that he was about to give a speech. Sheer incredulity made János pause as Antonio stepped out of the crowd into the empty no-man's land between the strikers and the strikebreakers.

"The time for negotiation is well past." Dimitri had reappeared at János's elbow. "They will not be listening to reason."

"We have no weapons!" Antonio shouted. "This is a peaceful strike. All that we want is fair pay for a day's work, which we have not been allowed. Edward Emerson is wealthy and wants for nothing, and yet we live in squalor. Nothing else do we—" Antonio's speech was cut off when a well-aimed street cobble impacted heavily into a grey-coated Agency man, who crumpled into the dirty snow.

János dusted his hands off with a certain amount of grim satisfaction. Antonio finally seemed to grasp that this was not a situation for talking. To his credit, he did not flee in the face of the enemy, but actually turned his back on the massed strikebreakers, and walked back to the picketers' line. There was a moment of watchful calm after this. The only motion the snow falling gently between the lines.

At some unheard signal, the Agency line charged, ploughing into the ragged ranks of the workers. Everywhere people were running and screaming, some trying to get away from the Agency's truncheons, others pushing toward them. To János, it was the fourth battle of Isonzo all over again. Later, he could remember only small moments, such as wrenching a truncheon out of an Agency thug's hand and backhanding him with it. The man went down, spitting blood and teeth into the wet mush underfoot.

He caught a glimpse of Dimitri amid the shoving panic, stepping back from a grey-coated form, a bloody knife in his hand and a razor-thin rictus of triumph on his face. He stumbled across a knot of three grey-coated figures hammering at Antonio, who cowered on the ground, covering his head with his arms. The three attackers didn't see János until his stolen billy club snapped one of their wrists. The subsequent scuffle was brief but intense, leaving János alone over the cowering form of the Italian. Antonio was bleeding from several cuts to his face, his hands were bruised black as a coal miner's, and several of his fingers pointed in unnatural angles. János set Antonio's limp form across his shoulders, the way he had learned to carry a fellow soldier.

Burdened with the unresponsive union leader, János bulled his way through the shrieking, shoving mass of bodies. More and more union men were fleeing the Agency's merciless onslaught. The strike was truly broken now. How long the death throes would take depended on the determination of individual strikers, and how long the conquering forces cared to break heads.

Someone was thrown against János's legs and he stumbled, Antonio's weight keeping him slightly off balance. He reached out and steadied himself on the factory's iron fence. The fight was behind him. Before him were only those who were running. He felt drained and cold, and he ached from unremembered blows. He fell in with the fleeing current of workers, somewhat slowed by their leader.

He caught a glimpse of Mr. Emerson himself, surrounded by a cloud of managers and yes-men, their fine coats making them look like a parliament of great, black birds. János gave them the briefest of glances—staring would only draw their attention.

After seven blocks, János was breathing hard. He turned into an alley and put the Italian down as gently as he could manage. The Agency men showed no inclination to pursue, apparently satisfied with smashing the strike. János leaned against the soot-blackened brick of the alley, his arms, ribs, and head aching from blows and the frigid November cold. Bruises visibly darkened on Antonio's face as he panted for breath. The union leader groaned, touching a lump above his left ear, then stared at fingers that came away bloody. Quickly wiping his fingers in the dirty snow, the Italian struggled to his feet, learning heavily against the brick wall.

"How did it go, János?" Antonio's voice was strained and ragged.

"They broke us, Antonio. People ran." The Italian nodded, wincing as he did so.

"The strike is broken, but the union is not. Return to work tomorrow, János, and let them know." János nodded and turned away, but the Italian grabbed his coat. "They have to know. We must keep their hope strong. You must be the strong back of the union, János."

Antonio pushed off from the wall and stood on his own feet a trifle unsteadily. János reached out to assist, but Antonio knocked his hand away. He took a few steps and, gaining confidence in his own strength, strode out of the alley, leaving János alone to consider the price of pride. With Antonio gone, he leaned against the wall himself, cold, aching, and now alone. The snow was falling more thickly, and there was nothing for him to do but go home.

János could hear his daughter's wails echoing down the hall of the tenement building. He opened the door to their small apartment knowing what he would see. Anna-Maria huddled on the couch, pale and small under an inadequate quilt, her beautiful eyes red-rimmed from lack of sleep, failing to quiet their screaming child. Her face was thin, the bones sharp under skin stretched too tight. To see her weak and frail like this was like a knife in his chest. Anna-Maria had been so full of life, so loving, so joyful. Birth had not been kind to her, and even afterward, Elizabeth had been a great strain. If they had been in the old country, her parents or his aunts could have helped. Although people like Dimitri and the widow Beattyrzek upstairs lent a hand when they could, they were not family. János's heart ached. He should never have left her, should never have gone to the strike. And yet, if he did not bring home money, how would they eat? How would she keep up her strength?

"She keeps choking." Nearly in tears, Anna-Maria spoke Magyar.

"English, Anna-Maria, speak in English. Do you want our daughter to grow up speaking Hungarian in America?"

She gave him a venomous look, and thrust the squalling Elizabeth at him, who shrieked as if she were being dangled above coals. Dimitri's comment about his beautiful daughter cut at János as he looked at his daughter's face. Little Elizabeth's upper lip split like a rabbit's, the fissure running back into her mouth, so Anna-Maria had to be very careful when she nursed. Little Elizabeth often choked, and often did not get all the milk she wanted. Crying was the only way she could make her displeasure known, and she did so constantly.

"Stop her," was all that Anna-Maria said. When the shrieking babe was safely in János's grip, she rose from the couch, wrapped her blanket around her, and stalked into their small bedroom, slamming the door. She could not sleep when the baby cried, and somehow, Elizabeth would only calm down for her father.

János held his small, fragile daughter in aching arms bruised by truncheon and cold. Her little head fit into his palm. Tiny fingers grasped his forefinger, and tried to move his finger to her mouth, wailing for comfort. With great tenderness, János found another blanket to wrap her in, mindful of the apartment's chill, and snuggled her to the warmth of his chest.

He sang softly and rocked her gently. He did not sing the songs he knew from the old country, the songs of his childhood. For him these conjured up memories of the war, the prison camp, and fleeing Béla Klun's Communist thugs. Hungary was of the past now, and America was the future. He sang his small store of hard-learned American songs of American dreams, letting his deep, powerful voice soothe her. By the time he was through 'The Big Rock Candy Mountain' she had stopped crying. When he looked down, she returned his gaze with expectant, sleepy eyes.

She was the reason for the strike, to make life better for Elizabeth. She would grow up speaking English, and not stumble on American words like he did. America was a land of great opportunity, but she did not promote her adopted children if they did not speak good English. Elizabeth would go to school and she would not have to work in the woolen mills. She would get a good job, maybe even at a university. He had failed her today. If he had been stronger, he could have held the Pinkertons back, and forced Emerson to bargain to have the factory open again. He could have saved the extra money to send her to a good school.

By the time he had finished 'Wabash Cannonball' she was asleep, heedless of the tears that silently flowed down her father's face.

In the following week, work slowly settled back to normal at Emerson's washing machine factory. The supervisors were more spiteful and demanding, and quotas were increased to make up for lost time. Despite this, it was in many ways a relief to get back to work. János no longer had to worry about what Emerson was going to do next—the owner considered that he had won. Like a sated wolf, Emerson would wait a little while longer before trying to wring more money out of this factory. János surreptitiously passed the union signal around the factory, a clenched fist held at stomach height, and got many responses. Antonio had been correct—the strike was broken, but not the union.

Two weeks passed between the morning of violence and the next union meeting. János took the precautions Antonio had said to, by making sure that no one followed him. This meeting was supposed to be only of the trusted inner circle, those whose dedication to the cause was beyond question. They met in a small cellar, with only one way in or out, and everyone had to be identified by the two door guards before they were let in.

"—not pleased with you, Mr. Petricelli." Nikolas Theonotos was already complaining when János came through the door. He was a big Greek with piggy, untrustworthy eyes who always had something to gripe about. He seemed to think that he deserved to run the union, even if he couldn't read a word English. "How is it that Emerson was able to hire Pinkerton thugs?"

The bruising on Antonio's face was fading to green, making mottled patterns that shifted in the muted light. Nikolas, by contrast, seemed to have escaped the battle unscathed.

"I don't know." Petricelli was deadly calm. His hand gestures were easy to follow in the dark because of the white gauze that enveloped one hand. "If I had known we were going face them, I would not have insisted that we strike unarmed."

"It is not like Emerson to spend so much money." Dimitri was abruptly at János's elbow.

"I agree," Antonio let out a tired sigh. "Emerson has never used professional strikebreakers before, at either of his factories. I don't understand why he has done so now."

The crowd mulled that over with some dark mutterings.

"Something has changed with him. And we need to find out what before he again applies his new-found iron heels of tyranny and destroys the glorious dawn of the workers' era."

János shook his head. Antonio was a fine man and a good speaker until he started talking about the workers' revolution. Dimitri just pursed his lips and looked away.

"What I will need is a pair of volunteers to follow Emerson. We need to find out if he has any new friends or associates. I would do so myself, but I fear that the Agency knows my face. The union will, of course, compensate the volunteer for their time."

"János and I will take this duty." Dimitri was quick to take advantage of the offer.

"We will?" János had been thinking of Anna-Maria and Elizabeth. Although the union was supposed to make their future better, he begrudged the time he had to spend away from them. His wife was growing more short-tempered every day, and János worried about her even as his helplessness frustrated him. What could he do?

"We will," Dimitri was definite.

"Are you sure, János?" Antonio's gaze was penetrating, even through his glasses.

János considered carefully. He wasn't sure what Dimitri had in mind, but he recognized the crafty look on Dimitri's face. Spying on Emerson sounded dangerous, and yet, Dimitri had never led him wrong.

"Yes, Dimitri and I shall follow Emerson."

That brought a rude snort from Nikolas, who had likely wanted the extra money for himself. With seven children at home, he was usually quite happy to stay out late. Several other members of the crowd made their own disgruntled noises, but none seemed to want to say anything directly to János or Dimitri.

Outside the meeting, Boston's bitter winter wind cut at János's exposed flesh. He hunched his shoulders and thrust his hands as deeply into his pockets as he could. Dimitri pulled on fingerless wool gloves, falling into step beside his friend.

"I will not do anything criminal, Dimitri."

"Dietrich is still in the hospital with a broken arm, Donovan may never walk again, and Pavel still can't use his right hand. Was *that* criminal?" Dimitri did not look at the larger man walking beside him, remaining inscrutable as they passed through shadows.

"If we act illegally, we are no better than the Pinkertons."

"The rich have made the laws, little brother." János had never heard Dimitri speak so bluntly about class struggle before. "Big bosses run this country, the same as any other, and they make police no better than thugs."

"Which is why we cannot afford to have any illegal activity associated with the union. Do you remember when Gustav came to the meeting smelling of pilsner? Antonio pitched him out on his ear! We conduct the union according to law, and so we do not invite a Palmer raid." Dimitri's refusal to look at him was beginning to grate on János. He was confused and becoming more frightened. Dimitri was a friend, it was true, but he was Russian, and how far could he truly trust a Russian?

János instantly regretted the thought. Dimitri was a good friend. He had left Elizabeth in the Russian's care more than once. And yet, he was not at all happy with being volunteered as a spy.

They did not speak as each paid their nickel and stepped onto a streetcar. It wasn't much warmer, but at least they were out of the wind. The silence between them was broken only by the rumble of wheels and the noise of the city as it passed them by.

"Why is it that men everywhere fear their government?" Dimitri's voice was soft, only carrying to János. "Even America, with her government 'by the people and for the people', men are afraid of attracting the government's attention." The lean Russian's eyes focused on something far away. Sometimes, János wondered if Dimitri truly believed that his ideas could change the world.

János huddled closer under his coat and said nothing. Dimitri had dared to vote against Harding just last year. The very thought of such interference with the workings of the government frightened him. Who was he to choose the next President, and what would be the reprisal if the President learned that Dimitri had voted against him? No, it was better not to vote.

"You worry too much little brother." The Russian did not smile, but mischief danced in his eyes. "I will follow Emerson and find out who his new friends are. You go home to your beautiful Anna-Maria and Elizabeth. They need you more than the union does."

János looked at his friend. Clearly, this was not all that Dimitri had planned.

"Then why did you volunteer the two of us?"

"So that you could find someone to watch Elizabeth and take your beautiful wife out for a night on the town. Not meaning to offend, but I can't think of anyone who is less suited to watching someone unobserved than you are."

János's started to get angry, but it melted away like ice on a hot day. While he had never shirked an honest day's labor in his life, even he had to agree that he was simply not built to be lost in a crowd, or even a medium-sized shadow. But taking money—especially the union's money—for something he wasn't going to do felt wrong.

Dimitri, sensing his turmoil, placed a small, clever hand on János's cuff as a gesture of reassurance.

"Little brother, there are things some men are made to do. You can lift washing machines into their crates all by yourself, something I will never be able to do, no matter how long I tried."

"I don't need your charity, Dimitri."

"Of course not. But you would not turn down a raise in pay if it were offered to you, would you?"

"As if it would be," János muttered darkly.

Dimitri gripped János's cuff in a surprisingly tender gesture. "It will be all right, János," Dimitri's voice was low, but intense. "I promise that it will be all right. I will do the spying. Go home to your beautiful Elizabeth and Anna-Maria."

János had nothing to say to that. Outside the windows of the streetcar, Boston's city lights slowly passed them by.

For the rest of November and into early December, János saw little of his Russian friend after work. Dimitri read aloud in the factory's din as always, keeping the workers from utter boredom. But when the whistle blew and the shift got out, he was never anywhere to be found. János worried that he had offended Dimitri. It was not like his friend to be so absent. He breathed small sighs of relief every morning when Dimitri walked through the factory gates.

It was the third of December before the union called another secret meeting. Again, the location was a small, cold basement, and two guards outside made sure no outsiders entered the room. By the time János arrived, the room was thick with smoke, and Dimitri was standing on the table.

"Emerson has joined a bourgeois pseudo Masonic group calling themselves the 'Hermetic Order of the Silver Twilight'. Truly it is just another drinking club for men, but these are the powerful overlords of this city: Deputy Mayor Daniel Parker, Chief of Police Elias Bicknell, and many other oppressors of the working man gather together in this lodge to laugh at the plight of the honest man as they smoke expensive cigars and guzzle illegal liquor, a single bottle of which would cost a month's pay to any man here." Dimitri's gestures were dramatic, making sure his imprecations sunk in on his rapt audience.

Despite the grimness of the news, János had to cover a smirk. Dimitri had obviously spent some time on his speech.

"This coven of industrialists is led by a revoltingly decadent specimen named John Scott, who styles himself the 'Noble Philosopher' of the organization. In but two weeks, Saturday the seventeenth, they will be having their Christmas celebration: A typically patrician orgy of expensive food and prohibited alcohol to celebrate their oppression of their fellow man.

"However, I have arranged for the two of us," Dimitri indicated János, "to pose as waiters for their Christmas debauch. When they are drunk and full of food, we will move among them and make the will of the people known." Dimitri's eyes flashed with fanaticism, his unsmiling face raised toward the light bulb above him, as if receiving a message from God.

Antonio frowned. "You are not planning anything ... untoward, are you, Dimitri?"

János looked down, remembering the bloody knife in Dimitri's hand during the Agency assault, and small, cold fish swam up his spine. He had never asked Dimitri about his past in Russia. He didn't seem like a dynamiter, but János had never met one. Could this small, older Russian be one of those socialists who gladly murdered their capitalist oppressors? He was so gentle with both Anna-Maria and Elizabeth. When he looked up again, Dimitri was simply Dimitri again, the small factory reader with a glint of harmless mischief in his eyes. No, János decided, those were not the hands of a murderer.

"I would not dream of harming a hair on their heads, Antonio." Dimitri's words were gentle, his expression open and disarming. "I simply intend to find out more about them, in an effort to counter their rigorous oppression of *honest* workers. If we could find something embarrassing to Emerson, we would be in a much better bargaining position. If we could find something incriminating against the entire lodge...." He let the sentence trail off into hopeful silence.

It was not long before the seventeenth of December came, and János found himself standing apprehensively outside a brooding three-story structure with an insignificant fence surrounding it, broken only by a small gate. Somewhere, a church bell was ringing the noon hour, the sound lonely and remote in the cold air.

János shivered, and not entirely from the cold. They were about to go into a bastion of the wealthy—surely no factory workers had ever been invited to join this club. For the past two weeks, Dimitri had drummed lessons on how to act into him, and it had become clear that the rich were as alien to him and his life as the yellow Chinese men and women who worked laundries. They might have a head and two arms, but they lived on a wholly different world and expected people to act very differently. And now the two of them were going to trespass into it.

In the street, in what János knew was going to be his last moment of freedom to speak and act as he wished for the rest of the night, he hawked and spat into the gutter. Dimitri once more smoothed the lapels of Janos's new tuxedo under his greatcoat.

"Remember what I have taught you, little brother. Most of serving the upper classes consists of shutting up and not dropping anything. And never forget that the rich will not act like you expect."

"Yes, Dimitri, I remember. Now stop clucking over me like a mother hen."

"And also remember that when the rich are full of drink, they can be very generous with their money. You could make more in tips in a single night here than you would working for three months at the factory."

János felt his jaw go slack. Three months' pay for a single night of work? Dimitri's eyes sparkled and he made one last brush at János's lapel.

"Did I neglect to mention that? Silly of me, really."

A quarter of a year's pay. János's mind whirled at the prospect. The things he could do with that much money—hire a nursemaid for Elizabeth, and allow Anna-Maria to get her strength back. They could both eat a good meal three times a day. He was rudely awakened from this dream by Dimitri, cadging at his cuffs.

"Don't spend all of it yet, little brother."

With a deep breath that steamed like a train in the cold winter air, János pulled himself together, and the two of them walked to the servant's entrance of the Lodge of the Hermetic Order of the Silver Twilight.

The interior of the lodge was more opulent than anything János had ever seen; he did not think that Emperor Franz Josef could have had furnishings this fine. The chairs were elegant, their dark, smooth wood carved with grapes and faces, the immaculate floor laid down in an intricate herringbone pattern. The linens were the finest things he had ever touched, the silver utensils better polished than any mirror János had at home. And no matter where he was, the smells from the kitchen were the most delicious mélange of scents he had ever known. It was all positively indecent, and yet, he felt the desire for such things rise in his heart. János tried to think of all the hours of sweat and toil such things were purchased with, and the misery of the no doubt underpaid craftsmen who made such beautiful objects, and still found himself wondering if he would ever be able to afford them.

The kitchen staff kept the two of them busy from the moment they walked in the servants' entrance, polishing silverware, carrying tables, setting places, and a thousand other trivialities. János thought he had done moderately well. All he received was the occasional sharp look and barked a command to move faster from the man giving orders. Waiting on the rich required more thought than his job in the factory, but aside from that, it was a lot less effort. He could get used to being wait staff, especially for what he was being paid.

Fear returned and chilled his enthusiasm when the first guests began to arrive. Large men doffed expensive, fur-lined coats and tall, silk hats, and when they shed these layers, they strode forth in evening wear that put János's new tuxedo to shame. Gold pocket watches, rings, cufflinks, and shirt-studs glittered on the fine suits of the corpulent gentlemen. The air of wealth clung to them like the smoke of expensive cigars.

Edward Emerson arrived with a crowd, and János tried to make himself scarce as the factory owner began to circulate about the room. He was relieved to see that the industrialist quickly met someone, and the two of them energetically shook hands and were immediately engrossed in a cheerful conversation punctuated with braying laughs. Unexpectedly, Dimitri appeared at János' elbow.

"The worker's blood is the lubrication for their friendship. That is Hamish Davenport, the head of the Pinkertons in Boston. This is a place for the wealthy to share plans for how to persecute the working man, and hatch their plans to unite into the iron heel that grinds us into the dirt."

János smiled blandly at the man in a tweed jacket who plucked a pair of oysters from János' tray, then turned back to the circle of better-dressed men he was addressing.

"Which is why the study of ancient civilizations is so much more difficult for American Universities. Gaining access to sites and records is a much greater expense which is disproportionately placed on History departments. It is therefore incumbent upon American business to step up to the plate, so to speak, and make sure that American universities do not neglect the heritage that Western Civilization has bequeathed upon—"

"You've been listening to Antonio for too long," János whispered to Dimitri. And yet, he was apprehensive. Something—perhaps even everything—about this Order of the Silver Twilight was wrong.

John Scott, the 'Noble Philosopher' came down to greet the first wave of guests. Dimitri had not told him of the man's strangely coarse, pockmarked skin. János did not like looking at him. Although Scott pressed the flesh and welcomed all his guests by name, there was another figure that caught János's attention. He was never announced or introduced, as Mr. Scott had been. János came out of the kitchen to find that he was simply in the lounge, as if he had always been there. After some time, he caught the name Carl Stanford. Stanford did not converse with many of the guests, and was never far from an unsmiling, hatchet-faced Mr. Reed, who János had no difficulty imagining as a Pinkerton leg-breaker or worse. While he was fetching drinks and carrying platters of oysters and canapés, János surreptitiously watched the mysterious Mr. Stanford, careful to never catch the man's gaze.

Occasionally, Scott would glance over at Stanford, as if seeking approval, or perhaps even in fear. And while Scott passed from group to group in the lounge, he did so alone. Stanford did not stay with any circle of conversation for long; in fact, they often seemed to melt away at his approach. What sort of organization was this, János asked himself in the brief moments when he was not too harried to think. In the now-vanished Imperial military, János had watched captains act as John Scott did now, and the generals acted like Stanford, with Reed as his attaché. This was not a military organization. What would this Stanford need for an aide at one of their own celebrations? The rich were different from the workers, that much was certain, but what sort of threat was this lodge protecting itself against?

These thoughts were pushed aside, but not forgotten, when the gentlemen were summoned to their dinner. János was amazed at the mountains of food that he was required to carry. He had only heard of people eating a ten-course meal, but he had never imagined that any person could eat so much in a single day, let along one sitting. First were the oysters and hors d'oeuvres, and when everyone was seated, a soup in a silver tureen came out. Fortunately, Dimitri ladled the soup with a marvelous dexterity; all János was required to do was hold the heavy bowl. To János's great amazement, not only was wine openly served, a *different* one was served with each course. All the names were strange and French to his ears, but Dimitri helped him sort out which wine to serve whenever he could. János would have felt guilty if the lean Russian had not been performing his duties with an effortless grace as if he had been born to service. Never had János seen Dimitri smile so much, but he also noticed that the smile never reached his eyes.

Next came salmon, then small medallions of beef, and when that was cleared away, roast lamb served with potatoes and a green vegetable. This was the food of the rich, the food he had always imagined that the wealthy ate; indescribable smells, food cooked to tenderest perfection. And there was more of it than he would have ever guessed; the parade of food seemed to go on forever. Next came punch in a great bowl, followed by squab cooked in orange. Next was something green and stalky that János didn't recognize. He didn't like the look of the grey, pasty material that followed, but Dimitri called it *'pate de foie gras'*.

The entire orgy of food and drink took nearly three hours, and the entire time János always seemed on the verge of falling behind. Fortunately, Dimitri appeared at his elbow whenever he needed help. In fact, Dimitri seemed to be everywhere at once, now refilling this man's glass, now helping János clear dishes, always with a smile and a polite nod. Clearly, there was much about Dimitri's past that János did not know.

Yet even as he served, the waste of the evening sickened him. Without exception, every gilt plate he cleared off had some food left over on it, which the kitchen staff simply threw in the garbage. János watched enough lamb, beef, and squab to feed him for a week get remorselessly discarded.

Finally, there was a choice of sweet deserts, and Dimitri assured him that the hard part of the night was over. Now the industrialist dogs would retire, and Dimitri's smile was vicious and angry as he told János that the captains of industry would be at their most vulnerable; smoking and drinking heavily to settle their enormous gorge. The more intoxicated they became, Dimitri said with a bright, hard gleam in his eye, the more generous they could be. They would also be freer with their secrets. Now more than ever, the Russian cautioned him, it was important to be quiet and allow the fat men to talk.

Great clouds of smoke rolled toward the ceiling of the lounge, born of a dozen or more fat cigars. In the gradually-increasing haze, Dimitri moved among the bulky men like a canoe among steamers, holding a match to the gentlemen's cigars, recommending a port or a whiskey, refreshing a glass, always smiling and bowing. János could not, however, rid himself of his uneasiness. While he was supposed to keep an eye and an ear on what Edward Emerson was saying, he found it difficult to concentrate on them while Stanford and Reed were in the room.

Stanford spoke pleasantly when approached, but seemed to pass his time watching and waiting, like a wolf sizing up a herd of deer. No, János decided, Stanford's gaze was not like a wolf's but more like a snake's. A wolf at least chooses which of the herd to chase down and devour, while a snake is just a cold machine looking for its next meal. János felt that same cold, impersonal indifference in Carl Stanford's gaze, and he couldn't help an involuntary shudder whenever that gaze passed by him. He did not know if he would be able to stand it if that penetrating regard ever came to rest on him. The man did not seem to drink. But neither did he act. He remained, watching, as the night passed. It was only when Stanford left, with his unsmiling hatchet-man in tow, that János felt comfortable enough to start to explore the lodge.

As the evening wore on, the gentlemen in their fine suits got more and more drunk, and became freer with their money. Fives and tens were left to be found under drink glasses, or were unexpectedly left in his palm when the fat men shook his hand in farewell. Others were less refined, and one extremely drunk guest shoved a fifty-dollar bill into the breast pocket of János's shirt. Even Emerson tipped him ten dollars, never suspecting that the Hungarian was one of his own workers.

After assisting a very drunk gentleman into his coat, Dimitri returned from the coat room and whispered that he had found a flight of stairs that ascended to the second floor. The way was unguarded, all they needed to do was slip away unnoticed. They went their separate ways around the lounge for another half an hour. The gentlemen drank, they talked, and the smoke from their collective cigars rivaled anything that came out of a smokestack.

János watched as Dimitri assisted another man with his coat, and followed on the same errand soon after. There, in the coat room, a broad set of stairs ascended to an unknown second story of the lodge. When the fat man had been properly swaddled in his fur-lined coat and gently tipped out the front door, the two conspirators quietly slipped up the stairs.

At the landing, out of sight from the first floor, Dimitri removed his shoes, tied the laces together, and then hung them over his shoulders. János did the same. Now in stocking feet, the two men could explore in relative silence.

They found the second floor to be much to their—or at least Dimitri's—expectations. A single room, more than twice the size of the dining room they had waited on, dominated the story. Yet it was as well appointed as the floor below, with expensive-looking paneling on the walls. To the left and right, the polished wooden floor made three broad, ascending steps, like a lecture hall János has once seen, with comfortable-looking chairs on each tier.

In the middle of the room stood a small block of wood like an altar, and beyond that a dais. Unlike the two platforms by the door, the dais at the far end of the room was larger, and emphasized long, blood-red drape that hung behind it. In fact, as János took in more details of the room, he noticed that the altar had a kneeling rail on it, so that the man who knelt there was also kneeling before the great dais with the red curtain. He did not like it. This was strange, and even considering Dimitri's assurances that the rich were not like workers, this seemed unwholesome, if not outright unholy. He could not think of a legitimate enterprise that involved men kneeling before each other. It was something men did to priests and kings, and this lodge seemed an unlikely place to find either.

From behind him, Dimitri let out a nearly-silent "Ah." János followed the sound into a small room off the landing that was full of books.

"You should look around, but quietly," Dimitri whispered. "Remember they are directly below us."

The room was quiet and oppressive, and János found himself unhappy to be searching the rooms without Dimitri's company. There was little enough to explore—two more small rooms, one of which was a neatly-arranged storage area, neither containing anything of interest. János returned to the large room, and gazed once again on the burgundy-colored velvet curtain that hung behind the large dais. The one to which members of this lodge knelt.

János was loath to approach that curtain, and for a fleeting moment, imagined that it concealed an enormous serpent, one with the face of Carl Stanford.

He shook the fancy off—he was a grown man, a strong man. He had no time for foolish fears. And yet, his hand trembled just a bit as he reached and slowly, silently pulled the curtain aside.

János let out a breath he hadn't known he'd been holding when he saw a second landing, with another set of stairs going up to a third floor. There was no sign of any sort of snake, nor of the fearful Mr. Stanford. János smiled at himself, trying to banish the specter of his childish fear. These men were rich and without soul, but they were not supernatural. He looked up the darkened stairs, wondering what was up there, when Dimitri emerged from the library.

"Nothing," his whisper was angry enough to melt lead. "Just books on Bacon and Marcus Aurelius, and *philosophy*. Nothing that tells us their true intentions." János wondered if his friend had expected to find a copy of the master plan for dominating and destroying the collective will of all workers, preferably signed in the blood of the oppressed.

"There is another set of stairs behind the curtain." Light and hope returned to Dimitri's eyes, and he gestured for János to lead on.

Determined not to show his childish fear to Dimitri, János pulled aside the curtain with a hand that did not tremble. The ascending stairs were dark and less used than the previous steps; dust had collected in the corners of the risers. At the top was a locked door, and János waited nervously as Dimitri knelt by the door. He could no longer hear the faint sounds of the revelry below them, but the silence of the lodge did not reassure him.

"Guilty secrets lie behind locked doors," Dimitri breathed as he carefully worked at the lock with a pair of thin metal picks. "Imagine the secrets in here." János stood still and quiet, trying to keep the fear from quietly creeping into him.

"Ah," was all that escaped Dimitri when he had finally opened the lock. They exchanged no words of triumph, but Dimitri's eyes sparkled. Were they a fanatic's eyes? A murderer's eyes? Dimitri certainly seemed to have skills that János had never known about.

The new corridor marched in a straight line, closed doors to unknown rooms on both sides, and ended with a closed door, also.

"Where should we start?" János whispered. There was something about this upper floor that did not like sound, and János did not want to attract its attention. Dimitri must have felt it, too, because he did not reply, but instead moved quietly to the first door on the left.

The door opened easily, giving them access to a small, darkened room. There were no windows, but Dimitri located a switch for the electric lights. Revealed before them was an unfurnished room, paneled on two sides, and great, scarlet drapes concealed the other two walls.

János looked behind one of the scarlet curtains—the wall was blank, but for a door at one end of the room. He approached it, but Dimitri gave a yelp that made the hair on the back of János's neck stand up.

He turned to see Dimitri on his knees, breathing rapidly. He had pulled the curtain aside, uncovering a large mural. János's first thought was for his friend, but the mural caught his attention.

From a clear night sky, a full moon looked balefully down on a ring of standing stones that crowned a hill. Within the circle stood a robed figure, dancing madly. Above it, rivaling the moon for brightness, floated a mass of weirdly glowing bubbles or spheres. Below the hill's crest were hundreds of decaying semi-human things that seemed to caper when János was not looking directly at them. And although János did not understand what the things in the picture were supposed to be, he knew it was the work of evil men. Nor could he look away until he had taken all of it in. Only then could he rush over to Dimitri, who seemed to be slowly recovering himself.

"We should not have come here," Dimitri whispered as János helped him to his feet. The small Russian leaned against him for a long moment, as if taking strength from the big Hungarian. János covered the mural with the scarlet curtain again, but he could still feel the horrible, baleful art, even though it was out of sight. Still, it was better than having to look at it.

"Should we go, Dimitri?" János could tell that Dimitri's fear had infected him. Though they did not have what they had come for, Dimitri was the smart one. János didn't even know what they were looking for.

"No, I'm all right." Dimitri was still visibly shaken, but he seemed to have taken strength from János's presence. "I'm all right," Dimitri repeated, although the Hungarian was not sure who the Russian was reassuring. "We'll see what's behind the door you found."

They entered what was obviously a library; the walls were covered with bookshelves, on which hundreds of books were neatly arranged. Dimitri looked at them with a connoisseur's eye, but János could to little more than read the titles. Many were in English, but some were in alphabets he did not know.

An old book bound in leather with five raised bands on the spine caught his eye. He took it down in a moment of idle curiosity, and then saw the title: *Les Cultes des Goules*. János did not know much French, but the title made him think of the decayed, half-human things that surrounded the hill in the awful mural in the room they had just come from. Silently, he handed the book to Dimitri, who seemed awed at the book, handling it as gingerly as he had Elizabeth. He seemed to understand some of it, muttering something about Sin Eaters and New York, since he lingered over the pages for long minutes.

Eventually, Dimitri returned the book to its slot, then ran his narrow fingers down the spines of the neighboring books, whispering their titles. "*The Thousand Dreaded Prophesies of the Eternal Chinaman*," Dimitri said, his voice filled with awe and dread. "*Cannibal Cults of the Andaman Islands*." When he turned back to János, his face was ashen pale.

"This is far worse than I ever imagined."

It was then that János heard footsteps on the stairs below them. Dimitri crouched noiselessly, leaning his back against the shelves of books. János simply stood, clenching and unclenching his hands with the need to do something. They waited as the sound of steps—János could tell there were more than two people approaching—came to the top of the stairs. They would simply wait the intruders out.

"Did we leave this door open?" Carl Stanford's voice turned János's blood cold. Dimitri's look was not angry, but defeated, and János knew that they had one chance to escape the clutches of Stanford. Noiselessly, he stole to the door, grasped the doorknob, and waited. Outside the library was silent now, and János could hear the blood slowly thudding in his ears. He held the doorknob firmly and waited, barely daring to breathe.

After some time, there came the faint sound of someone drawing aside the curtain on the other side of the wall in attempted stealth. János nodded for Dimitri to be ready, and the Russian crept silently toward the door.

János felt the grip of someone else's hand on the other side of the doorknob. He felt the other hand try to turn the doorknob against János's strength, and when he was sure they were gripping the knob tightly, he yanked the door open. The surprised Reed was pulled off his feet and fell sprawling on the floor. Something landed heavily on the polished floor, and János knew without looking that it was a pistol. But he had no time to think on that, the hatchet-faced Reed was already getting to his feet, and reaching into his coat. Without thinking, János slammed bodily into him, pinning him to the wall. His fist hammered into Reed's unprotected gut, and a killing knife clattered on the wooden floor. Reed pushed the Hungarian away and went for his pistol. János rushed in and caught Reed's collar by one hand. One, two, three, then more hammer blows smashed that hard, hateful face with all of János's his factory-bred strength. Reed went limp. Like a triumphant barbarian in the amphitheater of Rome, the Hungarian flung the lesser man's senseless body to the floor.

Outside the library, Stanford and Scott stood together. They had not acted, and were speaking nonsense and making gestures. János grabbed Dimitri's hand and hauled him out of the door. The two of them barged past the men in suits, and ran for the corridor. They had almost made it to the door when János was slammed in the back by a wrecking-ball. He lay on the floor a moment, dazed and gasping in pain. Dimitri's terror-etched face swam in his vision, and he heard the Russian's voice, as if from very far away, begging him to get up. The polished wooden floor was slick beneath his stocking feet, but with Dimitri's help, he got to his feet. All thoughts were gone but the blind need for escape as he half-scrambled, half-fell down the stairs, following Dimitri.

Stumbling clumsily through the red curtain, János's ankle went out from under him as he came off the dais. He fell heavily against the wooden altar in the middle of the room. He clawed his way to his feet as quickly as he could. But he wasn't fast enough. A quick glance behind him showed the silent, stalking figures of Scott and Stanford framed by the red velvet curtain. János saw John Scott gesture again, and an invisible weight crashed into his chest, and he collapsed.

His feet no longer worked. He scrabbled helplessly at the slick floor. There was a rushing noise in his ears. He fought the blackness that constricted his vision, his only thought to get away. Anywhere was better than under the terrible gaze of John Scott and Carl Stanford. His breath was labored and difficult but still he crawled. Someone was pulling ineffectually at his hand, saying things he couldn't understand. But unconsciousness would not be denied, and blackness closed over his vision like water over a drowning man.

He woke in blackness, and the cold of stone beneath him. He ached; his limbs from the penetrating cold of the surrounding stone, and his ribs from the impacts. He hugged his arms to his chest and rocked slightly, like an old man. His first clear thought was to worry about Anna-Maria and Elizabeth. They had been expecting him home, what would they do? How long had he been gone?

What had happened to Dimitri? His confused brain reassembled his confrontation with the masters of the Silver Twilight, and of Dimitri's steadfast but futile efforts to get him out. He ought to have run, János concluded mournfully. Perhaps then at least one of them would be free. Painfully, he stirred, and put his hand on the no-doubt ruined tuxedo jacket. The money was gone. It wasn't a real surprise, but the pettiness of it was another insult. Suddenly angry, János fumbled his way to his feet to find out what he could about his prison.

It took him less than ten minutes to find out everything there was to know about his cell. It was a circular shaft, with no door and no window. The cell was so small that he couldn't lie down, but had to sit with his back to the wall. The walls were too smooth to climb, and the ceiling too far up for him to touch when he jumped. With that done, there was nothing for him to do but sit and wait.

Time had no meaning in the black. He was hungry for a while, and then it faded. But his thirst grew. He slept from time to time, but there was little to differentiate the waking time from sleep, except for his growing thirst. The darkness was oppressive, as was the solitude. János could do nothing but sit, and wait, and worry. And grow thirsty.

An unknown time later, János glimpsed a light that filtered down through the overhead cover—which he saw was a good twenty feet over his head. He shouted out—more to hear his voice than in hopes of attracting his jailer's attention. And there came echoing back to him the gabble of voices. Quickly, it swelled in volume and rapidly became unbearable, the screaming, begging, and weeping of dozens of damned souls who had likely been down here longer than he. The sound froze János's blood as the realization came over him that these men had power, and they imprisoned whom they wished for as long as they wished.

The begging, screaming and screeching rolled through the cavern like thunder.

He watched the shadows through the lid of his cell as they grew shorter, and eventually, the light came to hover directly over his pit. The cover was removed, and János blinked and averted his eyes at the sudden brightness.

Max Reed's voice cut through the damned howling, like a drill sergeant's.

"If you do not do exactly what you are told, I will shoot you."

Another droplet of icy fear made its way into János's heart. Though the light burned his eyes, János looked up at the lantern-bearer. Max Reed was pointing a pistol down at him, while another man held the intolerably-bright lantern.

"I will do as you say." János's voice was dry and clumsy, and his tongue was starting to swell.

A crude wooden ladder was lowered into the pit, and János climbed out. Up close, he could see that Reed's face was still swollen from the beating János had given him. It was cold comfort—after the time in the pit, and the cold stiffness of his limbs. A second victory would be much more difficult, even if he could get the gun away from Reed.

His hands were bound with rope, and he looked around at the cavernous room, its floor full of pits like the one he had been taken out of. As they left, the shrieks and mixed gabbling of those they left behind subsided. János tried not to think about how many men were still back there. They walked briefly up a corridor and turned into an unexpected drawing room that was just off the darkened cavern.

The room was carpeted and paneled, just as the lodge was, the rear wall covered by an overfull bookshelf. Carl Stanford, John Scott, and another man that János did not recognize sat in comfortable chairs, dressed as if they had just come from a day at the office. Whoever the newcomer was, he fit in very well with Scott and Stanford; the same aristocratic bearing, the same practiced neatness. Their eyes were on him immediately as he entered, and he felt a chill pass straight through him.

"You see, Ambrose? This is the one we were discussing earlier." John Scott, the Noble Philosopher, could have been talking about his stock's performance, or a slab of beef, rather than the human being in front of him.

"Water," was all János could manage in the quiet that ensued.

With Stanford's permission, a glass of it was provided, and he gulped it down. His knees were weak with relief. Though his thirst was dulled, not quenched, János could feel some strength returning.

"We thought you might be interested to look at him, at any rate." Stanford's voice was detached and impersonal, but when he spoke, his eyes moved to the man he called Ambrose, and János much preferred that.

Ambrose stood, approached, and looked the large Hungarian over.

"Indeed, yes indeed," Ambrose's smile was knowing. "In this Transleithanian, gentlemen, we have the veritable physiognomy of the Piltdown Man. Observe the strong, nearly prognathous jaws, the lack of refinement in all aspects of his character—the thick fingers, and the depth of the rib cage and coarseness of the facial features. Surely there is more gorilla in this man's ancestry than anything else. Open up that thick skull and you will find a brain barely three-quarters the mass of a good Nordic one, and not half so well ordered."

He turned his back on János, making a theatrical presentation to Stanford and Scott.

"Gentlemen, you would not believe what I could make of this man."

"That's all very well, but you can't have him. We have promised one of our lodge members that we would make an example of him."

"You have the other, Carl." Ambrose carried his appeal to Stanford, rather than Scott. "How much of an example do you need to make?"

"We need them both." János knew that he was being haggled over like a piece of fish in a market.

"You would put the concerns of some industrialist peon before me? How long have we known each other, Carl?"

"As I recall, New York was the capital when we met, *Ambrose*." The name was a knife from Stanford's mouth. "But we all have our own gardens to tend. Don't suddenly come over genial simply because we have a toy you want to play with; it's beneath you. You can stay for the entertainment, or you can leave, but he is ours."

It appeared that wheedling was beneath Ambrose's dignity, and he returned to his chair without another word. Again, the room went quiet, and János almost flinched as all three of the seated men turned their eyes on him. Their eyes burned into him, and his skin itched as if they could see beneath it. He did not show defiance, but simply stood, arms bound in front of him, head down, as motionless as he could, trying not to do anything to excite their interest. Again he thought of Anna-Maria and Elizabeth. They seemed very far away.

Then it was Stanford's turn to stand and approach. Though he stood shorter than János, there was a commanding, almost imperial presence to him. Fear coursed through János as Stanford approached, and he tried not to flinch.

"My name is Carl Stanford, not that it will mean anything to you. I have saved you from the gentle ministrations of our Mr. Mogens because I have a special message for you to take back to your union." He stopped, and looked expectantly at János.

"What message?" His tongue was still thick, and he did not look up. They did not intend to kill him, then. His sense of relief was not great, however, since he did not doubt that he would be sent back to the union as an example. He tried not to wonder how long they were going to beat him, or many bones they intended to break. He tried to picture Elizabeth's little face, but Stanford presence was inescapable. János closed his eyes, so he wouldn't see anything coming.

"No matter how much you organize, no matter how many of you there are, you will never amount to anything." Stanford's voice was low—almost a whisper, but the words wormed their way through János's ears and into his brain. He could feel them. "You are the vermin of this world; blind, idiot creatures that crawl out of the darkness and return to it after a brief, confused period in the light. You cower from the truths of the universe, clinging to illusions of gods that might for some reason care what happens in your miserable lives that are but an eye blink in eternity."

Struck by the speech, János looked up and straight into Stanford's waiting gaze. The cold blue eyes were flecked with darker, almost black areas, and his pupils were like holes through which János could see the darkness between the stars. There was no pity in those eyes, no remorse, and no kindness.

"Hold my cane."

Stanford held out a curious brass walking cane. Stanford pressed the top into the Hungarian's hand, and János looked down to see that the top was shaped like a grinning skull.

There was a tingling in his hand where he touched it, something odd that János had never quite felt before. He wondered if this was what electricity felt like.

The tingling grew into a pain, but János would not be put off by some trick. He had endured worse. But then the pain changed, worsened, as if his flesh was sticking to the cane. The itching, irritating pain became the cold burn of frostbite. János tried to drop the cane, but Stanford's hands were suddenly around his, not allowing him to let go. The pain grew.

János had once had a bullet dug out of his gut with a knife

while the killing Alpine winds howled. He had been beaten by prison guards, strikebreakers, and Béla Klun's thugs. He had *never* endured pain like this. He felt an intangible *tearing* sensation, so profound that János could not believe that it hadn't made a noise, as if something had been removed from his gut, and a cold like the frozen wind off the Alps filled him. Abruptly, his hand was free, and János dropped the hellish cane and retreated as far as he dared, cradling his arm, though in truth, it didn't hurt. The frozen pain was inside of him, somewhere that he could not touch. He fell to his knees, and his eyes filling with tears.

"Reminds me of nothing so much as a monkey who is just learning that fire is hot, doesn't he?" Ambrose Mogens seemed unaffected by what had just happened.

"Bring in his friend," Scott said, and in a few moments, a guard returned with Dimitri.

The Russian fell like a burlap sack of bones at János's feet.

"No more, no more, no more," Dimitri whispered over and over, and János shushed him. Despite his tied hands, he cradled the small Russian to himself, as he would a crying child, letting the smaller man weep out all his grief, even as he tried not to think about how they had hurt him. How they would hurt János. After a time, Dimitri's words turned into silent weeping. He looked up at János, and the Hungarian was shocked at the flat, dead aspect of Dimitri's eyes.

His surprised gaze went to Stanford who was leaning casually on his evil cane, a look of smug superiority on his face.

"If you hold the cane long enough, I will let you and your friend go."

At that, Dimitri covered his head and whimpered. János shushed him again, and gently wiped the tears from his eyes.

He closed his own eyes momentarily, and imagined his Anna-Maria. Not as she was now, but before the baby—when she had been alive and full of life and love, of the day he had asked her to marry him. That day in the spring when they had been walking in the Boston Commons. The grass had been fresh and new, the tree buds had been bursting forth into fresh, green leaves. Early-blooming flowers were pushing up from the earth, and the city was shaking off her winter coat.

"Yes, yes, a thousand times, yes," she had said, and he had caught her up in his strong arms and kissed her, right there. She had smiled for the rest of the day, warm as the sun on a summer day. He had thought his heart would burst. He was so proud and in love. He held onto that memory, took strength from it.

With all the dignity he could muster, he stood, and did his best to loom over Stanford.

"No."

The denial of the deal seemed to genuinely surprise Stanford; for a moment, he lost his calm, almost bored look.

"What bargaining power could you possibly think you might have?"

János thought of Saint Stephen's admonition to his son Imre: *Be strong lest prosperity lift you up too much or adversity cast you down. Be humble in this life, that God may raise you up in the next.* He knew what sort of game this was—the bored prison guards who wanted to see a fight, had played it with the inmates at the POW camp. A vague promise of a reward, only to be snatched away as the hapless victim reached for it.

"I have your fun to bargain with. You may kill me, but you won't like that as much." He remembered his wedding-night and the first time he had seen his bride naked. Her blushing modesty, even in front of her newly-wedded husband, touched an unusual tenderness in him. How his heart ached with love for this small woman with beautiful curves and soft lines who had pledged to spend the rest of her life with him. That thought gave him strength, even before this court of cold and terrible men. He would be strong for her. He wanted to see her again.

A cold smile crossed Stanford's face.

"We could tie you down and simply lay the cane on you."

"Then you didn't have to bother bringing me here. You want to see me fight my fear."

Stanford hesitated momentarily. Apparently, he had thought himself unique in his cruelty. János knew from hard experience that his sort was all too common.

"You may be wrong about the sophistication of his brain matter, Ambrose." Stanford stroked his cheek with the skull-head of the cane. "Before we dicker any further, you should know that this really is tearing pieces off what you stupidly think of as your soul. And it won't heal, won't grow back."

"My soul belongs to God and myself."

Stanford's smirk made his blood run cold, but he tried his best not to show it. "May the lies of your ignorant little religion be a comfort as your soul is torn to shreds." He produced a beautiful golden pocket-watch, and dangled it loosely from the chain.

"Hold the cane for six minutes, and I will let you and your friend free."

"Two." János hoped that Stanford would honor his word. But what could he do if the man did not?

"Four."

"Three."

"Four."

Stanford spoke with a finality that let János know that his brief moment of control over the situation was spent.

"Four minutes," he conceded.

Scott and Mogens shifted briefly and then settled back into seats as if about to watch a good show.

"Four minutes," János repeated. Then, to forestall the fearfulness of anticipation, as the second-hand of Stanford's watch swept past the top of the minute, János snatched the cane from Stanford's hand.

The sensation began again with a cross between a tickle and an itch. It was of little comfort, though, since János knew what was coming. All too quickly, the thing was sending blinding waves of agony throughout his body. He just kept the picture of Anna-Maria in his mind, trying to ignore the pain, as Stanford stood calmly in front of him, watch dangling carelessly from his hand. János tried not to count out the seconds. He closed his eyes, and thought of his Anna-Maria. He could feel himself ebbing, as if the cane was drawing out his blood, his life heat. A sense of cold and weariness started around his heart, and he could feel it growing. He glanced at Stanford's watch.

One minute had passed.

After two minutes the agony had him on his knees, actually

leaning on the cane to support his body. He could no longer picture Anna-Maria, could not remember her face. There was nothing between him and the certainty that Stanford was right, that his immortal soul was being devoured, and that Stanford, Mogens, and Scott were all demons from Hell. But he kept his crushing grip on the cane, not letting go. The cold was building in him, and his limbs were shaking with fatigue. Despite the cold, he was sweating with effort. He opened his eyes for a moment, not to see the watch, but to glare his hatred at Stanford, but the force of that hate was waning.

The final minute was nothing but a blur of agony that lasted longer than any shift he had worked. And when, finally, the second hand swept across the twelve, he heard the cane thump to the carpeted floor, and the relief from his agony was so intense it was almost a new source of anguish. Without a word, he crumpled to the floor and lay, panting, his cheeks wet with tears.

The world was heavier when he opened his eyes again, and a chasm of weariness yawned in him.

"Get up."

János scrambled to obey, standing unsteadily before the three men in suits. He looked at the toes of his shoes, now hopelessly scuffed, and hoped they would not hurt him anymore.

"Get him up."

János pulled Dimitri to his feet. Vaguely, it occurred to him that once he might have fought the impulse to obey Stanford, despite being afraid of him. But that determination seemed like a cloud now; he could perceive it from a distance, but it melted from his grasp when he reached for it.

"I believe that's message enough for your little union." János stole a glance at Stanford, who was smiling. He hoped the terrifying man would not ask him to do anything else.

Stanford approached, putting a hand under János' jaw, forcing his head up. Stanford's waiting eyes were like cold, dark oceans that would freeze him long before he drowned.

"I think that will do nicely."

Stanford removed something from his own pocket, and placed it in János's hand—it felt like a roll of paper. Stupidly, he raised his hand, and discovered that it was a sheaf of hundred-dollar bills. Shocked, János could only look from the roll of bills to his unlikely benefactor.

"Why?" was all he could ask. Stanford gave an indifferent shrug.

"It's only money, my dear fellow. I suggest you use it to fix the face on that repulsive little brat of yours."

He nodded to Reed, who took them both by the arm, and steered them out of the room. They were escorted, none too gently, up a set of stone stairs and to the ground floor of the Lodge of the Silver Twilight. János recognized the servant's entrance they had come through, what seemed like half a lifetime ago.

Reed opened the door, and shoved Dimitri out. János made to follow, but Reed's grip held him back. The Hungarian turned to face the hatchet-faced bodyguard, and drew back from the unmitigated hate that seethed in that bruised face. Without warning, Reed's fist smashed across János's face, and the Hungarian stumbled down a few stairs and fell to the hard, snow-covered ground. It was a moment before he could get back up.

János supported Dimitri, and the two of them stumbled into the snowy streets huddling together for warmth. They had only their ruined tuxedos between themselves and cold Boston winter, János still clutching his bundle of hundred-dollar bills.

"I wish we had not come here, Dimitri."

From somewhere in the ruin that had been Dimitri, a sad and hollow apology formed.

"I should not have brought you here, little brother."

THE MASKED MESSENGER

WITH DAVID CONYERS

Harrison Peel counted the dead as more covered corpses rolled into the Marrakech morgue. They weren't really humans, rather the dissected remains of their flesh, bloody in leaking body bags. The sharp, coppery smell of blood filled the room, reminding Peel of an abattoir.

Lounging next to Peel was Fabien Chemal, a spook with Morocco's DST intelligence agency. Chemal mumbled something in Arabic about being inconvenienced by the gory spectacle. While he watched junior spooks and morgue attendants catalogue the grim remains, he offered Peel a cigarette. Peel refused, wishing instead for a good strong coffee.

"How many dead?" Peel wiped his sweaty hands on cotton pants. It should have been cold in this place. That's how they would have done it back in the NSA. Cold to keep the body parts preserved for proper forensic analysis.

Chemal shrugged, lit his cigarette. "We don't know yet. At least eighteen dead: five Americans, two Germans, one Spaniard. The rest were my people, but I guess your people won't care about that."

"I care." Peel said as he stood. The smell of death and smoke felt constricting from his seat in a corner. "The NSA care, otherwise I wouldn't be here."

Chemal raised an eyebrow. "I get the impression, Mr. Peel, that you were a little eager to come in person, rather than send a subordinate?"

Peel didn't know precisely what Chemal's rank was in the murky hierarchy of the *Direction de la Surveillance du Territoire*.

He knew that any time he didn't spend with Chemal he would spend being tailed. They were controlling him, and this would make his job here more difficult than it needed to be.

The morgue was in the basement of Marrakech DST offices. At least one more level existed beneath their feet, reserved for DST's prisoners and interrogation cells. In this building, the dead warranted more respect than detainees.

"Some personal reason perhaps, Mr. Peel?"

Peel ignored Chemal's question. The Moroccan's tone sounded *too* inquisitive, as if Peel were under interrogation. "You said you don't know how many died in the blast? How's that? And secondly, I'm not sure it really was a blast. To me the bodies look like they've been sliced to pieces. Thousands of pieces?"

"They were ... They still will be?"

Peel's stomach felt empty. He was confused, but then everything about yesterday's terrorist bombing in Jemaa el-Fna square lacked any resemblance to sense. The blast had been invisible, soundless. People were shredded where they stood in the Marrakech market. Yet their clothes, wallets, purses, souvenirs and the pavement beneath them remained untouched. It was as if invisible demons had mutilated their victims with razor sharp teeth and claws.

"Do you know that some of the victims died *before* the blast occurred, hours, even days before?"

"I don't understand?"

Chemal shrugged. "Neither do we... really." His burned-down cigarette hung precariously from his lip as he reached for another. Perhaps his need to smoke was only a need not to smell death. "Of the eighteen dead, two were market vendors who would have been in the square at the time of the blast, had they not been shredded three days earlier. The German pair were found in their homes two mornings ago in the same mutilated state."

Feeling anxious, Peel rubbed the back of his head where it itched. He saw a pattern now, and wished he didn't. Yet he'd been right to come so far, these people needed to know what he knew, if only they would let him help. "There's more, isn't there Mr. Chemal?"

"Yes." The Moroccan lit a new cigarette from the embers of the last one. "Three more have died in the twenty-four hours since. Same cause of death: spontaneous shredding."

"And none were in the square at the time?"

"They were when the blast went off." He caught Peel's stare with a sardonic grin. "You came all this way Mr. Peel, all the way from Maryland, U.S.A. Can you tell me what it is that's happened here?"

Peel wouldn't catch his stare. "You said the bomber is still alive? I need to speak to her before I can give you definite answers ... if I can do even that."

The DST agent glared. "Be my guest," he snorted, and waved to indicate that they should now leave.

He escorted Peel downstairs, past two Royal Moroccan Army privates, their Steyr AUG assault rifles and unblinking stares guarding the only entrance. Deeper in the smell was of shit and perspiration.

"What do we know about her?" Peel asked as the corridor grew dark and confining. He didn't look in any of the cell's peep holes, afraid of what he'd see. Even the air felt more constrained down here.

"Her name is Souad Benhammou. She's not talking, but we suspect she is a member of Moroccan Islamic Combatant Group. MICG, a terrorist organization as Wikipedia likes to label them. Our information suggests that someone from the West is funding them, in all likelihood, someone in the United States."

"You have evidence of this?"

"Nothing substantial. We do suspect she's related to the wealthy Benhammou family, although they are denying it."

"And who are they, exactly?"

Chemal laughed throatily. "The Benhammous? They're 'Arabized' Berbers who made their fortunes long ago in phosphate mining. A rare breed—wealthy Berbers I mean."

"Interesting?"

"Perhaps." He stopped outside a cell, took a large metal key from his pocket. "You really want to talk to her? She hasn't responded to any of our interrogation methods, *any* of them, and it's been over twenty-four hours."

Despite his misgivings, Peel nodded.

"Well good luck then." Chemal's tone was flat. He sounded like he wanted to be somewhere else.

The door was opened slowly, betraying its weight when Chemal pushed his whole body into it. Hesitantly Peel stepped inside.

In the tiny cell, a thin woman sat against a wall stained with trickles of dark water. Dressed in a black jellaba, only her face and cuffed hands showed. Dark eyes stared through Peel and the wall behind him. She looked like she'd been staring at nothing for a very long time. When Peel stepped closer he saw that her hands betrayed the usual third-world interrogation technique bruises, and several circular cigarette burns. It was Chemal's crushed filters that littered the concrete floor. Peel cringed, wondered who was the enemy here.

"I'll leave you to it." Chemal locked Peel in.

Peel sat opposite the young woman on the only other chair, where she had to stare through him unless she wanted to break her gaze. She didn't.

He spoke to her slowly in his disjointed Arabic. "My name is Harrison Peel. Once upon a time I used to be a Major with the Royal Australian Army, fighting terrorists like you. Now however, I work for America's National Security Agency as a consultant. I still work in counter-terrorism, but these days we're against a different breed of terrorist. Men and women who've made deals with dark gods, alien gods ... You know what I'm talking about: the real gods."

There was the briefest flicker of her eyes. Slight enough that if Peel hadn't been paying attention, he would have missed it.

"I'm here because you have a weapon, an explosive device that works outside our perceptions of space and time. A weapon beyond the limitations that you and I and everyone on this world is trapped inside, called cause and effect."

Her concentration broken, she looked at him through tired eyes. When she answered, it was in English. "What would you know of these things?"

"A lot more than you could imagine," Peel too switched to

his native tongue because it was easier for him, "perhaps, or perhaps not?"

"The weapon was a gift, a gift from the Masked Messenger."

Peel raised a questioning eyebrow. "Nyarlathotep?"

Her blood-shot eyes grew large, and she trembled. With that single word Peel had finally rattled her.

She spoke softly now, but there was no mistaking the venom in her tone. "It seems you are well versed in the shadowed world."

Peel gave a tiny smile, remembering his own haunted past, and where he'd read the name Nyarlathotep before, words that had left him cold. "Yes, unfortunately." He leaned forward, whispering. "Let's start at the beginning, shall we? I know you're not Moroccan Islamic Combatant Group as you'd like everyone here to believe. From some reading I did in a very old book, I can see that you're really a member of a secret sect which calls themselves the Sisterhood of the Masked Messenger."

She went back to saying nothing again. Chemal was right, she would indeed be difficult to break. He wasn't sure he had the will to break her, or if he really should.

"What I don't understand, Souad Benhammou, is how you triggered the bomb without being killed."

She permitted him one more flicker of her eyes, one more acknowledgment that he existed. "Who said I survived?"

It took Peel several seconds to notice his whole body had gone cold. He toppled out of his chair, stumbled backwards against the cell door, to smash his fists against its coarse metal.

"Chemal!" he cried. "Chemal!" he screamed.

He looked back to her.

She smiled for him, briefly. Then her face lined with a dozen crimson lacerations. Her shape seemed to fold, crumpled into her falling jellaba. Her heart, before it collapsed into a dozen slices with the rest of her meat, pumped one final time, spraying Peel with the last of her living blood.

A fist slammed into Udad Benhammou's mouth with a meaty thunk, nearly knocking him out of his chair. Only the handcuffs that fastened him to the steel table saved him from a fall. Fabian

Chemal looked around the small, dingy cell, as if seeking answers from anywhere but his silent prisoner.

"Your sister is a terrorist, Udad, and so are you. When is the next planned attack? Who is the target?"

Udad looked down at the scrap of tanned pig leather Chemal had placed in his lap. Earlier the interrogator had put on gloves and rubbed the unclean pigskin over Udad's bloody face. The man was a disgrace to everything holy, nothing but a Western puppet. Udad did not let his hatred show. He did not speak, allowing the interrogator to read what he wanted from Udad's silence.

There would be a reckoning, and this dog would receive his reward.

Chemal lit another foul cigarette, and waved the cherry-red tip threateningly close to Udad's eye.

"In the old days, we would have sewn filth like you into a pigskin and dropped you in the river. You are nothing but an Al-Qaeda puppet, a fool who wants to murder women and children for some ignorant interpretation of *Al-Qur'an*."

Udad did not react. He merely stared into a corner of the room. The red glow of the cigarette moved away from his eye.

"Unfortunately, we have a squeamish Westerner who seems to think he can walk into another country's affairs. Typical cowboy." He punctuated his annoyance by putting out his cigarette on Udad's forearm. Udad heard the sizzle of his burning flesh, but the pain was less to him than the itch of a mosquito bite.

Vaguely, Udad heard a scream, and then another. Chemal took no notice of it until a thickset man came through the cell door to whisper something in Chemal's ear. With a look of annoyance, they both left, and Udad was alone in the dirty concrete cell.

He'd barely had time to think before Chemal was back. He placed a boot on Udad's chest and shoved. The chair would have tipped over but for the cuffs that locked Udad's wrists to the steel table. Chemal leaned his weight onto his prisoner, and the joints in the Udad's arms protested.

"Seems our American got a little excited. I hope you weren't too attached to your sister."

"Souad?" Udad had thought himself immune to pain. Chemal's face became a mask of triumph, and Udad realized he had spoken aloud.

"She's a bit of a mess—you probably wouldn't recognize her anymore." He searched Udad's face before going on. "I don't know what he did, but the blood he got on the lightbulb makes the whole place stink."

Udad closed his eyes and tried not to imagine what the cursed mongrel had done to Souad, but the reek of burned flesh suggested too many things. She was in Paradise with the martyrs, but the assurance only brought him scraps of comfort.

Chemal gave Udad a spiteful shove that nearly dislocated his shoulders.

"Unfortunately, our enthusiastic but careless American has managed break what could have been a valuable source of information." He shrugged, then moved his weight. "You are, therefore, free to go." Chemal kicked the chair out from under Udad, slamming his face against the sharp edge of the table. Udad could feel blood slowly oozing down his forehead, and wondered how badly he had been cut.

Chemal stalked out of the cell. Some time passed before a hard-faced officer unlocked Udad's cuffed wrists. Less than five minutes later, the prisoner found himself outside police headquarters, back among the familiar busy streets of Marrakesh.

Udad stumbled down the road, his mind in turmoil, his body aching. He could not risk contacting the Group. Not even through one of the anonymous mail-drops at an Internet Café. Chemal must have thought him truly stupid if he believed that Udad would lead the DST to his comrades.

Through tired eyes Peel watched the red sun rise over the High Atlas range. He muffled a yawn behind his hand, yet felt invigorated by the clean air outside the ramparts of Marrakech, so different to the stifling medinas. "Where are we going?" he asked Fabien Chemal, who lit another cigarette from his perpetually-full packet. He too was red-eyed.

"Tamegroute, near Algeria."

Peel nodded, recalling that the town was situated on the edge of the Sahara not far from the Algerian border. Its location was about as remote as one could get in Morocco.

"Why there?"

"We've captured another Combat Group terrorist."

"Oh." He hadn't expected news like this, and wasn't certain if he should feel positive or cautious. He wondered why he hesitated, he'd heard the name Tamegroute before, but couldn't remember where.

He looked at the truck that was to be their transport, hired to a production company shooting a film in Ouarzazate. In the enclosed tray were stage lights, power boards and other electrical goods that Peel couldn't identify.

"The truck belongs to a cousin," was all that Chemal offered in explanation. "He needs it to go to Ouarzazate, and so do we. From there we can arrange further transport to Tamegroute."

When the two spooks were sealed inside the tray, the truck set off east into the High Atlas. Chemal was soon snoring. With no windows to enjoy the scenery, Peel opened his copy of *The Masked Messenger* to jog his memory concerning Tamegroute. He felt certain that the answer lay in the book.

Peel had bought this first English edition in Marrakech many years ago. At the time he'd used it to aid him with another similarly peculiar investigation in the Congo. Obtained from a scholar named Jamal Alhazred, this copy was a rare edition. Printed by Colombia University Press in 1930, it had been translated by the Professor Samuel Colbridge and then edited and compiled by Professor Rudolph Pearson. If the signature and bookplate were authentic, this had been Pearson's personal copy.

As Peel flipped through the pages, he unconsciously removed his bookmark, a photograph of Nicola Mulvany and himself relaxing on a pristine beach in tropical Queensland. They looked happy, and this brought a tear to his eye. Not a day went by when Peel didn't yearn to have Nicola again, to share more moments like the moment in the photo, for the rest of their lives together.

"She's very pretty."

Peel snapped the book shut, hiding the picture within the yellowed pages. It was a woman who had spoken to him, from the shadows towards the back. When Peel saw her clearly, he saw that she had long dark hair, deep grey eyes, and a smile that was seemingly both sardonic and understanding. Peel couldn't guess her age, but there was no doubt she was the most beautiful woman he had ever laid eyes upon. And yet he could not find it in him to feel attracted to her, as if there was an element in her chemistry that he recoiled from.

"I'm sorry I gave you a start Mr. Peel. I thought you were aware I was here."

"Who are you?" He blinked at her.

"My name is Ms. Rope." Her English was perfect. Her accent he couldn't place. "But most people know me by my first name, Lathanty. I work with Fabien Chemal in the DST. Didn't he tell you about me?"

Peel felt stunned, like he'd just walked away from a major road accident. "I ... ?"

"What, Mr. Peel?"

"I didn't know you were there. You just startled me—that's all."

She smiled thinly.

"What do you do Ms. Rope, I mean with the DST?"

"Let's just say I'm an intelligence analyst."

"Specifically?"

"Specifically, I advise on the obscurities in human relationships that are too subtle or too arcane for the average DST agent." She nodded to Chemal who still snored. "When dealing with suicidal terrorists, often they prove to be fanatical experts on their religious texts. Understanding them and their sources becomes an important tool in determining their motives, and to find them before they strike."

Peel nodded in agreement, even though he didn't believe her. Women in Morocco fared better than in most Islamic countries, but few women were employed in the Moroccan secret service. And yet Chemal must have known about her, because from where he sat he could not have failed to notice her before he drifted off.

"That photograph, is that your wife?"

"My fiancée," Peel explained. He slipped the picture from the book so Lathanty could look at it. Then he took the engagement ring from his pocket where he could touch it whenever he felt alone and lost. He showed her the ring, but didn't let it go.

"Beautiful."

"She died before I could give it to her, just over a year ago, so she's not really my fiancée." Peel explained quickly not wanting the unasked question to linger. "It was my fault. I got her messed up in this world of secrets and deceit, and it cost her." He didn't add that Nicola had been torn to shreds by an alien monster born in another dimension. A death all too similar to Souad Benhammou's passing. His trip to Morocco was stirring old feelings.

"You must miss her?" She handed back the photograph.

"Every day."

"What would you do to bring her back?"

"Anything," blurted Peel. Then he looked to Lathanty, intrigued by her peculiar question. "But she's dead. I just have to accept that, don't I? Move on. She'd want me to do that, not wallow in self-pity."

Lathanty looked to *The Masked Messenger* which Peel held tight in his sweating hands, as he slipped the photograph back inside. "That's an interesting book you're reading Mr. Peel."

"You've read it?"

"Let's just say I'm well acquainted with its content."

Peel didn't want to ask, but suspected she was implying knowledge of the original. That version had been written in Arabic in the early Eighteenth Century by a woman called Sharinza, the same woman who was supposed to have founded the Sisterhood of the Masked Messenger. A more chilling thought; Lathanty might have even read the even more ancient tome that had influenced the original *Masked Messenger,* a tome known in obscure academic circles as *Al-Azif.* That book would later inspire many translations and become famous as the most comprehensive and terrifying guide to cosmic horrors this world had ever seen, the *Necronomicon.* Not that Peel had ever laid eyes on any of these manuscripts; he knew them only by their fearsome reputation.

"It's an interesting book Mr. Peel. Five hundred fables, most of them concerning a dark god called the Masked Messenger, Nyarlathotep, and how she offers power and salvation to those who ask for it. There is, of course, always a price."

"I thought most of the protagonists died horrible deaths."

That thin, almost nonexistent smile again. "That's because most of them bargained poorly. Did you ever read the tale of Sharinza herself, how she walked into the deep Algerian desert in search of the Temple of the Masked Messenger, forgotten for eons, buried under the Saharan sands?"

Peel remembered. It was the very story that mentioned Tamegroute, the town which had been playing on his mind since their departure. It was also the first story in the book, a prologue of sorts. Sharinza had found the temple, met with a god, then returned to her homelands. She brought untold horrors back with her, horrors that unfolded into four-hundred-and-ninety-nine more tales of death, madness and destruction. Some of those horrors were not too dissimilar to the weapon Souad had used in Marrakech.

"You should read it again. Sharinza bargained for the life of her lover."

Peel felt his heart flutter. "And did she get him back?"

Lathanty looked away. "Read it again Mr. Peel, find out for yourself."

Udad wandered the streets of Marrakech seeking some surcease of his pain, finding none. He considered assaulting the Westerner, gunning him down like a dog in the street. But the police retaliation would be swift and certain. He would be a martyr, all his sins forgotten, but how would he know for certain that the man was dead? It occurred to him that he didn't even know the name of the butcher who had laid hands on Souad. Frustration welled up in him. What could he do?

Defeated, he returned to his small, sparsely-furnished apartment.

On his small cot was a cardboard box. There was no address, no note, simply the box, held closed with tape. Listless and sore from a day of volatile emotions and physical abuse, Udad opened the box without interest.

The book inside was old and beautiful. He ran his fingers over the raised, flowing script on the leather cover. *The Masked Messenger.* He had never heard of it. A small scrap of paper stuck out of the thick sheaf of pages. Udad opened to it. It was a note, unsigned, but in Souad's careful, well-practiced hand.

If you have the courage to avenge my dishonor at the hands of the Westerner, this is the key.

A cold thrill moved through him. She had known. She had known what would happen to her. Emotions warred in him. He had never been more proud of her, and yet his anger quickly resurfaced—he could not tell her how brave she had been.

He spent a sleepless night reading—starting with the page Souad had marked. Udad quickly realized that the forces of Hell were contained in the book. *The Masked Messenger* was clearly the work of the Great Deceiver, but the resources of the enemy could be used against him by a clever and righteous man. His comrades at the Combat Group viewed him as useful because of his money, but Udad knew he was destined for more than just providing funds for the revolution.

It was nearly dawn when Udad, his head spinning from the things he had read, collapsed on his cot and fell into a dark, dreamless sleep.

He was awakened some time later by a sense of motion in his room. Instantly, Udad was out of his cot, machete in his hand.

It was not a policeman that stood before him, but a woman. She held no weapon.

"Who are you?" He demanded with a strong, harsh voice.

"I cannot tell you who I am, but our aims are similar. We both knew Souad, and we both seek justice." Her voice was soft and mellifluous, like honey on the tongue.

He lowered his weapon, but did not put it away. In his small, dull room, he could make out that one of her eyes was covered with a white film. She was properly and modestly veiled, even though it was inappropriate for her to be in the company of a strange man unescorted.

"I don't trust you. You are probably a spy."

"I knew your sister, and I helped fulfill her last wish by getting you that book." She gestured toward the tome that was lost somewhere in the shadows.

Udad was torn. He'd heard strange rumors of a sisterhood of devil-worshipers but he refused to believe that Souad would have done anything so blasphemous. Whoever this woman was, he would have to be on his guard. If he kept his head about him, he should be able to use this woman even as she attempted to use him.

"I doubt that you ever knew Souad. I should kill you simply for sullying her name with your tongue." He made a half-hearted gesture with his machete.

"Souad spoke many times of her younger brother Udad, the brave boy who would stood up to his father when he was only fourteen. How she used to chase you round the yard after you snatched the book she was reading. And how you became serious and studious after a chance meeting with an Afghan *mujahid.*"

"Enough." There was nothing unmanly about tears, but now was not the time. "Say what you have to say, then leave."

"Come with me." She beckoned him to the doorway. "And we will talk."

Naked and bloody, bathed in cubes of sunlight dissected by the windows of wrought-iron grills, Peel screamed from the highest tower in the Tamegroute Kasbah. Every muscle in his body flexed and burned as another jolt from the car battery sizzled his flesh. In his time in the Australian Army he'd been trained to resist interrogation, but not torture. Fabien Chemal wanted information Peel didn't have, and he was determined to use any extreme to obtain it.

Peel's pain had hardly begun. To remind him that his current torture was nothing, a bucket of petrol wafted its acrid odors just out of reach, but just within eyesight. And Chemal liked to smoke cigarettes.

"Please, I told you," Peel sweated, gritted his teeth. "I don't know anything about the Combat Group."

Rope sat quietly next to Chemal, a delicate finger poised at her mouth as if she were watching nothing more than an engrossing film. Chemal wouldn't look at her, but Peel had little choice. She asked the questions while he administered the pain. Despite their roles, she was colder than he. Together they were formidable interrogators, and Peel was afraid he was not far from breaking, telling them all the lies they wanted to hear. And when he had branded himself a traitor, they would wipe their hands of him, a cheap and nasty death as his reward. They would abandon his body to the Sahara, never to be seen again.

"You were talking to me in the truck yesterday," she asked firmly, "discussing the terrorist organization, the Sisterhood of the Masked Messenger?"

"You were there, that is what we did."

Her eyes looked to Chemal, who was hot and bothered, then to Peel again. Her mouth hinted a smile, as if she knew a secret that neither man did. "You've heard of the Temple of the Masked Messenger, haven't you, Peel?"

"Yes," he tensed, hoping that his answer would not bring him another electric shock. Thankfully it did not. "You know this, so why do you keep asking me?"

"Do you know where this Temple of the Masked Messenger is? Is that where the Sisterhood is to be found?"

"I don't know exactly," his voice sounded hysterical even to his own ears. With every second he was expecting the next burning jolt of electricity. "All I know is that the temple is located somewhere in the Algerian Sahara, somewhere south of Tamegroute. Please, that's where you'll find the people you're after."

In a hurry to get to his feet, Chemal toppled his chair. He punched Peel in the gut, hard, and then again, harder still. Despite his bindings, Peel doubled over, grunting as air was expelled from his lungs.

When he could breathe again he sobbed. He didn't want to die, not like this, not upon a misunderstanding. "Why are you doing this to me?" He looked to Lathanty hoping that she might offer some compassion, but all she would do was smile thinly. He hated that smile now. "Please?"

"You bastard!" Chemal lifted Peel by his bloody chin. "You've confessed. There is no salvation for you. All I can do is put a stop to the pain, but only if you first tell me what I want to know."

"But I've answered all her questions."

"Her questions?" Chemal eyebrows crunched into a frown. "What are you talking about Peel? It's just you and me." The DST agent looked about the darkened stone room. He looked right through Lathanty Rope.

Peel became confused. Rope was standing right next to Chemal. Couldn't he see her?

"I've confessed to nothing. I've done nothing wrong. I'm trying to help you both!"

"Both?" Chemal stepped from Peel, took three deep breaths as he wiped his sweaty brow. He lifted the tape recorder still spinning on the cell's only desk, rewound it for a few seconds, and then pressed play.

Peel listened through bloody ears, and couldn't believe what he heard.

CHEMAL: When you thought I was sleeping in the movie truck, you risked a telephone call to your contact with the Combat Group? Don't lie now Peel, I heard every word.

PEEL: You were there, that is what we did.

CHEMAL: You're the western spy who's funding the Combat Group. You sold them the weapon.

PEEL: Yes. You know this, so why do you keep asking me?

CHEMAL: So how do you fund them exactly? I want names, places, accounts, and dates. Especially places.

PEEL: I don't know exactly. All I know is that the temple is located somewhere in the Algerian Sahara, somewhere south of Tamegroute. Please, that's where you'll find the people you're after.

The tape was stopped. Wiping sweat from his face Chemal drew a cigarette from his pack. His first smoke since the interrogation commenced. "That a confession Peel, if I've ever heard one."

Peel felt his gut blacken and knot. It was Chemal on the tape, not Lathanty Rope. How could they both be asking him questions, but he could only hear one of them, the single voice that wasn't recorded?

Then Peel understood.

Lathanty Rope.

An anagram of Nyarlathotep.

When he caught her eye, the smile she gave had grown large, and was nothing less than evil.

"You don't exist, do you?" She said nothing.

"You don't exist outside of my own mind, do you... Nyarlathotep?"

"I exist Mr. Peel, even if only you can see me. But that's how I wanted it. That's how I always wanted it."

"Who are you talking to?" Chemal's eyes glanced to the room's dark corners, his eyes frantic.

Peel ignored him. "What do you want with me?"

"What do I want? What do you want, Major Harrison Peel?"

Peel didn't see Chemal splash him with the bucket of petrol. The combustible fluids burnt his eyes, clawed at his nostrils and lips. His whole body convulsed. Fabien had his cigarette in his mouth. He lit it, drew upon its smoke. Now he had it in his hands, ready to flick it away. "Names Peel, I want names."

Peel screamed.

Lathanty slid close to him, whispered in his ear. "You want to escape this place, don't you?"

"Yes," Peel sobbed.

"Give me the names," roared the DST agent.

"You'll agree to do something for me," Lathanty spoke over Chemal, "just like the Sisterhood promised to deliver something to me after I gave them that weapon. In return I'll save your life, and perhaps I'll bring your fiancée back."

"Anything," Peel sobbed again, "anything."

He didn't want to die like this, not to be burnt alive in some forgotten North African town in a country where no one would miss him, where no one would even acknowledge his passing. And the pain, he couldn't even begin to imagine what it would feel like, to wail as his skin and flesh melted from his bones.

Chemal puffed his cigarette, allowed the flaming embers to grow. "I won't ask again Peel."

"Please?"

Lathanty's face lost all its beauty, ran with streams of acid, burning away her coarse grey flesh and dark hair. Her clothes smoldered. When her eyes widened, they reflected the entirety of the cosmos itself. With a flick of her hand acid splashed across the Moroccan's face.

Chemal screamed, held his hands to his melting eyes only to have his fingers dissolve to the bone. Sockets without lids smoked upon a skull without skin. Blood and caustic fluids mixed and boiled, and Fabien Chemal screamed louder than Peel ever had.

His lit cigarette fell from his bone tips as he crumpled upon his knees, and fell towards Peel.

Nyarlathotep caught the red ember mere centimeters from ignition.

In the shadows, Chemal's skull cracked and dissolved exposing his brain, and finally the DST agent died.

All the while the dark god held the captured cigarette close to Peel's face. "We have a deal Harrison Peel." It wasn't a question.

Peel looked into the grey face, burning with the same acid that had killed Chemal, but caused her no pain. "We have a deal," he sobbed. In the shadow's Chemal's corpse was nothing more than black smoldering bones and bubbling corruption. It could have just as easily been him.

The Masked Messenger extinguished the cigarette between her index finger and thumb. Then she touched the ropes binding Peel's hands and feet, dissolving them effortlessly. Too weak to stand, Peel collapsed on the floor.

She threw a bucket of water over him, invigorating him with its cold. "Get dressed," she pointed to his clothes, "the desert awaits."

Udad found the mysteries contained within *The Masked Messenger* profound and difficult. For all that they appeared simple, the book's stories unfolded before the educated man, revealing disturbing possibilities. The power of it made Udad's head spin. Surely, he had lost his job by now. He had not left his apartment for days, and could not tell if his lightheadedness came from the dizzying insights of the book, or because he could not remember the last time he had eaten. But just as prayer was better than sleep, *The Masked Messenger* was more nourishing than food.

He stood, and the floor spun treacherously under his feet. He understood the dangerous and unreliable nature of reality now, the fundamental betrayal with which Shaitan had deceived nearly all of creation. Udad had mastered those esoteric truths, understood that the web of lies had holes in it, and knew that acts supposed impossible could be accomplished if one perceived both the deceit and the truth.

He ran a rough hand through his sweat-soaked hair. His apartment was stuffy, smothering. In the days since his interrogation, the pain in his shoulders had eased, but the burn-scars on his forearms still bothered him.

"Udad?" The call was a harsh whisper, and he looked around, unable to locate the voice. Had he imagined it?

"Udad are you there?" Her voice drifted faintly through the door.

He jerked the door open to find the same women who had given him the book. She looked at him with a boldness that was unbecoming to her sex. And still, he moved aside and allowed her into his small, shabby apartment.

She looked him up and down, her good, brown eye seeing merely him, but the milky orb was piercing. "You have read the book. And now you see the world with new eyes."

Udad could only grunt in response, his voice dry and cracked from disuse. Again, he wondered at her temerity, not only willing to speak with him alone, but to address him as if he were her student. She stood, back to him, looking over his barren apartment, betraying no signs of apprehension. She was unlike any other woman Udad had ever known, with the possible exception of Souad.

The memory of his sister was still a hot dagger in his heart.

"You do not know the risk I have taken in giving you that book." The woman—whose name he did not know—was looking at him now. "Souad said that you were trustworthy, that you were the sort of man who could get things done."

"Get them done, yes," he echoed her distantly. His mind felt disconnected, jumbled, as if it were sand that had once been stone. "Is it true what the book says about the temple near Tamegroute, the one that Sharinza visited?"

"No." She said it in a gasp, and fear glimmered in her good eye before she turned away from him. So, she was a woman after all. "You do not want to go to that temple. We ... we need you. You were not given that book for your own—" He cut her off with a glare.

The weariness, the uncertainty, and the feeling of distance all faded, replaced with a sense of purpose. A plan, half-formed and cloudy until now, roared through him.

"You said Souad was a valuable member of your ... organization." He almost said 'cult.' "This will be my trial, then. If I can reach the temple, then both Souad and I will return to you, and you will be stronger for having both of us. If I fail, then this book is only lies and blasphemy."

She looked at the floor, understood his threat.

"The book does not tell everything. Some secrets were left only with trusted servants of our order, so that no one who only has the book would know the whole truth." She glanced up at him, only to flinch away from his hard stare. "The temple of the Masked Messenger is much as the book says it is. But Sharinza's story does not mention that there must be an offering to access the power of the temple."

"And what does the djinn of the temple prefer? I expect it is not exotic incense."

"No. A soul must be offered."

Udad nodded, turning this profane act over in his mind. "What else?"

She tried to look at him, and again flinched away.

"Peel, the Westerner who murdered your sister. He has a copy of *The Masked Messenger*, and he could be headed toward Tamegroute."

"He is an ignorant American who doesn't know what must be offered, even if he can understand the book." Udad felt the heady rush of power course through him. Even if Peel wasn't headed for the temple, it would not be difficult to kidnap him. "Still, it would be best not to make him wait for his destiny."

Udad could see no greater justice than to burn the soul of the Western unbeliever who had murdered his sister in order to light her way back from death. And if the temple did not work as the book claimed, he would at least have revenge.

"Is there anything else?"

"Just being near the Temple is dangerous, Udad." Her small hands plucked at the air. "Time and space are distorted, and can drive a weak-minded man mad. You could see your past or future."

Udad was unimpressed.

"I don't fear the future. Is this why you need a man to go? Someone without womanish fear?"

She dropped her gaze to the floor.

"Then you should go," he said. "I need to prepare."

Clearly cowed, she left. When the door was safely shut behind her, Udad pulled the clothing out of a chest, revealing the AK-47 hidden beneath.

It was nothing for him to steal a pickup truck and turn it south. It was a long drive that took him across the Atlas Mountains and into the burning, trackless Sahara, but his desire for vengeance burned hotter than the pitiless desert sun.

Peel sped into the mighty Sahara. He'd crammed Chemal's Landrover with bottled water, canned food, and petrol drums in the back. He needed to be prepared as drove out of Tamogroute and to the south, where a vast lifeless world opened to him.

When he made an illegal crossing into Algeria nobody noticed. When he reached the Bechar to Tindouf road, he crossed it without thought and drove into the mighty sea of sand dunes.

It was then that the Masked Messenger appeared.

She sat next to Peel, in the passenger's seat. She wore only a dirty white robe. Acid perspired from her pores, dissolving the fabric of her robes and the car seat, but never enough to completely erode either. She smelt like drain cleaner.

Peel ignored her for three days.

Only when he was lost, when he was convinced that he'd

been driving in circles for the last forty-eight hours, did he deign to talk to her.

"What exactly do you want of me?"

That thin smile again, but no answer.

Later they stood together outside the stationary Landrover, on the rise of a dune. Peel peered into the vast expanse of still yellow waves searching for a landmark to drive towards. He guzzled another water bottle until it was empty. It was so hot he felt that he sweated most of the water before it reached his stomach.

His unwanted companion required no sustenance. Outside the hot wind gathered, swirled her robe about her slender form as if it were a living entity. She continued to drip acid, an endless supply carving canals in her flesh. Where the acid fell upon the sand, glass formed.

"Are you going to speak to me … Nyarlathotep?"

She pointed south. "There's a sand storm coming."

"What does that mean?"

"It means you're about to lose your vehicle."

Bottling his anger, Peel fashioned a makeshift turban to protect against the encroaching winds of coarse sands. When the storm hit he worked hard, dug through the rest of the day and right through the night. But the sands were too fast, too persistent. Without really remembering when it happened, the four-wheel drive was swallowed by the dunes. He'd only managed to save an AK-47 assault rifle, a knife, his map, five liters of water, and his copy of *The Masked Messenger*.

"Fuck you!" he yelled into the night, for Nyarlathotep had long abandoned him. "I said fuck you!"

Exhausted he wrapped a shawl about him, sat with his back to the violent winds, and waited out the storm.

In the morning when the winds had died, Peel marched. He held off from drinking the last of his water for as long as he could. He trudged south only because his map said that a water pumping station lay somewhere in that direction. But in the desert, there were no landmarks to keep his bearings, and when his mind was rational, he knew he was lost.

Time passed and eventually his water was no more. The sky

swam, blistered with gusts of heat like invisible demons sent to torment him. Eventually he tumbled down the side of the dune. When he crashed at the base, his mouth and eyes stung with the sand that filled them.

"I'll do it!" he called. "Whatever you want, I'll do it."

The ground began to rumble. Huge layers of sand slid down the dunes, forcing Peel to continuously climb upwards. Just beyond the next crest a gigantic cloud of sand billowed into the sky. He spied enormous stone blocks rising in its chaotic fury.

Peel clambered up a shifting dune. A great temple was rising from the Sahara, greater than any structure built by humanity. Sand ran off its mighty roof like waterfalls. Hollow reverberations like the echoes inside an enormous cavern rang to announce its materialization. Peel could only wonder at its size, for it was at least three hundred meters in height, with four sides a kilometer and a half long.

Upon its square roof were gigantic statues of faceless winged demons. In mighty alcoves arranged around its base where impossibly large statues of octopoidal-bat hybrids, each carved from a single piece of stone.

In a daze Peel walked up to its base, stood at its mighty steps. He could not be sure he wasn't hallucinating until he clambered upon the first mighty stone block. When he reached the lower balcony, exhausted and sun-burnt, a single stone entrance awaited him. In his heart, he knew that an infinite darkness lay beyond, and that he must enter if he was to find answers and salvation.

Peel staggered into the temple, his weapon slung under his arm, his sheathed knife within easy reach in his belt.

The portal was more than a doorway, for he found himself transplanted across the gulfs of space and time, and perhaps into another universe altogether. This was no longer the Sahara, but a vast alien city of buildings and towers carved from single pieces of rock. Each structure was connected by a web of passageways, balconies, tunnels and bridges joined at conflicting angles that only Escher could have imagined. The sky was a brilliant green tapestry of stars and galaxies. Half the horizon was dominated by a tremendous gas giant, its swirling atmosphere of browns, oranges and whites clearly visible. Peel could make out six satellites of varying colors, populated with oceans, mountains, volcanoes and ... writhing tentacles.

In a stupor Peel walked to the edge of one balcony, peered over its lip. Hundreds perhaps thousands of kilometers beneath him was the surface of a purple world decorated with pink clouds and pasty-grey mountains, and a sea which frothed like bubbling acid. This city reached heights so great, Peel could see the curvature of the moon upon which it was built.

Feeling vertigo Peel stepped back.

Now the Masked Messenger waited for him. She wore an elongated mask of bronze, with two dark eye-slits and no mouth piece, so slim that it should have been impossible for her face to hide behind it.

Beyond the Masked Messenger lingered two muscular naked humans, a man and a woman. Their faces were blank stretches of featureless skin. They waited motionlessly like bodyguards.

"I'm insane, aren't I?" Peel asked.

The Messenger approached, removed her mask revealing the normal face of Lathanty Rope, now hairless and disfigured by her caustic blood.

"So where am I then? Am I to be another one of your tales?"

"You're in my home. This is Sharnoth, the Court of Nyarlathotep beyond the universe. All things can be learnt here, for a price." Her mask had transformed, as she handed him a bronze jug lapping with clean water.

Peel didn't hesitate as he guzzled its entire contents. "Including the knowledge on how to bring Nicola back?"

"All things are possible."

His eyes caught movement, not from the faceless watchers, but from a distant man running between passages, darting across bridges, and peering into windows. He too carried an AK-47. At times Peel could see the man more than once, as if he could glimpse the man in his past, his present and his future all at the same time. Like Souad's weapon, in this world time and space were unaligned with cause and effect.

"Who is that?"

"The man I want you to murder."

Peel lifted his Russian made weapon, firm in his hand now that he was no longer delirious with dehydration. The Masked Messenger in her infinite planning had arranged for everything.

"Who is he?"

"He is Udad Benhammou, brother of Souad. He is here to kill you."

Because of the water in his gut, Peel felt alive again, more clear-headed. But that was exactly how Nyarlathotep wanted Peel to feel, because she had a job she wanted him to do.

Peel had killed enough times in his life, and he regretted every one of them. The faces of the dead kept him awake at night. His only solace was that each killing had been in self-defense, or to protect against alien intrusion that they worked to allow. But to kill in cold-blood for a selfless purpose, Peel wasn't certain that he had it in him, or if Nicola would even want him to.

"Why, what do you get out of it?"

Again, Nyarlathotep gave Peel that sardonic, all-knowing, omnipotent line-thin smile. "Nothing that you could ever possibly hope to understand."

Udad clenched his AK-47. It was his closest link to the real world. Most of the time, the gun's steel retained some heat from the desert outside. Sometimes, however, it was cold beneath his fingers. Udad clenched his teeth until the warmth returned. He did not like this palace of the *ifrits*. The sky was unnatural, frightening, and made Udad nauseous just looking at it. The temple around him was no relief either.

His other anchor to reality was his hatred of Peel. Udad had seen tracks leading to the mighty temple, and they could not have belonged to anyone but his sister's murderer. There was a symmetry to all this, the poetry of fate.

Udad crept across the strange interior, keeping his head down. He tried to ignore the grotesque, ungodly statues. The carven abominations mocked everything that was sacred and decent, and their imagery preyed on his mind. Two days of driving in the hot desert night and sleeping during the worst of the Sahara's blistering heat had left him exhausted and parched, but still determined.

He crept through the dark interior of the temple, searching, unsure as to how long he had been doing so. Time seemed elastic and strange, wrapped around itself. Several times, he could not tell how many, he found himself in places with no memory of having arrived. Experimentally, he made a single pass with his hand in front of his face. His hand appeared to flicker randomly before coming to rest where he had intended. On the second pass, he tried to change where his hand would stop, but somehow, it ended up somewhere else.

Fate, it appeared, was strong here. All the better for him.

After an uncountable time of stealth and waiting, Udad saw Peel and a bald woman standing together on a raised dais. Anger surged through him. If he had been betrayed by the Sisterhood, he would hunt them all down. Then he would be the sole master of the temple and its power. Peel had a reliable AK-47 slung off his shoulder, like the one Udad held.

He found a dark corner, next to one of the immense carven blasphemies. As quietly as he could, Udad worked the action of the AK-47, chambering a bullet. Neither Peel nor the woman seemed to notice. As Udad watched, she gave him an urn, and Peel drank. It was too much to hope that it was poisoned.

As he brought his sights to bear on Peel, the figures on the dais flickered and vanished. Udad cursed under his breath. He should have been faster. His sister's spirit cried out for vengeance, and he had been too slow. What evil magic was this?

Even as he remonstrated himself, someone—Peel—was back on the dais, alone. Udad could not make out his features, silhouetted against the nauseous green light from outside, but the distinctive assault rifle with the curling magazine slung off one shoulder was all the confirmation he needed.

Peel turned. He appeared to hear the shot just before Udad squeezed the trigger. The weapon's chest-thumping retort was immediately swallowed by the strange geometry of the temple. There was a chunky spray as the bullet caught Peel in the head, and he collapsed like a sack of grain.

In his triumph, Udad did not rush his pleasure. He walked casually up the stairs slinging his weapon over his shoulder. His sister was avenged, and the sacrifice had been made. The powers of the temple were now his to command. But first, he wanted to see the face of the man who had murdered Souad.

He reached the top of the dais, but no body and no blood awaited him. The polished grey-yellow stone of the dais was dust-free as if it had been polished.

He glanced back to where he had come from and saw himself, weapon aimed. The retort of the shot reached him a split second after his own bullet smashed through his skull.

The offices of the French oil prospecting company, although still deep within the Algerian Sahara, were a welcome sight for Harrison Peel. He drank their water, ate their food, and used their amenities until he felt refreshed and human again. Then he commandeered their telephone to call the United States.

"We all thought you were dead, Peel," said the distant voice of Jack Dixon, Peel's NSA contact back in Maryland.

"I should have been, mate. I should have been."

"Well glad to hear that you're not."

"A geological survey team found me in the middle of nowhere, brought me here. Unbelievable really, the chances of them finding me were astronomically low, but they did."

The open office plan was pristine and clean, with desktop computers and notice boards. A young woman sat at one of the computers, her keystrokes even and unbroken, otherwise Peel was alone. From where he stood he couldn't see her face. She didn't seem to be eavesdropping, so he let her be.

"Get yourself to In Salah. We'll have a passport and a flight out waiting for you."

"Thanks Jack, I owe you one."

"You always do." He laughed and then hung up.

Peel sighed, feeling as if he could actually relax for the first time in weeks. He made himself coffee in the minuscule kitchenette. Instant was all that was on offer, but it tasted good regardless.

The silent woman continued to tap away. Only her fingers

moved.

Peel's mind was drawn again to the horrors he experienced inside the temple, and its bizarre and terrifying secrets. He'd told the Messenger that he would not kill Udad for her. As simple as that, he had walked away, out into the Sahara, expecting to die.

Even now he wasn't certain he hadn't imagined the whole thing. Was the Masked Messenger really a cosmic god that made all the decision on when and how the universe evolved? Or was she entirely a fabrication of his fevered mind?

His copy of *The Masked Messenger* was all that had survived with him. His knife, the gun, the water, even his photograph of Nicola and their engagement ring had been consumed by the sands. Why had the book survived?

The tapping had ceased without him even noticing it.

"Harrison Peel." She wasn't asking.

He turned, faced the young woman staring at him. She was pretty, until he spied her milky white eye.

"Yes?"

"I have something for you." She handed him a vial with a metal stopper. Inside swished a pristine transparent liquid that turned turquoise and amber depending upon the angle of the light.

Reluctantly Peel took the vial. "What is this?"

"The Messenger keeps her promises."

Peel did a double-take as he stared back at the woman. Was she one of the Sisters? Was their organization real? Did the Masked Messenger actually exist?

"Drink it," she explained. "And it will take you back in time and space, to be with your lover once again. But only some experiences of your past will change. You'll still return to Morocco. You'll still become lost in the Sahara and find the temple, where you will fulfill the Messenger's plans."

"But I ..." he stumbled. He wasn't sure whether he should dismiss her, or interrogate her. "What? I didn't kill Benhammou."

"We never expected you to."

"Then what did I do, to deserve this?"

"You've read the book Mr. Peel, the first story? After her servant sacrificed himself in the temple—a fact not recorded in the book—Sharinza returned to her home, and in doing so bridged the dimensions between our world and that of Nyarlathotep, and then ..."

"... and then forty-hundred-and-ninety-nine tales of destruction and madness plagued the world," Peel finished.

He put his head in his hands. He'd been little more than a pawn in a game he barely understood, and couldn't have affected the outcome any more than a grain of sand could have stopped the sandstorm that had engulfed his truck.

All he had to show for it was the vial. He looked at it, wondering if it was everything the woman had said. Was he ready to go through the past year again, face all those horrors and watch so many of his friends die? Only he'd have Nicola by his side, and what a life she would make for him again, or would Nicola become a hollow reflection of her former self? Perhaps he could even defeat Nyarlathotep, by refusing to walk into the desert to find her temple, and save the world from whatever horrors awaited. Perhaps he could do any of these things ... or could he? Would he even remember that he was to live that last year all over again?

He looked up to ask the woman that very question, but she was gone.

On the long bus trip to In Salah, Peel threw the vial into the uncaring sands. Quickly it disappeared from his sight, and more importantly, his reach.

GOD OF CHICKENS

Len lay on his belly, overlooking the chicken man's huddle of filthy shacks. The ammonia reek of chicken shit was like sandpaper up his nose. He nudged Jess with his foot.

"Which one does the chicken man live in?" Len whispered, trying not to disturb the warm evening quiet.

"The fuck should I know?" The setting sun turned the surrounding Loblolly pines into black prison bars.

"How many chickens do you think he's got down there?" Jess asked in a flat, bored voice.

"Supposed to be a couple hundred. Gran'ma Black says he never sells any, and never sells eggs, neither." Len was still whispering.

"Your Gran'ma talks to fucking angels. Your family are all retards."

Len could feel the hot flush of embarrassment climb his face. He pointed to the filthy, feather-strewn ground below them.

"I think he's coming out."

In the gloom, the slapped-together collection of lumber, construction leavings, hubcaps, and bales of hay somehow added up to five huge chicken coops. Dark shadows swallowed everything else. Chickens clustered in odd groups, and occasionally pecked at the ground.

Len had chickens at home. They were filthy, stupid creatures. He'd helped his momma cut their heads off, then pluck their feathers. Eating them didn't bother him at all. Maybe he could convince Jess to just steal a couple. They could spit them over a fire. Jess would want to kill them slow, but that was better than messing with the chicken man. Len was afraid of the chicken man.

Jess had just opened his mouth when the shack's door shifted. He caught his breath as the chicken man lurched into view. He was over six feet, with broad shoulders. A flabby gut hung over his worn belt, his hair a tangled nest, the sunken face old, lined, and filthy. He moved with a lurching hobble. That was good, if they had to run, he wouldn't be able to keep up.

He brought a pair of sawhorses out of his shack, then set a big sheet of plywood on them. With a strange bit of ceremony, he spread some sort of stained cloth over it. Len heard the scritch of a match, and the chicken man lit a pair of hurricane lamps, one on each end of the cloth-covered table. The wan light from the two lamps showed the chickens, which should have been roosting in the dark. Instead, they crowded around the circles of lamplight, clucking quietly with the hushed tones of a church congregation.

Len held his breath, not daring to disturb the turgid atmosphere. The darkness crowded in on them, and he thought about how far away home was.

"Buk *bawk*!" The chicken man screamed, and the assembled chickens swayed. From the thronged mass of birds, there was a stir, and a rooster strutted out of the crowd. It stood in the yellow pool of light and for a moment, man and chicken considered each. The rest of the chickens shrank back, like they were holding their breath, or praying.

The chicken man seized the rooster's neck in one thick hand. Len expected him to crank it around his head, the way his momma did. Instead, he savagely bit the feathered neck. Blood sprayed all over the chicken man's filthy face and clothes, and onto the makeshift altar. The rooster's wings beat convulsively until the chicken man's powerful hands ripped its body in half. Len bit his finger hard enough to draw blood as the rooster's guts landed on the altar with a squishy *plop*.

"Cool," Jess breathed. The chicken man devoured the rooster raw, crunching the bones in his powerful jaws, leaving the oozing, bloody lump of guts untouched on the altar. Hundreds of shining bird eyes reflected the flickering light of the two hurricane lamps.

When the chicken man had finished his meal, he clucked

and muttered to himself, then hobbled into his shack. In the light of the two lamps on the bloody altar, Len watched the chickens disperse to their roosts.

"We should go." Len felt like he wanted to cry.

"No way. This is going to be fucking cool." Jess's eyes were bright and crazy, like the time he came up with Toad Golf. Then he was sneaking down the hill, and Len was debating whether he wanted to follow or stay alone in the dark. After a moment, he followed.

They skirted the light as much as they could, keeping to the deep dark. The chirp of crickets and the buzz of katydids hid the sound of their sneakers on pine needles. Len froze when an owl hooted somewhere in the darkness. Owls were bad luck. But Jess kept on, and soon they were at the chicken man's rickety shack.

Len looked at Jess, wondering if he really wanted to go through with this. As if in answer, Jess kicked the door to one side.

"You chicken-fucking freak!"

The chicken man turned in surprise, his broad, filthy face filled with fear—or was it? Then Jess rushed him, Len following. They knocked the big man to the ground and started throwing punches and kicks.

"How do you like that, you sick fuck?" Jess screamed. Len wasn't hitting as hard as he could, but Jess was wailing away and screaming like the guy had called his momma a whore.

"Noooo!" The chicken man curled into a ball, protecting his head with his arms. Jess hammered some spiteful shots into his face anyway, and his fists started coming away bloody. Len worked his fat belly until his shoulders started to burn. He stopped, even though Jess was still kicking. The chicken man didn't look that hurt, big and blubbery as he was. Just cowering.

Jess was still screaming that the chicken man was a freak who had no right to live. He stopped gasping for breath, and the chicken man lurched to one knee, then the other. Standing, he towered over the boys, a filthy titan in the confining darkness.

"Not chicken man!" His rumbling bass filled the shack like a roll of thunder.

"Not chicken *man!*" The blood trickling down the side of his face made him appear terrible and menacing. He looked more angry than hurt, and Len was already thinking about running.

"*God of Chickens!*" He roared it so loud that Jess was thrown to the filthy, feather-strewn floor. Len, still on his feet, turned and ran, scrambling out of the shack and into the sane black of night. He managed five running strides before the chickens descended on him. Angry beaks and flying talons clawed at him. Blinded, Len stumbled and went down under a smothering blanket of pecking and clawing chickens. Far away, Jess was screaming.

Len fought his way to his knees. He caught one last glimpse of Jess, staring at him, blood pumping from a great raw wound where the God of Chickens had bitten his neck. The chickens had stopped attacking. Jess made a single, spasmodic gesture, then sagged to the filthy ground. Through blurred eyes, Len watched the God of Chickens pick up the Jess's unresponsive body and carry it to the bloody altar.

Len cradled his head with his arms so he wouldn't see what came next. He felt the chickens' attention focus on the altar. He didn't think to cover his ears until he heard the snap of bone, and the repulsive wet *thud* that followed. He covered his head and rocked himself, waiting for the end.

The stump of heavy feet approached. Len closed his eyes and huddled into himself, not wanting to see the God of Chickens' huge, bloody teeth coming for his neck.

Instead, something hot and wet brushed across his forehead. He opened his eyes to see the God of Chickens towering above him, his right hand holding something dark and raw. Len swallowed a convulsive sob.

"Tell them I am coming." The God of Chickens' voice was resonant, commanding. "It will do them no good now."

Len sobbed, huddling into himself until the heavy, uneven tread of the God of Chickens receded. When he looked up, the lights were guttering, and even the chickens weren't paying him any attention. And then Len was running through the darkness, not caring which direction he went so long as it was away from the God of Chickens.

Len screamed himself awake to the pale grey sky of oncoming morning. He was curled into a tight ball, shivering against the chill, wet with his own sweat and morning dew. His dreams had been filled with teeth and blood, and the wordless scream of a lost friend's unending terror. In the wan morning light, he found neither cheer nor comfort. Len rubbed his forehead, and his fingers came away with black flakes under the nails. His arms were covered with scabs from being pecked and scratched. He ached. Jess was gone. Forever.

The memory was like a fist to the gut.

Alone, cold, and nearly weeping, Len wandered in the forest as the sun made its cheerless appearance. It was close to noon before he got clear of the trees, and realized he was on the Connolly's land.

The sight of the familiar old farmhouse brought him no renewed sense of reality. The God of Chickens was out in the woods somewhere, and Jess was gone, and Len would never be the same. Not even if he were a thousand miles away.

Len skirted the tall corn, green and thriving in the now-warm summer morning. He moved past the old farmhouse toward the cracked and ill-paved road. He froze when he saw a chicken in the front yard. It made no move to attack, or alert the other chickens. Instead it stood, immobile as a statue, staring at him. Len looked up and saw other chickens, dark-eyed and still, watching him. As Len moved, their heads swiveled to follow him.

He wondered how long it would be before the God of Chickens knew where he was.

Len had no plan beyond getting back to town. Home was not a place of comfort, and no one was going to believe him when he warned them about the God of Chickens. What was he going to do now? His despair came with the memories of teeth and breath that reeked of blood.

He didn't hear the cop car until came to a halt just in front of him. Len groaned—the only cop in Rocky Bottom was Bobby Sherman—Jess's dad.

Bobby was tall, hard-muscled, with close-cropped dark hair

and bright blue eyes. His black and grey uniform was always creased and pressed, right down to his tie. He got out of his car and gave Len a once-over. Len couldn't look him in the face.

"You look like shit, Len."

Len nodded, feeling hollow.

"Jess didn't come home last night." Len closed his eyes and felt a dizzying abyss swallow him. What use were words when there was a God of Chickens?

"He's coming." It came out a croak, the desiccated voice of a hundred-year-old man.

"Who's coming? Jess? Where's Jess?" Bobby grabbed Len's arm hard enough to hurt. "Who's coming, Len? Were you two getting fucked up in the woods last night? What's on your forehead?"

Len stared down a long tunnel at Officer Bobby's face. He should feel something. He was Jess's dad, and a cop. Someone in authority, someone he used to know. But that time was gone. He'd seen the God of Chickens and everything was different. Len tried to free his arm, but Bobby hung on, his grip crushing Len's skinny arm. The line of Jess's blood on his forehead was burning hot. Len started to cry.

He gasped out a few words between sobs. "Jess... chicken man... God... Jess's blood... so awful."

"What are you talking about? Where's Jess?" Concern and worry lined Bobby's face now.

Len wiped at tears and snot with the back his hand.

"He's dead, Bobby."

"You'd better be lying." Bobby lips were white. He lifted Len's chin with one hand until Len had nowhere else to look but those intense blue eyes. "Were you getting fucked up in the woods last night?"

Something broke in Len's heart, and the story came tumbling out of him. He didn't make much sense in his own ears, but he didn't care. Bobby just shook his head.

"You weren't just smoking weed last night, were you? Are you two getting into the hard stuff?"

Len let out a bitter, exhausted bark of disbelief.

"No, it was the God of Chickens. He did it. He killed Jess."

Bobby used his thumb to pry Len's eyelids wide, first the left one, then the right.

"Looks like it's out of your system, whatever it was. Are you talking about the Chicken Man?"

"We weren't on anything last night, OK?" He touched the hot, flaking mess on his forehead. "This is Jess's."

The muscles stood out in Bobby's cheeks. Then he sighed and let go.

"We're going to see the Chicken Man."

Len froze.

"No. I don't want to go."

"Don't do this to me, Len. I need to find Jess."Len saw the determination in Officer Bobby's face, and unexpected pity washed through him. Bobby would never find what he was looking for.

He put up a hopeless, half-hearted fight as Bobby shoved him in the cop car's back seat.

As they drove, Len stared at the faded Naugahyde of the seat. He smelled old cigarettes, sweat, and puke. There were no handles on the inside of the doors. Pressure was building up in his head, like someone was inflating a balloon behind his eyes. By the time they turned on to the dirt road that lead to the God of Chickens' ramshackle coops, he was aware of little else but the overfull throb of his head.

The car ground to a halt, and Officer Bobby pulled Len out of the car.

They weren't alone. Half a dozen cars had pulled off the road, parked in a haphazard fashion among the Loblollies. Bobby ignored them.

"Now, where'd you leave Jess?"

Part of him was still a pile on the filthy altar, and Len couldn't get the image out of his head. He didn't know what to say to Officer Bobby. Bobby pushed Len ahead of him, and they walked toward the God of Chickens' filthy huddle of shacks. The reek of chicken shit was strong enough to taste, and Len's head was exploding in slow motion as he rounded the small hill.

He stopped so suddenly that Officer Bobby ran into him

and gaped. Where before there had been chickens, now eight or nine people were sweeping, cleaning, and shoring up the dirty coops. Nowhere could Len see any chickens. The God Himself stood near the altar. Behind him, the unspeakable pile of organs buzzed with a torrent of flies.

"What the Hell?" Bobby gaped for a moment, then moved around the immobile Len. He grabbed Mary Dickey by the arm. She blinked and shook her head, as if clearing it.

"Mary, what are you doing here?"

She looked back at him with blank incomprehension, then at the rake in her hand.

"God's work." She said it with a spaced-out, hippie sort of way, like she'd been smoking dope. Bobby gripped her arm tighter.

"Have you seen Jess?"

She didn't answer, but shook her head and tried to turn away. Bobby's hand squeezed her arm, as if he could crush what he wanted to hear out of her.

"Jess is no longer here." The words rolled across the small clearing. Bobby's head snapped around to look at the God of Chickens, and he let Mary go.

"I've never had any trouble with you, and we've left you alone like you asked." Officer Bobby's voice trembled just a little bit. "Jess is my son, and you *will* tell me what happened to him."

The God didn't speak. Instead, he threw his head back and laughed, a deep booming like someone kicking a kettle drum. Len shuddered and covered his ears to keep his overfull skull from exploding.

Bobby's gun was in his hand, and trained on the God of Chickens. The other people were taking an interest, letting their chores wait as they watched the confrontation.

"Where's my son? What happened? Did you hurt him?" Bobby was shouting now, his voice with a hysterical edge that sounded like Jess's.

The God stepped forward, and Bobby stepped backward. The gun shook, and he braced it with his other hand.

"He is no longer among us." The God of Chickens' voice was rich, commanding. Len wanted to follow it forever.

Mary Dickey, Constance Millington, and Kevin Hoover all stepped forward, but the God waved them back.

"This is someone else's job," he rumbled.

"Tell me where Jess is!" Bobby screamed. He was breathing hard, his knuckles white on the pistol grip. The God of Chickens stepped forward again, and Bobby retreated, now within an arm's reach of Len. Len's head was a blaze of agony, like a balloon taut with water. The slightest touch would make it burst. But all he had to do was give in, and the pain would stop.

He punched Bobby in the head, as hard as he could.

The gun went off with a deafening roar, and Len was pushed aside, dazed, as the God of Chickens rushed in. Officer Bobby was strong, and he struggled against those massive hands to control the gun. The God of Chickens thrust his head forward, powerful jaws snapping like a bear trap. Cartilage popped as the stained teeth sank into Bobby's neck, and this time Len didn't look away. With a wrench like a dog killing a bird, the God of Chickens pulled his head away, tearing off a mouthful of flesh. Officer Bobby held his hand uselessly up to the gaping wound, blood jetting between his fingers like the cut end of a garden hose.

He gurgled and fell, his blood a pool spreading beneath him like a sticky red carpet. For a moment, his fear-filled eyes met Len's, and he watched as the life drained out of them. And then the pressure in Len's head was gone.

The God of Chickens cradled the still-warm body in his arms and brought it to the altar. His small flock followed, including Len, and formed a small circle around the altar. Len looked up at the faces he had known for years, the people of Rocky Bottom. He saw the light in Mary and Constance's and Kevin's eyes, their faced upturned and blissful.

The sound of snapping bone made him close his eyes, and he knew to expect the wet thump that followed. And then the people were jostling him, moving around the makeshift altar. As each person approached the God, they knelt and mumbled something, and He smeared some blood on their forehead.

When it was Len's turn he knelt and whispered, "Bless me, God of Chickens."

The God laughed again, a terrible sound like a chugging locomotive. Len looked up to see a wide, terrible, mad smile spread over the broad, filthy face.

"God of Humans, now."

N IS FOR NEVILLE

(FOR WILUM PUGMIRE)

"Thank *Christ* Simon kept the goth crowd out. Whenever they show up, everything's just a *disaster*." Lise Endicott dangled a champagne flute from her hand. "They're all so irredeemably dull; not one of them knows any language but English, most of them wouldn't know the *Malleus Maleficarum*, let alone a truly esoteric work. And the sex..." Her gesture toward the heavens was plaintive. "No time for romance or seduction. Just a mopey hello, their Myspace page, and then they're naked and needy."

Neville pursed his lips, gazing at her tantalizing low-cut bodice. The rich red brocade perfectly complemented her chocolate coloring. But madness lay that way. In bed, Lise gave more directions than his car's GPS. And in about the same flat tone. With clothing to separate them, he liked her company. She knew books, even if she didn't share his passion for them.

Simon Townsend's occult parties cut across all social strata. Not six feet from Neville, a wealthy dealer in illegal antiquities, dressed in flowing silver and grey silk, was deep in conversation with a greasy-haired street-corner prophet who smelled like a dumpster. Beyond them, laughter erupted from a conversational knot as a local scribbler of horror tales, well-known for his home-made Bishop's mitre adorned with a picture of Barbara Streisand, held court. The same crowd which had been attending for years, and the same tired conversations.

Neville did not believe in any god or divine power, but he longed to find something beyond mere humanity, some evidence of existence after death. He did not think he would find it in these nouveau religions with their sixties-holdover hallucinogens and shabby rockstar showmanship. Answers would come from authentic ritual, with roots that went back centuries or millennia. Simon felt the same way; old and forbidden ceremonies from the dark corners of the earth were the centerpieces of these parties.

Neville scanned the room with dispirited gloom. Aside from Lise, no one interesting was here. Then he brightened.

"Who did you come with?" he breathed.

"I haven't seen any new or interesting faces. Who are you talking about?" Lise asked.

"He's dark. Dark and gorgeous, wearing a white silk shirt, black jeans, and demi-boots with silver buckles."

"Sounds delicious. Point him out." Lise looked in the direction of Neville's gaze.

"Standing near Jane."

"Jane Waite, the slut overflowing her corset?"

Jane displayed her expensively-sculpted breasts like a jeweller's best diamonds. She would use them to attract the lowest life-forms she could, preferring ex-cons, morgue assistants, and child molesters. After a rushed, sticky assignation in a dark corner, she would go home and tell her husband all about her evening.

"His head is shaved. He's wearing tight black jeans, with a bulge that is either wool socks or proof that God plays favorites." Neville could feel the week's listlessness falling away. Of course, the gorgeous man would open his mouth and ruin everything by being inane. But Neville would savor impossible hope until then.

"Who is he talking to?"

"Nobody. He looks like he's waiting. Right now, he's the only person not laughing at whatever Jane just said."

Lise craned her neck.

"I can't see anything delicious in Jane's circle. Why don't you engage this lollipop, so I can see him up close?"

Neville threaded through the crowd while Lise went in search of more champagne. Neville appreciated her patience. She didn't have to snatch at a piece of candy the instant she saw it.

The good-looking stranger was still on the fringes of Jane's conversational circle. She was laughing over a cutting remark at the expense of a former lover, her court echoing her. All except the stranger.

"Good evening," Neville said with all the charm he could muster.

"Good evening," the dark man echoed. Was there a hint of surprise in those lustrous mahogany features? His voice was rich, with a hint of gravel. His eyes were so dark that Neville couldn't tell where the pupil began and iris ended. He stopped searching before it became staring.

"Neville Bicknell Winthrop, at your service."

"I would introduce myself, but our host is eager to do so later this evening. I see that you are a great reader, Neville."

"Well, yes. I own more than twenty thousand volumes, many of them rare. I couldn't live without books."

"You've read Ludovicus Prinneaus' *De Vermis Mysteriis.*" The stranger showed pearly white teeth. Neville tried not to quaver. The gorgeous man knew incunabula.

"I own a copy. The hideously dull 1490 Blackletter edition, printed in Düsseldorf. Very rare and expensive. Blasphemy did not made for a lasting legacy until the twentieth century." The pride of Neville's collection was locked safe and untouchable by all but himself in a temperature and humidity-controlled vault, away from unappreciative eyes and unwashed hands.

Neville saw Lise approaching. He clenched, afraid that she would ruin the fragile intimacy he and the dark man had built. When she was close enough to be included in their conversation, she stopped. The feared torrent of words and attention-whoring never came. The stranger didn't say anything either. He spared Lise a momentary glance, then turned those dark, bewitching eyes back to Neville.

"I have leads on a few related volumes, if rare and esoteric books interest you." Neville would tell any silly, stupid lie to get this man into bed. He ached with need. "A collector in Beirut is selling a copy of Antoine-Marie Augustin de Montmorency-les-Roches, le Comte d'Erlette's infamous *Les Cultes des Goules.* And I've heard that a copy of Friedrich-Wilhelm von Junzt's *Die*

Unaussprechlichen Kulten was recently sold at an invitation-only Hong Kong auction. Rumors say the purchaser was from New York." The last at least was true.

Again, a flash of white teeth, this time a predatory snarl. Neville took a step back and glanced over at Lise. She stood, drink in hand, a blank expression on her face.

"She can't see me," the stranger offered. "No one can but you. Because they haven't read what you have."Neville waved his hand in front of Lise's face, but she didn't react. She was breathing, but she didn't respond. When he turned back to ask what was going on, the dark man was gone. Neville's heart sank. It had been some time since he had been dismissed so abruptly. Had he come on too strong?

He turned to Lise and discovered a sly smile on her face. "When do we find this tasty newcomer of yours? I'm dying for some variety—"

She stopped when she saw Neville's dumbfounded expression.

"And I'm guessing that you can't find him either."

He caught her by the shoulders. "What just happened?"

"Are you having a flashback? You're not your usual intelligible self." She shook his hands off.

"Tell me about the last five minutes."

"You said you saw someone yummy over here. You walked over, I followed discreetly. When I got here, you flaked out and asked me what just happened."

Neville was silent, searching his memory. How could she have missed the handsome stranger? She had stared at him for more than two minutes. He looked in the direction the man had gone, but couldn't find him in the shifting mass of people.

He had seen the man. Spoken with him. He could not have imagined the vivid impression, the hint of musk that the dark stranger had left in his wake. So, what had happened to Lise? She had looked at him, didn't remember him, hadn't heard a conversation not two feet from her. Impossible.

"Would you happen to know what the big to-do will be this evening?" Lise intruded on his thoughts.

He should leave, go home. Something inexplicable had just

happened, and Neville's skin prickled. But leaving would mean losing his chance to find the dark man. Could he go home, retreat to his books, give up on ever seeing the luscious man again? He couldn't bear the possibility.

"Simon is playing this one close to the vest." Lise continued in the face of his silence. She glanced in the direction of the locked and chained door off the library.

Nouveau religion bored Neville. Sixties-holdover hallucinogens and shabby rockstar showmanship were no substitute for authentic ceremony. The centerpiece of Simon's occult parties were old and forgotten rituals from the dark corners of the earth. And though Neville did not believe in any god or divine power, he longed to find something beyond mere humanity, some evidence of existence after death.

"Do you think tonight will compare to the Mithraic baptisms?" Lise asked.

Despite his turmoil, Neville smiled. How many people could say they'd been showered with gallons of hot bull's blood? While the experience had been primal and powerful, he couldn't say that he'd touched the divine through it.

"Simon mentioned that he'd brought a Yale anthropologist this evening. I may feel the need for stimulating conversation about erotic Moche ceramics." Lise was determined to keep the conversation going.

Neville sighed, and gazed down at the century-old cherry floor. Perhaps some absinthe would make the night more comprehensible.

Simon walked into the center of the library striking a small chime to produce a clear, piercing note. After three peals, conversation subsided.

"Your attention, please. Everyone's attention." Simon wore an embroidered smoking jacket, which was odd. He was a fashion victim, and this look was ancient. When Neville spotted the stem of a briarwood pipe peeking out of Simon's pocket, he realized the smoking jacket was an attempt to look collegiate. He was trying to get into the Yale anthropologist's pants. Neville smirked, turmoil fading from his mind.

"Ladies and gentlemen," Simon continued. "I intend for this

evening's entertainment to climax at the Witching Hour, and it will take a bit of preparation. Those of you wishing to partake, please make your way to the locked room off the library. The rest of you, well, go back to whatever you were doing."

Not that anyone would miss this. Partygoers flowed in Simon's wake, into the library and the mysterious locked room beyond. With all eyes on him, Simon took a dramatic second to search for his keys. This was the moment he lived for, more than the occasional tumble with an anthropologist. He drew out the slow, sexual insertion of the key. With a turn, the lock jumped, and Simon pulled the overly-theatrical chains off the door handles. With a push, antique doors stolen from an Italian abbey groaned open.

The crowd pushed into the newly-revealed ceremonial room. The walls were murals of an Alpine sunset, rose and gold with dark mountains looming in the distance. On a skeletal lectern of curling wrought iron sat an enormous black folio.

"Tonight, we perform some special tantra." Simon caressed the tome on its lectern; eighteenth century European was Neville's assessment from this distance. "We shall take a page from Friedrich-Wilhelm von Junzt, who travelled far and wide, a seeker after mysteries, like us. *Die Unaussprechlichen Kulten* holds rituals described nowhere else. Tonight, from a lost lamasery at the roof of the world, we will indulge in a ritual to summon ... " he paused and glanced down at a small card in his hand. "Alasya Paramatattva, the Crocodile of Ultimate Truth."A hot prickle crept up Neville's neck. They were going to perform something from the *Kulten*? Strange Roman and Zoroastrian ceremonies were one thing, but this might be going too far. And hadn't the gorgeous stranger mentioned its sister grimoire *De Vermis Mysteriis*? The convergence disquieted him.

And yet, what if it worked? To be present for evidence that something existed beyond the mundane and prosaic world, even if it were the terrors von Junzt and d'Erlette wrote of. To call a god down, regardless of what god it was, would be a spectacular triumph.

"None of my tantric studies involved sheet music," Lise said, scanning the page that was handed to her. "But that was to satisfy my inner demons, not summon them."

The entities described by Prinneaus and Le Comte resembled demons in the same way that ostriches resembled sparrows. But Neville reminded himself that he didn't believe in them. So, what would be the harm?

The ritual consisted of a strange rondel of four different choruses that chanted unpronounceable words in different time signatures. Simon accompanied the cacophony with a weird, monotonous tune on a *kangling,* a Tibetan trumpet made from a human femur. Neville could not laugh off the bizarre chant and grotesque music as the usual ritual garbage. Something insidious and perniciously inescapable lurked in the sound, as if it had been orchestrated by someone who had never experienced music.

The noise continued for some time, the auditory chaos magnified with each repetition of the chant. On top of the din was a jarring, off-key layer, as if from a flawed or broken flute. No one was playing such an instrument, it must have been an auditory hallucination brought on by the atonality.

In the midst of the ear-torturing noise, Neville spied the gorgeous dark-skinned man in black and white standing on the edge of the crowd. As far as occult entertainments went, this was a bust. If Neville had wanted to sing nonsensical music he would have joined a church choir. At least he knew the dark man wasn't a figment of his imagination.

Even as the thought crossed his mind, the crowd drew back from the stranger. The chanting died away, and the audience stared.

"You have called, and I am now here, without noise or inconvenience." Neville remembered that voice from their all-too-brief conversation, but now it flowed with naked power. The assembly gasped, and Neville recognized the quote from the *Grimoirium Verum,* a book of prosaic conjurations. What was this man playing at?

"I see that congratulations are in order. Despite your ignorance and fear, and you have pierced the Outer Darkness and finally arrived at a truth." The haughty words stabbed like shards of ice. Had the summoning truly worked? The thought was enormous and terrifying.

The man swept the room with his chill gaze, and no one was able to meet it. Men knelt before their gods because no one wanted to look them in the eye.

"I see. A collection of charlatans looking for the truth behind their own lies."

The crowd reeked of confusion and fear. Although the words were full of contempt, Neville was awed.

"This audience is brief, but you shall have the truth you seek." Then, like a magician, he vanished.

For the next week, Neville retreated to his vault, with only his beloved books for company. He tried to concentrate on the familiar pleasures, but memories of the exquisite dark man would not leave him be. What was he? Magician, trickster, demon, God? Neville was drawn to his treasured copy of *De Vermis Mysteriis*. What about the book had allowed him to see the Alasya Paramatattva? He pored over the fragile pages, wondering which of the shuddersome horrors described might wear the guise of the Crocodile of Ultimate Truth.

After days of wading through Prunneaus' dense Latin, Neville was exhausted and wrung out. In a moment of weakness, he paged through a newspaper, hoping the mundane prose would rest his tired mind. Instead, he discovered that a Yale professor of anthropology had killed himself by leaping out his New York publisher's window.

The story was lurid enough to quote several witnesses. The anthropologist, normally reserved and polite, had emerged from an elevator and charged straight for a tall window. After bloodying his nose and then fists in a frenzied attack on the unyielding glass, he had grabbed a chair and shattered the window. Without a second's pause, he threw himself out the new aperture, killing himself and a pedestrian ten stories below.

Disturbed, Neville called Lise to ask the name of the Yale professor at Simon's party. When she didn't pick up, he left a message. Lise, normally eager to trade gossip, had not gotten back to him by the time Neville went to sleep.

Nor did she call the next day. Was she out of the country?

Neville tried her number several times, and each time her cold, remote voice mail recorded his worried tones.

He was finally distracted by a call to his cell phone. He picked it up, and someone was breathlessly telling him that Jane Waite had strangled herself.

Neville could say nothing. He hadn't liked Jane, but it was a blow to realize she was dead. Lise was still not responding to his calls, and he worried that something had happened to her, also.

Jane's funeral was a solemn, closed-casket affair. The whispered undercurrent that flowed through the pews said that her husband had found her and loosened ligature, only to watch in helpless horror as she screamed "Alasya Paramatattva" and tore at her face. Only death had stopped her convulsions.

Neville scanned the mourners for the dark, sardonic god, but did not find him.

He spent two anxious days alternately worrying over Lise and studying Prinneaus' recondite Latin. His diligence was rewarded with a name. Nyarlathotep, called the Crawling Chaos, and the soul of the Outer Gods. This mordant, mocking figure who sometimes appeared as a dark pharaoh sounded like the Crocodile of Ultimate Truth. But this identification did not bring any comfort or protection. He brooded on this for hours, scouring the book for any hint as to the entity's weaknesses. He found none.

Helpless, Neville tried calling Lise once again. To his surprise, the line was picked up.

"Hello?" The voice was not Lise's, but older and matronly.

"Um, hello. Is this Lise Endicott's phone?"

"This is her phone, and I am Sister Mary-Lucia."

"*Sister*? Lise ran away to a cloister? Don't you have to believe in God to become a nun?"

"She asked if I would assure you that she was alive if you called. She did not want you to worry."

"Can I talk with her?"

"I am sorry. She is in seclusion at the moment, contemplating the new life before her."

"You have to be fucking kidding me."

"I assure you we are not. This order has been the salvation of many troubled young women…"

Neville hung up, his mind spinning. The god. It was hunting them down one by one and… doing what? Jane Waite had long played dangerous sex games. He didn't know anything about the anthropologist. But Lise was as cynical and world-weary as anyone he had ever known. She hadn't prayed to anything but her own appetites in the eight years he had known her. How was a retreat to a convent some sort of truth that the Crocodile shown her?

He needed access to the *Kulten*. There had to be some sort of defence, some way to understand this thing before it came for him. He called Simon, and as expected, got his personal assistant Zelney.

"You haven't heard?" The fear and shock in Zelney's voice let Neville know he was too late.

"No." Neville felt hollow. The pursuing doom was consuming his friends. "Tell me he's alive."

Zelney choked a little, and gave him a hospital room number. Then hung up.

Two hours later, Neville was pacing outside the designated door, an abyss yawning in his stomach. It couldn't be as bad as he imagined, could it? Anticipation had to be the worst part. Had to be.

With a bracing and surreptitious sip of brandy, he opened the door. Simon lay on a bed, hooked up to a couple of leads. A large bandage obscured the left side of his head, including his eye. Simon's expression was not the familiar, knowing smile Neville had come to know, but open and empty.

"Simon?"

The patient's one good eye blinked rapidly.

"Hello?" His voice had changed into something lonely and forlorn.

"Simon, it's Neville. Can you see me?"

The person, and Neville couldn't decide if he truly was Simon anymore, squirmed as he tried to get a better look. His usually fine motor skills were gone. Considering the head trauma, that wasn't surprising. Simon, if he was in there still, faced a long period of recovery.

Neville approached, and Simon's good eye followed him. With a sinking feeling, Neville realized that Simon's eye was empty, all personality lost.

Oh God.

"What happened? Who did this to you?"

"I did." The simple statement was flat, final, and chilling. Simon mimed snipping something with his trembling right hand, then jammed the fingers into the dressing over his ruined left eye.

Neville wrestled Simon's hand away from the bandage. Simon resisted for a moment, straining to reach his eye, whipping the threatening fingers back and forth. Then the frenzy was over, and Simon relaxed back into the bed.

"Why? What happened?" Neville was nauseous with fear. What could make a man stab himself in the eye with scissors? Had he really destroyed his own forebrain, lobotomized himself?

Simon's blank eye regarded him, and the monotone voice came from somewhere unimaginably distant.

"I didn't want to think about Him anymore."

Him. Of course, Him.

"Nyarlathotep?" Neville whispered the name.

Simon exploded in a screaming fury, hands clawing at Neville, fingernails digging bloody furrows into his face. Neville tried to fight him off, but Simon had a madman's strength, leaping off the bed. The monitors screamed, mingling with Simon's animalistic yowl. He slammed Neville into the wall. A hand came up under Neville's jaw and his skull cracked against the plaster wall once, twice, and the third time something gave way.

Then they were surrounded by a horde of white-clad figures. Simon's fingers were pried off Neville, and Simon was dragged, screaming and thrashing, into the bed. Neville reeled out of the room, his last glimpse of Simon being held down and pumped full of chemicals.

A card waited for him when he got home. It sat, perfectly centered, a cream square on his dark blue table cloth. The door was not broken in, and the locks hadn't been picked, as if the messenger had appeared out of thin air, dropped the envelope, and vanished.

He stared at it, not sure what to do. The entity destroying his friends had no need to warn him or command his appearance. And yet, something told him the envelope was poison; if he didn't touch it, Nyarlathotep could not touch him.

What if he just wanted to talk? What if he wanted more than talk? The possibility of gazing into those dark eyes, of touching that perfect skin... he tore the envelope open.

Flawless copperplate writing invited him to lunch at an outdoor café at eleven A.M. the following day. Neville sat considering the card. Avoiding the encounter was absurd. The Crocodile of Ultimate Truth did not need to wait for him in a café. He considered running, hiding himself in Bangladesh. But what good would it possible do? How could anyone run from a god, or the truth?

He spent a sleepless night among his books. What would happen to him? What could Nyarlathotep reveal to him? What would happen to his books if he went mad and destroyed himself?

He tried to imagine what it would be like to be dead, to not exist. The only image he could conjure was a terrifying eternity of hopeless, disembodied drifting. But proof of god, no matter what god, was evidence of immortality of the soul. Wasn't it?

The café was empty when Neville arrived. Grey clouds loured above him. Across the street, a broken-winged pigeon flapped at the foot of Saint Francis' statue. Neville tried not to glance at his watch too often. He buried his nose in the menu, hoping that it held no special significance.

He had not yet made up his mind when the chair opposite him shifted. He lowered the menu and the Alasya Paramatattva sat down. His spotless white suit was exquisitely tailored. Neville was consumed with longing.

"Try the curried chicken salad. You'll like it." His voice was even more masculine and commanding than Neville remembered. What should one do when the Crocodile of Ultimate Truth suggested a lunch item? *E. coli* was not a truth, was it? Neville put his hands on the glass-topped table to keep them from shaking.

A pert waitress smiled at them both, and took Neville's order. He could not persuade his guest to order, even though he volunteered to pay. Then she was gone, and they were alone. Neville dared to look into the empty black eyes, and found himself in the uncomfortable position of staring into a bottomless abyss. He tore his eyes away, realizing how wrong Nietzsche had been. The abyss does not stare back. The abyss merely is; cold, uncaring, eternal.

The silence grew, until Neville had to say something or scream to fill the emptiness.

"Would it be impolite of me to ask questions?"

"You are free to do as you please, Neville, just as I am." The flash of teeth was as friendly as a tiger's snarl.

"Who are you?" Neville asked in a whisper.

"I have a thousand names, am perceived a thousand ways. I have been called the Black Pharaoh of Khem, and the Blind Ape of Truth." With each claimed title, Neville was granted a vision. He saw the dark man with a blue and gold Egyptian *nemes* on his head, two columns of perfumed smoke rising before him. This shifted to a wildly-flailing yellow baboon with a golden collar and empty pits for eyes. "Men have worshipped me as the Howler in Darkness, and the Bloated Woman." Neville saw an unutterable monstrosity with cancerously tortured skin and a bloody tentacle emerging from its grotesque head. The vision faded to an inhumanly obese woman with an elephant-like trunk and two side-facing mouths screaming in triumph over a field of bloody, eviscerated corpses. "I am older than this planet, more ancient than the eons before the stars were kindled. I have seen civilizations, races, and aberrations of reality that would drive you mad. I am not some anthropomorphic projection, I am entirely different from everything you could ever conceive of."

Neville reeled at the visions and the words. What slumbering horror had they awakened? What hubris to attract its attention.

"Your little group of friends summoned me in order to alleviate their boredom." If there was emotion in the voice, it was alien to human experience. "I considered many ways of sharing my irritation. A nearby supernova to irradiate this planet to lifeless rock, or perhaps inspiring some terrorists to a nuclear detonation in this city. But, interesting as fusion is, I decided that your assemblage of seekers deserved something for their accomplishment. They sought truth. Their reactions have been entertaining."

Neville looked up, and was trapped in the all-encompassing void that was the Alasya Paramatattva's gaze. For an instant, Neville glimpsed a black protoplasmic horror with bloody fangs and razor-edged tentacles that howled from a limitless ocean of carnage, of unstoppable fury like an endlessly-erupting volcano, and hate so cold it could snuff out stars. He gasped, the vision so clear and present that he cringed.

Oblivious, the waitress set his salad down. Neville caught his breath. He thought about looking for a reaction from the mahogany god, but would not risk being swallowed by that terrible, empty gaze again.

He pushed a trembling fork of salad into his mouth and chewed. It tasted of nothing. He had to escape, to get away from the horror in barely-human form that sat so frighteningly close. With a trembling hand, he put his credit card on the table between them.

"I am here to give you the gift of truth, Neville."

He clutched the table and choked back a moan.

"You have always wondered how you would face death. It is such a contradiction to this culture, so divorced from your daily existence, and yet such an obsession. There is an excellent chance that in six months, you will put the barrel of a cheap revolver in your mouth and pull the trigger."

Neville tried to shut out the words. He would shoot himself? What could drive him to that? He opened his mouth to protest, to ask, to curse, but Nyarlathotep silenced him with a raised finger. Neville rocked for a moment, his inner turmoil a physical churning in his stomach.

The little waitress returned, and handed Neville's credit card back to him.

"I'm sorry. You've been declined."

Neville started. The dark man reached out and tapped the bill with a finger. The waitress nodded, smiled at him, and left.

"Your trust fund is gone, and your credit account is over its limit, your stock holdings have evaporated. All the money you have left is in your wallet."

Neville's mind reeled. Death was too great an unknown to contemplate, but poverty was all too real.

"Of course, you could live comfortably if you sold your books," the dark man said.

Sell his books? He would sooner kill himself.

The Crocodile's mocking laughter rang in his ears. Far too late, he understood something of the otherworldly horror they had stupidly attracted the attention of. He had his truth, for all the good it did him.

Dear God, Neville prayed, let there not be an afterlife.

NOT AN ULCER

Dudley hated taking the bus. It was full of niggers, faggots, retards, and worse. He tried to bury himself in his book, shutting out the press of degenerate humanity. What the hell was wrong with people that they had to yak on about what they'd seen on TV last night? Were their lives so empty? Couldn't they shut up for a minute? Dudley gave up trying to read and stared out the bus window. With the sun down, the city lights passed behind his reflection.

Late as usual, the bus dropped him off, and Dudley walked his slow way back to his apartment. He turned on the TV as soon as he got in the door. The babble helped push back at the empty silence.

He ate two packages of mac and cheese while flipping channels. When he was done, the remains of the evening stretched out before him. He tried to return to his book, but couldn't concentrate. After an hour of fidgeting, the idea of visiting the park seeped into his head. He turned the television back on to drown the thought. The park was poorly lit, some part of him reasoned. No one would know. Angry, Dudley poured himself a few fingers of Jim Beam, and confronted himself in the bedroom mirror.

"You don't need to go." The Dudley in the mirror looked him straight in the eye, not at all cowed by his authoritative tone. "You've been working hard. You're well above the monthly quota, and it's not even the 20th."

Dudley-in-the-mirror wasn't impressed. There was something suspect about him, something soft, almost feminine. Dudley wiped at the mirror, hoping to change the image. His other self stubbornly remained the same. To dispel the illusion of weakness, he rolled up a sleeve and flexed his bicep. He could not form the rock-hard muscle he once had.

"You don't need this. This is the sort of bullshit that gave Cheryl an excuse to leave. It's a weakness, something we should have left behind long ago." But the man in the mirror didn't want to listen.

"Please," he whispered, wheedling now that command and anger hadn't worked. "Please, I don't want this." It was a lie. The hated part of him wanted it in a deep-down way that words couldn't touch.

A second shot of Jim Beam strengthened the rebellion. Dudley glared at the mirror, which had somehow gotten the better of him again. Fuming, he pulled out a cheap wallet without identification, and stuffed a $50 into it.

He dropped his regular wallet on the table, along with all his change, keeping only the key to his apartment. He pulled on a dark overcoat, despite the summer night's warmth, and locked the apartment door behind him. Letting out a deep breath that was both of determination and longing, he walked out to meet the pretty man-boys who only came when the sun was down.

He returned some forty-five minutes later, furtive and out of breath. Tired but relaxed, he took a shower. His belly seemed larger than usual, the skin taut. He couldn't even see his toes over his distended gut. God, he was fat. His mouth hardened into a disapproving line and he scrubbed himself harder.

Out of the shower, his skin pink and raw in places, he laid down on the empty flatness of his queen-sized bed. He pulled out another bottle of Jim Beam, who lived in a drawer next to his bed. Three swallows burned his mouth, and soothed the jagged edges of his bitter self-recrimination. He glanced toward the mirror, but the angle was wrong to catch a glimpse of the satisfied image that lived in it. Safely alone with his guilt, Dudley surrendered to unconsciousness.

On the bus the next morning, Dudley still felt weighted down. He was getting weaker, not stronger. He'd spent more than two hundred dollars at the park in the last three weeks. As he stewed over this thought, a great fat bulk, like a primeval mastodon, squeezed its ponderous mass down the aisle, brushing him as it passed. The bus swam around him as the reek of too many bodies engulfed him. Gasping for air, he pulled the cord and escaped the bus.

He regretted the move as soon as he put foot to pavement. He was fully five blocks from his office, which stood on the crown of a steep hill. Jogging turned the fat on his belly to lead before he had gone a single block. He really should get a gym membership, he thought, feeling his heart thunder in his chest. Not too long ago, he would have been able to run up this hill without breaking a sweat. Now, he was almost out of breath, and the hill seemed to get steeper.

He arrived at work at quarter past eight, his button-down shirt plastered to his sweaty torso. The receptionist looked at him with slattern-eyed condescension.

"You're late—oh, you're sweating, Dudley. Are you OK?" She had the effrontery to use his first name, as if they were friends.

"I work harder than anyone in this office," he snapped. "You'd think I might get a little slack as to my time of arrival." She bowed under his verbal assault, and looked back at her computer screen.

"I just wanted to make sure you were all right." Her voice was meek.

"I had a *year* in *college*," his hiss was cutting. With nothing left to say, he stalked past her desk and onto the main floor of the call center, with its rows of grey cubicles. At work, there are no mirrors.

He sat down and booted up his computer. How could it only be Tuesday? He saw the day stretch out before him. Beyond that was the work week, and beyond that a month that was an endless hill of paperwork for him to roll the mighty stone up. This was what made him fat and unhappy, the endless grinding days to make no difference? Dudley Gerritson looked upon the mighty work ahead of him, and despaired.

The sun had set by the time he left the office. Somehow, the tide of paperwork had receded, and he'd made a few sales on top of that.

The commute home was strange. People were looking at him. His guts were ropy. He must have eaten something bad. Angry, he stomped into his apartment and picked a good boxing match on pay-per-view. Jim Beam helped him sleep.

On Wednesday morning he was sluggish. His stomach still bothered him. No longer leaden, his guts squirmed as if infested with maggots. Breakfast didn't help, and the nausea stayed with him through the trial that was his morning bus ride. He caught furtive glances from the loathed people on the bus. What was wrong with him? He checked himself in the bus windows. Hair neatly combed, tie on straight… but he didn't look good. His cheeks were hollow, his eyes sunken. How could he look so wasted when his belly was so large?

He spent the day in a state of heightened alertness, which he told himself was not fear. Drinking to get sleep was leaving its mark on him. What choice did he have? Without a few swallows of Jim Beam, he could toss and turn all night. His worries faded as he fell into the rhythm of his work day, calling people, convincing them they needed new windows, then filling out the paperwork for the sale. He stayed late, finishing up, dreading the bus ride and the silence of his apartment.

He survived the commute with little more than a feeling of disgust, until he came to his stop. Nausea roiled up as he waited for the door to open. As he doubled over to keep from puking, someone shoved him from behind, and he spilled out onto the sidewalk.

He hit the bottle hard, unable to shake his fear. Tension and whiskey made his head throb like his bloated and painful stomach. He felt disassociated and powerless, an ineffectual ghost in his own apartment. He slept fitfully, awake every few hours.

Thursday's ride home was a horror show. Crammed together like niggers in the triangle trade, the stench of pressed-together bodies was overwhelming. Dudley shrank away from the spic standing next to him. He closed his eyes and tried to wish it all away, but the stink was inescapable, and his flesh burned to touch that sensual, dusky skin. The bus lurched, throwing hot bodies together. The rest of the ride was spent with clenched fists, breath hissing between his teeth. He arrived at his apartment bleary-eyed and exhausted.

He ordered a meat-lover's pizza for one, flipped channels while he ate, then shut the TV off. The comfort food did nothing to settle his rebellious stomach, and he could not get the feel of the Latin man off his skin. The clock said seven, too early to go to bed. He cleaned a little, then settled back in his reading chair. He couldn't concentrate, his mind always returning to that stolen touch on the bus. He threw his book down. What would he do for the next three hours? The answer he did not want came immediately. Setting his jaw, Dudley poured himself a whiskey and went to confront the bedroom mirror.

"I am not a faggot!" he screamed at his reflection, then clamped a hand over his mouth. He took a deep breath, dropped his hand, and began to reason with the Dudley in the mirror.

"I get that you're lonely." He knew his own tone of false sincerity. He had a lot of practice with it. "I get that. But isn't there something else we can do?"

"If wishing worked, you'd be paying women." Dudley's hand went over his mouth again. He never responded when he was lecturing himself. God, what was he coming to, arguing with his reflection? His paunch gurgled and roiled, echoing his turmoil.

"It's not just about me. Think of what this would do to Dad."

Harold Gerritson loomed tall and stern in his son's memory: distant and unsmiling, his perpetually disapproving mouth set in a hard line. Harold wanted a son who was wasn't a pussy, who could fight and drink and play sports like a man. He'd bought thirteen-year-old Dudley a subscription to *Hustler* to help him grow up right. And yet, when Dudley had gotten his lacrosse scholarship, it hadn't been good enough. He should have gotten one for football, and at a better university. Not that any Gerritson before Dudley had gone to college.

And if he'd been disappointed then, how could Dudley even contemplate something as shameful as... wanting men? The stern spectre of his father's unforgiving features was far too easy to imagine, even as Dudley admitted to himself that he couldn't remember the last time he'd called home. Had it been months? Nearly a year?

"It's your life, not Dad's."

"Shut up." Which side of the argument he was on? To cover, he took a swallow of whiskey, only thing that seemed able to settle his disaffected stomach.

"So what are we—am I going to do? I can't keep on like this." He eyed his reflection, daring it to come up with a reasonable solution.

"We could find a guy we don't have to pay—"

Dudley slammed a fist into the glass. Blood oozed from his knuckles, and a hundred fractured Dudleys stared jaggedly back at him. His eyes stung. God, he was so alone.

He staggered over to his first-aid kit. He splashed some Jim Beam on his knuckles as an antiseptic, and took a few gulps as an anaesthetic. Dudley felt like he was plucking the glass out of someone else's hand. Once he had wrapped the hand in gauze, he finished off the bottle, then stumbled into bed.

Something flapped and flowed its way into his dreams, a lean, figure capering madly to an unrecognized, fantastical tune. The figure filled him with a terror built of hope and longing. He wanted to get close, although whether to join in the dance or murder the dancer he didn't know. And then it was gone, the haunting melody replaced by the dull shrill of his alarm clock.

Dudley didn't risk a look at his fractured bedroom mirror. Sleep hadn't refreshed him. A swallow of whiskey got him to the bus on time, but it didn't stay with him. By eleven, despair hovered over him like a personal thundercloud, and his belly was bloated to the point of bursting.

He couldn't leave. People judged him by his job and family. Dudley had already screwed up a marriage, he couldn't make a mess of his job. What would he be then? One of those damned bums that whined and cadged change on the street corner.

Dudley could feel the panic rising in him as the hollow futility of his existence crashed in on him. He ran to the bathroom and locked the door behind him. Only then, with a solid door separating him from the unfeeling world, did he break down weeping on the cold tile floor. Long, uncontrolled minutes passed before he could stop.

He eventually stood, and for the first time that day, looked at himself in a mirror. Dudley-in-the-mirror's eyes were haunted, his hair unkempt, clothing dishevelled. He already looked like one of the faggot bums that peddled useless shit on the street. The future unrolled itself before him, where he slept under a bridge and muttered to himself, collecting tin cans in a shopping cart so he could buy a two-dollar bottle of booze. But was that existence so different from this one? Wade through filth so he could reach the goal, the weekend or the bottle of booze? Both goals were illusory; the weekend and the alcohol were both gone too quickly to provide any lasting satisfaction.

From somewhere, he found the strength to claw back from the brink of despair. He could pick up the broken pieces of his life and turn them into something worth living. If he worked at it, he could make himself a worthwhile person. He would need to be strong—stronger than he had been. Be a man, throw out the empty wallet, move away from his apartment with easy access to the park. He looked his reflection in the eye. He would survive this. And the first thing he would do was get rid of his damned fat mid-section. Maybe then his stomach would give him some peace.

Dudley's eyes were dry by the time he left the security of the bathroom, his movements stiff and uncomfortable.

His bitch of a boss was waiting at his cubicle, and Dudley knew he would get raked over the coals. Rebecca avoided all contact with her underlings, except to chew them out.

"Can I have a minute in my office?" she asked, sugar-coating the axe Dudley knew was about to fall. Panic pumped bile into his throat. The air was hot, his shirt collar too tight, but his hands were inexplicably cold, and he could feel himself sweating.

"Sure." He was in no condition to argue. Without another word, he lurched toward her office.

Panicked heat flashed through him when she closed the door behind them. He would not go quietly. No one had served the company longer or with more devotion than he had. Perspiration beaded on his forehead, and the office walls loomed close.

"Are you all right?" She asked it with quiet concern, and he stared at his feet, unable to gauge the strength of his response if he opened his mouth.

"Dudley?" she persisted.

"It hasn't been a good week." His tone was strangled. Trying to find anything but her lying brown eyes to look at, Dudley settled on watching the lines bounce across her computer screen.

"Your work has been slipping for the last couple of days, Dudley, and you're not looking healthy. Is there anything we can do for you? You're one of our best people, and this is unlike you. Do you need some time off?"

He tried not to laugh. She'd stab him in the back and fire him when he was away. It happened all the time. He thought about telling her to shove the entire company somewhere that he had no doubt was tight and cold. Instead, he said nothing.

"I know you're proud of your attendance record. But you've got so much vacation time built up that it shouldn't make any difference." Rebecca oozed cloying, insincere sympathy.

"No, that won't—" he started, but he felt something like a hand move in his belly. Nausea boiled up in him, and he leapt to his feet. He distantly heard Rebecca ask "Dudley? What's wrong?" He took three hesitant steps toward the door, before collapsing to his knees. All he could think was that he wanted to throw up outside her office if he could. Then, abruptly as it had started, the attack was gone. Dudley tasted bile.

"Look, you're obviously not having your best day." She dripped with saccharin kindness. "Tell you what, I'm going to send you home, but it won't count against your personal time, all right?"

Head buzzing, guts roiling, Dudley knew he would not make it through the rest of the day.

"If there's anything—" she began.

"No." He cut her off, unwilling to hear any more of her simpering lies. "I need a little time and some space, and I'd appreciate it if you didn't crowd me."

She held up her hands to show that she was leaving him alone, and he left her office without another word.

The bus ride was strange at noon. The harsh sunlight was

not kind to the interior of the bus, nor ill-bred mob in it. At least there weren't many of them, and Dudley took a seat far away from everyone else.

He stared out the window at the passing city, trying to sort out his life. His stomach was bloated like a pregnancy, the skin taut as a drumhead. God, could it be cancer? Maybe it was something as simple as an ulcer. He worked too hard, and he'd gone through a divorce, and he was having those... feelings. No wonder his body was rebelling.

He rubbed his belly, hoping to calm it. Poor thing, so tied up in knots with his confusion. His fingers slipped into indentations. Dudley screamed and leapt up, tearing at his shirt. For a brief second, he could see the impression of a skull, pressed against the inside of his skin. It opened its mouth briefly, then pulled back. Screaming, Dudley fled the bus, nearly falling to the asphalt in his haste.

He sprinted into traffic, dodging cars as horns blared. He ran until he was out of breath and lost. What would he do if this wasn't just an ulcer? He was too young to get cancer. Lost and empty, Dudley wandered, cracked pavement moving beneath his feet, grubby and soot-streaked apartment buildings hemming in the sky. What was happening to him? Cancer didn't make skulls pop out of your belly.

Sodium streetlights made sickly pools of yellow light on the sidewalk when something kicked his gut from the inside. He rushed into an alley, looking for a garbage can to puke into. He only got a little way in, and then fell to his knees. The pain was excruciating, but he held on, crawling and holding his belly.

Dudley heaved like he had drunk bad tequila. What emerged was not vomit, but some sort of pinkish solid, as if his organs were coming up. Horrified, he tried to clench his mouth closed, but the purges were too violent to be stopped. Eventually, the agonizing heaving eased, and Dudley flopped onto his side, too surprised that he was alive to react to the outside world.

He lay, panting and exhausted, until he heard the uneven shuffle of bare feet on pavement. Dudley opened his eyes to see a tall figure capering in darkness not five feet from him. He stared at it with repulsed fascination until it turned, and he could see the raw, wet, bipedal thing, all ropy muscles and too-tight mottled red and yellow skin. Dudley did not want to look at the twisted limbs, or the horrifyingly familiar face.

In the midst of its dance, it caught him watching. It stopped, facing him full on. Dudley held his breath, not daring to move. The thing born of his vomit laughed a long, terrible while, then did a beautiful pirouette in the dark shadows of the alley.

"Hello at last, Dudley." The thing's speech was a burbling rasp, as if it were unused to speaking, or its bones had not yet hardened. There was something familiar about the voice.

The two stared at each other, and Dudley was the first to look away.

"What are you?"

"Don't you recognize me? You've seen me, even argued with me." It had a manic grin as it stooped to press its face near Dudley's. "I'm all the parts that you tried to strangle. I'm everything about yourself that you have rejected." The uncanny eyes bored into Dudley's. "There's a lot more to me than you thought, isn't there?"

Dudley felt his eyes grow hot. "Not really." His repressed self crouched over him, a rail-thin grotesque in a disgusting alley, wearing a filthy blanket like a cloak.

"We both have what we want." The thing cocked its head, birdlike. "I'm free, and you're rid of me."

It stood, and Dudley struggled to his knees. There was an emptiness in him, as if a weight had been lifted. A void that ached.

The creature—the other Dudley—surveyed the dark alley as if he were a prince exploring his new kingdom.

"I think I'll go dancing, maybe. Go out and have a good time. Find a man I can love."

"No! You can't!"

Dudley's hands were around his twisted double's throat, desperation loaning him the strength he needed to seal off his warped twin's air.

"You can't!" He shrieked, wrenching his other self's head around. "You aren't me!"

The grotesque fought back with surprising strength. Fingers

fumbled at his face, but Dudley kept squeezing the scrawny throat. The creature grasped at his hands, and loosened one. Dudley grabbed it by the ears and slammed its head into the brick wall. After the second blow, he could see red spatter. Fuelled by a savage loathing, the red stains only spurred him on. After several impacts, the thing went limp and slid bonelessly to the alley's filthy concrete.

He'd done it. He'd purged himself of everything he'd hated. Yet Dudley felt no sense of triumph. In fact, he felt nothing. No rage, no bitterness, no joy, as if he were just the empty, emotionless shell of himself. What had he done?

He gazed down at his twisted reflection, pitiable now in death. He knelt, and gathered the strange corpse in his arms, desperately wishing it back to life. But he didn't feel it. He felt nothing at all.

THE NEIGHBORS UPSTAIRS

The people who lived upstairs had parties that went late into the night. Everything seemed polite, quiet, fun; and if Jeremy hadn't had insomnia, it would all have been fine. But he lay on his bed, eyes open in the inky black, listening to muted talk, music and clatter of silverware on dishes. People sometimes laughed too loud, but how were they supposed to know he was sitting below them, staring at the ceiling?

When his clock glowed 2:28, most of the people had left. Jeremy lay in the insomniac darkness, listening to the murmurs and whispers that drifted down from above. What else was there to do? It sounded interesting, and in the dark loneliness of his bed, Jeremy hoped it might lead to something more … intimate.

With a thump, the conversation stopped. In the silence, Jeremy still listened, and when that provided nothing, he stood on his bed, and trying to hear more. No more conversation, no more noise at all. He was wondering if there had been an accident when he heard something being dragged. Toward the bathroom.

Following the sound, he stole toward his bathroom, directly under theirs, quiet as he could. Was someone hurt? Had they gotten drunk and fallen over?

Somebody grunted and what sounded like a pile of books slammed into the bathtub upstairs. After that, silence, and the sound of blood hammering in his ears.

The long, empty hush was broken by a black and hateful laugh. And then a sloppy sound like a jowly Saint Bernard working its way through a trough of chopped meat.

Nauseated, Jeremy stared up at the darkened ceiling. What was going on up there?

Despite the lack of sleep, Sunday was ordinary. Routine. Jeremy heard nothing strange above him. He wondered if he had dreamed it all.

That Wednesday, as he was brushing his teeth before bed, a scent tickled his nose. Something smelled. He breathed into his hand to make sure it wasn't him. It wasn't. Maybe it was coming up from the pipes. Sometimes that happened; the drains got clogged with all the people living so close together, rats crawled into tiny pipes and died. He ran some extra water down the sink to see if that would help.

It was still there on Friday, just a waft of the rot. He thought back to Sunday night, with the sloppy eating sounds, and shuddered. He called Ray, the landlord, who promised to look into it. Ray had been good to Jeremy, but sometimes didn't take him seriously. This time it worked. By Monday, the bathroom no longer smelled.

The upstairs neighbors had another party the following Saturday. Jeremy sat in his darkened bedroom, listening to talk and music. He tried to stay up to hear how it ended, but the party went slowly, and his eyelids closed before one o'clock.

What could have happened while he was asleep? In the grey morning light, he stared up at the quiet ceiling, and wondered.

During the week, Jeremy took the bus to and from work, and watched all the people hooked up to their digital phones and MP3 players, ignoring everything around them. The sight of their blank faces, floods of ones and zeroes overwhelming their senses, made him shudder.

Wednesday night, he was surprised by a knock at his door. Looking out the spyhole, he saw a couple in white tennis outfits. The man wore a sweater over his white polo shirt, while she was in a short-skirted one-piece. Who were they?

Despite his uncertainty, Jeremy opened the door. Her skirt was shorter than it had seemed, arrestingly so. Did he glimpse a tattoo high up on her buttermilk-smooth thigh?

"Hello Jerome," the man said, snapping his attention away from her legs.

"Uh, Jeremy, actually." His correction was mild.

"Yes, I'm sorry. Jeremy."

He smiled, showing broad, blunt, sparkling-white teeth, and extended his hand. Jeremy took it.

"I'm Daniel, and this is my wife Susan."

"Hello."

Brother and sister, they could have been. Same noses, same pale, flawless skin, same feathertouch eyebrows, same smiles.

"Ray called and said there'd been come complaints about our parties. So, we figured it would be best to go around and introduce ourselves, and apologize if necessary."

He told them. Hot rage rushed up Jeremy's spine. *Ray told them I was the one complaining, that rat-fuck traitor!*

Jeremy forced a smile that he knew was unconvincing. He wanted to scream at them, fly at them in a fury.

"You throw parties?"

They laughed like those two stoners on TV. *Exactly* like them.

Susan showed more teeth in a condescending sneer—*no*—a smile.

"Well, we're very *socially*" (she said it like *sexually*) "active. Most weekends we have a small get-together at our place. There's talk, a little game-playing. We mingle, relax, and have a good time."

Lying murderers. Jeremy wanted to cut them with his pure, righteous words.

"And since we know you now," Daniel cut in. "You are certainly welcome. Saturday nights, starting around five. We provide a nice nosh, so you don't have to eat before you come." What sort of food? Jeremy pictured the smiling couple chatting brightly as they carved meat off a former guest's leg, and served it as roast beef. God, they weren't just murderers, they were *cannibals*! Only wait, cannibals ate their own species, and he wasn't all that sure about Daniel and Susan. What were they then? Man-eaters, like sharks or lions.

Where had those thoughts come from? Jeremy checked his watch. He was overdue for his medication.

He smiled at Daniel. How was it the man was so much shorter, more compact than Jeremy, so much more fit?

"I would love to come. I'll have to check my schedule, to see when I have a free weekend." Which was all of them.

"We look forward to seeing you, then." Susan teased her pink tongue along her teeth. Her hand found his and gave it a warm squeeze that tingled all the way to his groin.

Then they were gone, and Jeremy latched the locks back into place and sagged against the door. The apartment felt empty with them gone, as if they had leached the color out of his everything. Not that there was much to his apartment, but it seemed so gray and sad now.

Jeremy went to the medicine cabinet. He should have taken his Symbyax and lithium twenty minutes ago, and he could already feel the bad thoughts creeping in. Maybe it was the stress, and maybe it was them, with their creepy, identical smiles.

He washed the two pills down with water, and counted out twenty-five deep breaths. When he was done, the world was still in focus, but the bothersomness of the details was greatly reduced. He could ignore the nagging strangeness which was not real.

The Jeremy in the mirror looked back at him. What had really happened during that conversation with Susan and Daniel? Most of his suppositions had been his bad thoughts. They were not cannibals, they would not serve human meat to their guests. Susan was not coming on to him. She might not even have a tattoo.

Then again, she might.

Jeremy sighed and looked at himself again. Thirty-five, starting to slide a bit. He wasn't Hollywood material, but he wasn't hideous, either. What if she had been flirting with him? What if it was one of *those* sorts of parties? He felt the flush creeping up his face.

What about the smell from their bathroom, another part of him asked.

Jeremy ignored the party the following Saturday, going so far as to go to bed early. The soft music and susurrus of muted conversation put him to sleep quickly.

It backfired when he woke at ten past twelve, and couldn't get back to sleep. He stared into the darkness above his bed, listening to the dwindling conversations. He got out a book, but couldn't bring himself to put on any music, or leave the room. After an hour, he gave up all pretense of reading. By then, there seemed to be a single conversation going on.

One voice had a high-pitched whinny of a laugh, often bracketed by the Daniel and Susan's TV stoner laughs. The squeaky laugh came more and more frequently, more uncontrolled, as if she were drunk and getting more so.

And then it stopped, and the silence crashed in on Jeremy. After less than a minute of nothing but quiet, he scampered to the bathroom.

The wall tiles were cool, the room dark. He did not turn on the light. He stood, listening, waiting, barely breathing. What was he listening for? This was ridiculous.

The lapping of a large animal slurping at a wet meal, seeped down from the ceiling. Quiet, surreptitious, but definitely there. What was happening? Why the bathroom?

Because the tub will catch all the bloody drippings.

He forced the idea away. Those were his bad thoughts, they weren't real. Daniel and Susan weren't eating a drunk girl above him, weren't using the bath tub to catch the fluids that leaked out of her horribly mutilated body as they was chewed it beyond recognition.

He stood, groped his way to the sink, and opened the medicine cabinet. He found his thick bottle of medication by feel. It hadn't been this bad for years. With a twist the top of the bottle was off, and he gently shook a pill into his waiting palm.

From above, the sound of bone snapping, followed by a low moan of pleasure. Pills scattered on the bathroom floor as Jeremy scrambled to the phone, frantically punching in Ray's number.

Dr. Meacham stood just outside the door with his brown coat and benevolent brown eyes. Behind him loomed a police officer.

Jeremy was nervous around police officers. They carried guns that sometimes went off for no reason.

"Good evening, Jeremy," Dr. Meacham said. "Ray was a little upset over your call concerning the upstairs neighbors, and asked if I could talk to you about it. He also wanted me to have Officer Anders meet you, which I agreed to because it would allay his fears."

Jeremy nearly choked on Ray's betrayal. He had called Dr. Meacham before, when he thought Jeremy was having trouble. But to think he needed a police officer?

He unlocked the door and let the pair in. Remembering his manners, he invited them for some juice and a seat at the dinette table.

Officer Anders accepted a glass of apple juice with surprising grace. He was young, probably in his late twenties, although his close-cropped hair made him seem younger. His eyes were tired, and he was starting to show a little gut.

"Can I start, Jeremy?" Classic Dr. Meacham.

"Go ahead, since you know what, uh, Mr. Anders wants to know."

"Jeremy, I'm going to share a little of your case history with the officer, so he understands you better. Is that all right?"

Jeremy looked from Dr. Meachum to the officer and back. He'd been attending Meacham's group sessions every week for more than six years. They'd established some trust. He nodded.

"Jeremy is an intelligent man with both a Bachelors and a Masters. Would you tell Officer Anders what you used to do?"

"I was a teacher. I taught High School Social Studies for three years."

"And why don't you teach anymore?" Dr. Meacham prompted.

"I smashed a television in front of my class."

"And why did you do that, Jeremy?"

Jeremy pressed his lips together for a moment. The officer was looking at him with bland interest, as if he wished he was chasing muggers or something. It was so humiliating to confess his bad thoughts. He deflated a little.

"I thought there were subliminal messages in the digital

broadcast that told the boys in my class to tear off the girls' panties and have anal sex with them."

"And was that true?" Dr. Meacham coaxed.

Jeremy closed his eyes, embarrassed.

"No, it was not."

To the officer's credit, he didn't laugh. Jeremy hated being laughed at. Anders just made notes in his little notebook.

"I have adult-onset schizophrenia," Jeremy volunteered. "I keep it under control with a strict regimen of medication and some behavior therapy when I am agitated. I have controlled my disease for seven years, and I have not had any violent outbursts or episodes of self-injury. In many ways I am lucky because my disease is controllable, and I am able to live a fairly normal life."

Dr. Meacham nodded his approval at this little speech, but Officer Anders was looking around the apartment. Jeremy seldom had company, and it wasn't at its best.

"You don't see a lot of VCRs these days," Anders commented, nodding toward the old CRT television surrounded by a cityscape of black videotapes.

"Re-taping helps me set my mind at ease, Jeremy conceded. "Watching digital media makes me nervous, so I tape the DVDs I buy."

"You don't think there are subliminal messages in DVDs and digital music anymore, do you Jeremy?" Dr. Meacham was using that gentle, sympathetic voice he reserved for asking the most difficult questions.

He wouldn't lie to Dr. Meacham. He wouldn't.

"No. But digital media makes me nervous. I figured I could either stop watching television, or I could re-record DVDs onto videotape, which is analog. I buy my DVDs, so I'm not making copies of anything I don't already own. Watching something on tape doesn't get at me the way a DVD does. It's part of keeping myself calm, since I'm more vulnerable to my illness when I'm flustered."

He looked from Dr. Meacham to Officer Anders. He was the only person in the room without some sort of title, he realized.

"Jeremy, is there anything specific about the upstairs

neighbors that puts you on edge?" Officer Anders asked.

He thought about Daniel and how much he looked like Susan. And how attractive she was. It had been… a long time since he'd been on a date. Did he really think they were eating people?

"Nothing really. Maybe I resent them because they seem to have everything; good looks, happiness, and their mental health."

"I think we all understand that. Why don't we talk about that in our next session?" Had Dr. Meacham made any statements today? It seemed like he had only asked questions.

Jeremy turned to the policeman. "Officer, I read the newspapers. I know it seems like every other week someone goes off his medication regime and does something unfortunate. I want you to know that I'm not that guy."

"The undiscovered fear is always greater than the one we know." Dr. Meacham stated, and Jeremy realized he'd thought too soon. "If Jeremy here can perhaps spend some time with his upstairs neighbors, I think he'll come to realize that they are perfectly ordinary people."

"You're the doctor," Anders said.

"Jeremy is an intelligent man, but he has never shown any sort of aggressive behavior towards other people. Even his episode with the television, expensive as it was, harmed no one."

Anders flipped his notebook closed, which seemed to be a signal. They stood and wandered toward the door, still talking.

"I really don't think you have to worry, Officer." Dr. Meacham said. "We'll go talk to Ray, tell him that Jeremy's been under some stress, and that he's no danger to himself or the Millstons."

"I agree. Jeremy, you have been very polite, and thank you for the juice and your time."

Anders extended his hand, which Jeremy shook. After they moved out the door, Jeremy latched it tight. For a long time, he stood staring at the bland walls of his apartment. Go to their party? They seemed to have one every Saturday. Did he dare? Yes, the pair of them were creepily alike, and yet… he couldn't remember them saying or doing anything overtly strange or threatening.

And then his thoughts moved to Susan, her trim figure in white, and how smooth her strong legs were. Her eyes had sparkled, really lit up her face. And that barely-glimpsed tattoo. He would like to get a better look at that tattoo.

At the same time, he couldn't believe their last name was Millston.

Saturday evening, right at six, Susan opened the door. Jeremy tried not to stare at the tiny pink nipples that strained against the translucent silk of her sheer blouse.

"I'm so glad you came!" In an instant, she was hugging him, crushing her hot breasts to him.

She released him after a moment, and he realized he still hadn't said anything.

"I know, it's all a bit overwhelming. Don't worry. Just come in and be yourself. We're an eclectic crowd and we enjoy all sorts of things. And we all love a fresh face to show off for."

She pulled him in, and closed the door behind him. Her hand was warm as it traveled up his arm, across his shoulder, and flicked some suspected dust off his chest. Her touch was electric.

She pulled on his collar, and he let her bring his head down to her.

"Mingle and make some new friends." Her voice was liquid and breathy in his ear.

She released him and melted into the crowd. His nerves were singing. Couldn't he just follow her around all night? Would that be bad?

Daniel was suddenly at his arm, his smile showing too many teeth, sweeping him through the clusters of people. He lost sight of Susan immediately.

"I'm a bit of tech geek," Daniel was saying as he navigated them through the crowd. "And I kind of want to show this off."

"Of course," Jeremy mumbled. They halted in front of a flat-screen panel with a phone attached to it.

"That's a Sony docking station holding my sixteen gig iPod,

transmitting to hidden speakers in every room," Daniel beamed, proud as a new parent. "That way, the music is pervasive without overwhelming the conversation."

Making the digital music inescapable. A muscle in Jeremy's cheek twitched. Meaningless (*or were they?*) patterns swirled on the video display on the tiny screen. Digital music, why hadn't he considered that? He let out a ragged sigh. There weren't subliminal messages in digital music. He didn't believe that. Not now. Those were bad thoughts, and he had kept himself under control for seven years. This was only for one night; he'd be able to handle it.

Daniel was looking at him, little lines of concern between his brows.

"Just admiring it," Jeremy lied. "More like envying it. You've got quite the set-up."

Daniel smiled, mollified.

"Well, if there's anything you're hungry for, just let me know." He clapped Jeremy on the shoulder. "Definitely try some of our goulash… we're quite famous for it."

"*Goul*-ash." He hadn't intended to say it aloud, let alone emphasize the first syllable like that.

"Now you're catching on." Was there a knowing twinkle in Daniel's eye? Before Jeremy could think of a response, his host had been swallowed by the crowd.

He shook himself and looked around. The Millstons had bought two apartments and knocked out a few walls between them. Their place made a spacious contrast to Jeremy's own closed-in rooms. Somehow, the soft music and light decor made the rooms seem larger than they were. And they were filled with people. They seemed like urban sophisticates, in recent fashions and edgy haircuts that made him feel shabby.

He looked around, wondering who to approach first, when his attention was grabbed by the kitchenette. Food. Food was safe.

The counters were strewn with a variety of cheeses interspersed with bowls of pineapple, grapes, peach slices and tiny pears. Beyond them all was a forest of wine bottles. He wouldn't touch the wine, but the cheese seemed like a good idea.

The first plate he came across had a crumbly substance on it that smelled like feet. He decided to pass, only to stop at a large bowl filled with that looked like a minced abdomen. Suspicious tubules like chopped intestines sat with unidentifiable meat chunks in a blood-red sauce. The goulash, he realized, as horrible as he had imagined.

Just behind him, Daniel whispered, "The secret ingredient is human neurons."

Startled, Jeremy whipped around. The closest person was more than eight feet away, Daniel was nowhere to be seen. Had it been bad thoughts? Was the digital music already getting to him?

He closed his eyes for a moment and regained his breathing. He had kept himself under control for years. He was not going to break that streak now.

Cheese. He was going to have some cheese. He was reaching for a Double Gloucester when he realized the plate sat in front beautiful cutting block.

Jeremy watched as his hand drew one of the knives. The steel was patterned, with a Japanese character on the thick part of the blade. It felt so good in his hand, like it had always wanted to be there. Like it should have been there. He ran the edge across the tip of his thumbnail, nearly slicing it down to the flesh. Sharp as truth. Sharp as hate.

Susan's bright blonde hair was making its way toward him, a shark's dorsal fin cutting through her guests. He shifted his grip on the knife. Had anyone noticed? He looked around, but he didn't want to take his eyes off her.

She emerged from the crowd talking with a small, dark-skinned woman with short, tight-kinked hair. They touched each other as they spoke, their eyes too intimate for mere friends.

She had lied to him. Had been lying the entire time. She didn't want him to see her tattoo. She was teasing him, enticing him, luring him in, but to what end, he wasn't sure. He would expose her, and Daniel too. He would show them up in front of their smugly complacent friends.

After two strides he swung the hatesharp knife slicing through Susan's cheek as the other woman fell back and screamed.

Flesh parted, but no blood spurted. Under Susan's skin was something grey and slick, with monstrous sharp carnivore's teeth.

The room was quiet, all eyes on Susan and the flap of skin that had fallen away from the side of her face, and the inhuman horror revealed below. With a shake of her head, like a terrier snapping a rat's spine, her human skin fell to her feet. Revealed, she was a dog-like abomination, rail-thin and wiry beneath her rubbery grey skin, long fingers terminated in thick, tearing claws.

She grasped his shirt and hauled him close. A prehensile tongue snaked out of her mouth and nuzzled his ear.

"I love an aggressive man." The word slurred out of the monster teeth overfilling her mouth. "God I'm turned on."

IN THE HOUSE OF MILLIONS OF YEARS

Intef floated, free, in the current of the great lightless river. He had peace; no worries or cares, no regrets, no ambitions. Past and future were far away, inoffensive. Calm suffused him in an omnipresent, timeless now.

Something caught at his attention; a speck of light. He let his drifting turn him away. A tiny sound, a chant, annoyed his ears like the whine of a gnat. With the first effort since he had arrived in this non-place, he ignored it. The drifting, the now, the peace, was everything.

The sound got louder, more insistent. His eyes burned as the pinprick of light grew, like the golden bark of Amun-Ra surmounting the horizon. He again tried to turn away, to let the dark encompass him again, but the noise and the light would not let him go. The droning chant grew, became sinuous, entwined him like a snake. He was dragged to the light, away from the comforting calm.

"Mighty Pharaoh?" Hands touched his face. "Golden Horus?"

Intef felt old. His muscles and joints ached. He opened eyes that felt parched as a thousand years of drought. Akhetsau, High Priest of Amun-Ra, stood before him, flanked by two strangers. They chanted the damnable, snakelike spell that had called him from…somewhere. His memory of where was fading like a morning mist.

"What is this?" Intef croaked.

Now that he was awake, everyone on the room bowed before him. In the sudden quiet, the braziers hissed, billowing out noxious smoke. With slow effort, he worked himself into a sitting position, and discovered that he was in a sarcophagus.

His coffin, with his name enclosed in the spells.

"Have I been ill?"

Akhetsau bowed his shaven head, unwilling to look directly at his god-king. Frowning, Intef searched his memory. What had happened? Where had he been?

The battle had been long and difficult. His men tired from their long march, the pretender's troops fresh, their supply lines short. But the enemy was weak, without much stomach for the fight, where Intef's men were fighting for their true god-king.

The arrow had struck him cross-wise, entering his right shoulder. Intef curled in on himself, as the phantom of pain rushed through him. He remembered the confused shouting of his men as he was hauled from the battlefield, the arrow an agonizing brand.

The stench of remembered rot filled his nostrils. He read the truth in the grim faces of the royal physicians, that he was dying with his great work undone. He had sworn to unite Upper and Lower Egypt under one throne, as they had been a hundred years ago. Only then would the Empire be as it should, the most glorious in all the world. Would his son be a true son of Montu and take up this costly, difficult war to finally unite the Two Ladies?

Intef shook the past off and peered into the gloom that surrounded him. He was not on the Bark of Amun-Ra. But where was he? He knew the smell of the room; salt and strange, bitter herbs. He was in an embalmer's chamber. Though he could not focus on them, two indistinct figures, dressed neither as embalmers nor priests of Anubis, stood by him.

"Gods above, what have you done?" His voice was strange, a dry croak.

Akhetsau glanced at the dark figures. Intef could see a great, ashen stain on the High Priest's normally immaculate white robe.

"We have brought you back from the brink of death, Golden Horus." The man behind Akhetsau wore a black, concealing robe that was a mockery of the priest's pure white. "We were High Priest Akhetsau's last hope, and yours as well. You wish for more life, do you not, Great Pharaoh?"

His words were oily, and Intef disliked him.

"How long has it been?" He spoke to Akhetsau, ignoring the men. "Are my armies in disarray?"

"We have performed ceremonies over your holy body for more than ten days, mighty lord. Your armies returned you here, and remain encamped outside the city." The man's unctuous voice worked into his ear.

Intef turned a baleful eye on the men. "And who are you?"

"Heriabgher and Tehenraau, gracious lord."

"Where are we?"

"Thebes," Akhetsau cut in.

Only now did Intef realize how exhausted he was, as if he had been in battle for days. His limbs ached, his head was as heavy as lead. He knew that he should show himself to his troops. Let them know he was not dead. But the prospect wearied him. He had been in the field, chasing the pretenders and laying siege to their cities—his rightful cities—for years.

"Leave us." He did not care if this was Heriabgher and Tehenraau's home. He would not show weakness in front of them. Glancing at each other, they bowed, and left.

"Home." Even uttering the word was tiring.

"Golden Horus?"

"I don't wish to spend more time in this place of death. Take me to my wives and children."

He reached out, and Akhetsau took his hand. The High Priest of Amun-Ra helped him from his coffin, supported him out into the cool night as if the God-King were a common drunkard.

Intef drank in the sight of his palace like cool water in the desert. His wives, his children were there, beer and good food. Gleeful shrieks erupted from the serving girls as they went running to fetch his wives. Intef stood on his own, feeling his strength returning. He clapped the priest's shoulder.

"Thank you, Akhetsau."

The priest bowed low, then straightened.

"I endeavor to serve Pharaoh and the gods with my every breath." Akhetsau let out a troubled sigh. "I was afraid Egypt had lost her true King, the only one capable of reuniting her."

"Afraid enough to let two strangers work spells on me?"

The priest looked away.

"What choice did I have? To leave the land divided, with the madmen of Henen-nesut in power for another hundred years? I had to grasp the straw they offered me, no matter what the cost. With you restored, Thebes shall be the seat of power forever, the Two Ladies reunited."

Intef smiled, some of his weariness lifting.

"There is a still a lot of work to be done. I shall reward you as you deserve, Akhetsau. And the two strangers, even if I do not like them."

Light was coming down the corridors, and the gabble of voices as his wives and their ladies-in-waiting all tried to call him at once. The priest bowed and retreated as the tide of Intef's wives washed over him. There were nerves to soothe, rumors to lay at rest, attention to distribute, and he had missed it all desperately.

After his wives had been reassured, news exchanged, he chose his fourth and youngest wife Enehy to pass the night with. She was his youngest, married to him less than three years, as beautiful and flawless as anyone the gods had made.

"Intef, is that truly you?" She asked when they were alone, her khol-smeared eyes larger than usual.

"Truly me, daughter of Nefer."

Her smile brightened.

"Then you have tired of the company of your men?" Only she would dare tease him in such fashion.

"My empire is my work. You, my wife, are entirely my pleasure."

"Everything my mighty God-King, strong as a bull, wishes." Her murmur was breathy. Her linen dress slipped to the floor, and she stood before him clad only in the golden pectoral he had given her when they married.

Her delicate hand reached out and touched his chest, and her face clouded over.

"What happened to your heart?"

She took his hand and placed it over his heart. There was no beat. His chest was as still as stone.

"It changes nothing," he said to buy time. Nothing was wrong with him. He felt the same as he always had. Didn't he?

Almost concealing her fear and confusion, she touched him again, stroking his sides, avoiding his chest. He watched her with unwanted detachment. He had desired to be reunited with her more than anything else. She had never failed to arouse him with her youth and beauty. He had hoped for, longed for her while he had been on the campaign. Now, he felt nothing, as if her hands and mouth were touching another man. His body was like stone, incapable of reacting. Hoping against hope, he let her continue, but no pleasure came. She redoubled her efforts, as he watched, unmoved, incapable, until he pushed the tearful Enehy away.

Her failure betrayed not only him, but all of the kingdom.

"Sobekari!" He called for the night guard who kept watch over his bedchamber.

"Mighty Horus?" Sobekari bowed as he entered.

Intef looked at the pathetic weeping woman, huddled in the corner. He thought of the stillness in his chest, of her failure. All he had wanted was to return to his wife, and she had failed to elicit his interest, or his pleasure.

"Throw her to the crocodiles."

Sobekari was a loyal subject. He glanced to the weeping woman and back to Intef.

"Dread lord?" His voice quavered.

"She had failed as a wife, and I have no more use for her."

Again his eyes flickered to her. He bowed again.

"As Pharaoh wishes."

A scream tore itself out of her as Sobekari's large hand closed around her arm. Intef felt nothing. She screamed again, and now the palace was alive with the shuffling of bare feet on stone. Whispers flew, and people watched wide-eyed as Sobekari dragged Enehy along.

He led them, and a small crowd gathered in their wake, to the temple of Sobek, where the sacred crocodiles lolled sleepily in the night's cool air. If her screaming didn't waken them, the scent of a good meal would.

The priests came scampering out of their small cells, prostrated themselves before the terrible presence of their Pharaoh. The musky, reptilian scent that emanated from the enclosure was unmistakable, as was the carrion reek from their previous meals.

Intef strode to the stone lip of the enclosure, gazed down on Sobek's sacred predators. They were groggy from the chill air, but the scent and hubbub had woken them. Enehy knelt at the verge of the muddy pit, her flawless skin pale in the moonlight, arms mutely raised to him, begging for mercy.

Sobekari paused, his hope-filled eyes on his Pharaoh.

Intef placed a hand on his chest, felt the stillness. Enehy and Sobekari were breathing hard, but he was not. He was not breathing at all. His body was completely silent.

She sent him one last, imploring look. When he did not respond, she closed her eyes. She landed in the mud, and for a breathless minute, blunt, scaled muzzles snuffed the air. Then they were in motion.

Enehy was done with screaming. She stood, naked in the knee-deep water, her golden pectoral gleaming dimly in the starlight. As the crocodiles closed, she walked forward to greet them. Sobekari turned away, but Intef stood, watching. He could remember her touch, but not why it had thrilled him. The crocs tore into her soft body, her screams brief and then gone. Blood roiled in the water as the beasts hissed and snapped at each other, trying to steal another portion of bloody meat.

Intef could see the fear and hopelessness in Sobekari's eyes. For himself, he felt nothing.

With his heart still and his breath gone, Intef found that he could not sleep. He closed his eyes and laid his head to rest, but it did no good. After long hours, he simply paced the dark and empty corridors of his palace, waiting for Amun-Ra's golden touch to warm the land. The cold hours seemed endless, without his heart and breath to keep time. How had he not noticed his body's silence? Why did he feel nothing, when he had thrown his beloved wife to the crocodiles?

Across the silent morning came the chant of Amun-Ra's

priests welcoming the god's life-giving rays, and Intef knew what he was. After endless, tortured darkness, the Golden Bark finally rose above the horizon, chasing the cold shadows from the land. But it did not warm him.

He summoned his scribes, and ordered them to take down his words.

"The necromancers Heriabgher and Tehenraau are to be treated as criminals. They have robbed me of the breath of life, and now I have no place in Ma'at. They have violated the sacred precepts of Ma'at by knowing what should not be known. I have no living heart to be weighed against the Feather of Truth. These traitors have done injury to their pharaoh."

"Find them and impale them on stakes. Find their families, and do the same. Destroy their houses, leave no brick standing on another. Burn what you find within, scatter the ashes on the Nile. Raze the villages they were born in, and allow none to escape. This knowledge is an abomination which must not be allowed to continue. No sacrifice is too great, no hardship too unendurable to bring lawful death to these men."

He paused. "High Priest Akhetsau brought these men of corrupt knowledge to his dying Pharaoh. He is to share their fate.

"This proclamation is to be sped to all the provinces of Egypt, even those in rebellion against their rightful king."

Intef had a tomb carved to inter his first life. Intef Seher-tawy, Maker of Peace in the Two Lands, was no more. He put away his wives, became Intef Wah-Ankh, the Strong in Life. And strong he had been. Untiring when his soldiers dropped in their tracks of exhaustion, never hungry, never thirsty, and unwearying in battle. His campaign against the rebels of Lower Egypt progressed, but always, somehow, victory slipped from his grasp. Taken cities rebelled, governors thought loyal betrayed him.

Fear was the common element. Fear of him. His body, withered by the rays of the Aten, had become a shrunken horror, detestable and inhuman. No one confronted with such a face would believe it was that of the Golden Horus, Pharaoh, Lord of the Two Ladies.

Intef had a golden mask made to hide his hideous visage,

and buried his second life in a new tomb. He re-named himself Nakj-tneb-tep-nefer Intef, the strong and beautiful champion.

His scribes told him he had been on the throne for only seventy years. His work was nearly done, the land close to united. But Intef had watched the burning sun rise on more than twenty-five thousand days, and wandered sleepless and alone for twenty-five thousand endless nights. His children had all grown old, withered, and been buried. Their children had done the same as the hateful tyranny of years ground on.

Intef stood before the assembled crowd of his courtiers, as well as the people of Thebes, the light of Amun-Ra's glory reflecting off the golden mask which hid his features.

"Egypt, the long work we have begun is nearly complete. The Two Ladies will come under a single crown, but this work is not for me to finish. The gods have another task for me." He gestured to the resplendent figure of Mokhtar, High Priest of Amun-Ra, standing by his side.

"The gods have sent me clear signs," Mokhtar's rich voice filled the court. "The Pharaoh Nakj-tneb-tep-nefer Intef, the strong and beautiful champion, now has other duties to perform, higher duties that only a god such as himself may attend to. He is to become a priest of Amun-Ra at the House of Millions of Years at Karnak, the holiest of holies, and worship them for the peace and prosperity of all the land. In years to come, should a Pharaoh wish to consult Intef's great wisdom, it shall be preserved and cherished at Karnak." In truth, Intef had begged the priest to find some way of releasing him from the unendurable bondage of rulership. Mokhtar had received this timely command from the gods.

"I present to you Mentuhotep, child of my body, to rule over you as Amun-Ra is king of the gods." Intef stepped back, bowing his head. Mentuhotep stepped forward, already fitted with the double crown of Pharaoh. He was in the glory of his prime, with strong arms, muscular shoulders, and a resonant voice. Men would follow him to their deaths.

"My long work is ended." Intef imagined he heard a breath, long held, finally exhaled as he stepped into the shadows behind his great-grandson.

Intef was taken by litter to the House of Millions of Years, and he looked forward to a new day for the first time in decades.

Karnak was beautiful. A temple worthy of the gods, spotlessly clean, blinding white limestone in the glory of Amun-Ra's light. Intef found some solace there, his days now filled with the endless rituals, singing the hymns of praise, and washing the statues of the gods. But even the priests' life was centered around the bodily needs he no longer had. The sacred brotherhood ate twice a day, times during which Intef could either watch, or remain alone. During the nights, they slept.

The long, still nights left time for holy contemplation and study of the temple's library. He wondered what had become of his Ba, his animating force. Sleep was for whole people, and he was an empty Khat, a body without soul. He looked on living men with envy and a sense of loss. Had his Ba been set free to join the gods and his ancestors? Did it live on without him? Or had the necromancers destroyed it? Was this shriveled body all of him that existed? When that was destroyed, would he cease to exist? His names were still carved on his tombs, and priests still said prayers in his honor, but without a Ba to receive them, were they worthless? He should have extracted answers from the necromancers before having them executed.

Intef was seldom consulted by Pharaohs; they preferred to honor him from afar. What had been a single holy structure was now a complex with outbuildings, layer upon layer of pylon gates, enormous columned pillars, a towering facade, and enclosing walls. But the Pharaohs who built these new structures were not merely bringing glory to Amun-Ra, Montu, and themselves. They were erecting barriers to contain that abomination that dwelt in the holiest of holies, the thing whose dead heart would never be balanced against the Feather of Truth. Him.

And yet, the names of the Pharaohs were carved into the walls, where he would eternally see them, and by reading their names keep their memories alive.

He was abandoned, alone, unique. Every day Amun-Ra's Bark came over the horizon, and he bowed and scraped before the remote gods, hoping some favor would be granted him. As the endless days stretched into years and the years to decades, then to centuries, he heard nothing.

"Ever-living God, there is a visitor who wishes to see you." Intef had just finished the Celebration of the Awakening of Amun-Ra. Time had worn him down like a road rutted by stone wheels. He did not even know the name of the priest who spoke to him.

The newcomer was dressed strangely, and his accent atrocious. But he knelt with proper respect.

"Mighty God of the Golden Mask," the man mumbled, awestruck.

"I am." He'd had another name, once. The grinding of years had abraded that memory to nothing.

"I… I did not believe you were real."

"And yet you sought me out."

The man tried to recover himself.

"You are said to an undying god, as old as this holy temple."

The God considered.

"I have watched more than eight hundred thousand days dawn in this House of Millions of Years. I have seen more nights than there are grains of sand. The Persian Darius came to murder me, thinking it would be as easy as slaughtering the apis bulls. He beheld me, and fell down in worship. As I watch, Pharaohs die, their children die, and dynasties pass into nothing. Nations have been born and passed away, and I remain."

"I have a son, Deathless One. His heart is quick, and I will send him to train as a scribe next year. He is a good boy who does what he is told, who will help his father any time that he can. He has a good heart and is the joy of his mother and beloved of his siblings.

"He fell from the rooftop as he was playing. The bleeding has stopped, but he has not woken for three days. The doctors mumble that there is nothing to be done. I came for a priest, but—" a choking sob interrupted him.

"Could you not spare him a portion of your eternal life? Only an eyeblink to you, twenty or thirty years. Or use my own life and give it to him? Please Great God, please."

The man wept, his shoulders shaking with his misery.

Intef knelt next to him.

"You are chained to your burden of years like an ox to its cart. Hope is a heavy burden to carry over such a stony road. Kill your child in the most painless way possible. Let your son go, and begin to heal your heart."

The House of Millions of Years was crumbling around him. Worn stone showed cracks at the once-perfect seams. The statues were no longer washed in the sacred lake, the priesthood had fled. This temple, the holiest of holies, was falling to ruin. The people sang only the praises of Osiris, only with a strange, foreign name. They had scrawled new pictures over carvings more than two thousand years old. He alone chanted the praises of Amun-Ra, whose wrath could shatter the world. Even stars had changed positions, so ancient was he.

"Dread God of the Golden Mask?"

He focused on the man who stood, fidgeting and frightened, before him. He wore a strange bastardization of Egyptian and Roman clothing. How long had it been since someone had come to speak with him?

"What do you want?" His voice was dry as the desert around him. Though he kept up the rituals, he had not spoken to anyone for close to a hundred years. The new worshipers ignored him out of fear. Even it its crumbling state, the sprawling temple complex was large enough to share.

"We are invaded, Dread One."

"I am neglected and ancient as the dust on the floor. The Greeks and Romans plundered the black land and no one consulted me."

"A family legend says that my many-times grandfather once spoke to a deathless god as old as this temple. When I heard of these Arab invaders, I thought that you could help us." His eyes were wild, like a panicked horse's. "Surely, none may stand against you who are deathless."

He pulled a sword from its scabbard and offered it. The god's wasted, leathery hand closed around it. He had not borne a sword since... the impossible remoteness of the past made it cloudy. Not something strange like this one, but a proper khoepesh. This felt Roman; light, short, strange. But it would do.

He had welcomed the dawning of Amun-Ra more than a million times since coming to the temple's confining walls. The world outside had changed little, the small huts men lived in were much the same, as were the men who tended their small farms and water lifts.

They still bowed before him, too terrified to look at the golden mask he had never removed. His enemies would also cower before him. All men did. This was no army. They were a rabble, peasants determined to resist invaders. They had heart, but only the messenger who had spoken to him even carried a weapon. Any disciplined enemy would leave them trying to stuff their intestines back into their mutilated bodies.

And yet, these people needed him. For the first time in his sleepless ages, he felt needed.

He would lead these farmers to victory, for the preservation of sacred Egypt.

"Where are our enemies?"

An enormous snake of men slouched in along the road. Mounted riders flanked them, keeping the soldiers in line.

A rider spotted them, and spurred his horse in their direction. Intef, the Undying One, stood his ground. Yes, that had been his name: Intef!

He roared his recovered name to the skies, and the horse reared, nearly throwing the rider.

Intef lifted his sword and took off at a lope, unsure if his withered body would take a full run. The horse shuffled its hooves and rolled its eyes in fear as the rider fought for control. When they were dead, he would slaughter the entire army. He was Intef of Three Thousand Years, God of the Golden Mask, strong like a bull, the Undying. None could stop him.

The rider got his mount under control, and charged across the dry sand. Intef felt the ground shake as the iron-shod hooves thundered toward him. The God of the Golden Mask braced for the impact, timing his sword thrust to take the rider full in the chest.

The rider whipped his curved sword up, knocking Intef's sword into the air, then swept downward. Intef spun to the ground, and saw, through the tilted eyeholes of his mask, his decapitated body collapse.

The horseman swung around, approached at a slow trot. Feet landed next to him. Rough, uncouth fingers grasped his neck, and Intef was hoisted into the air. With a wrench that tore his skin, he was pulled from the golden mask. A face considered Intef in one hand, the golden mask in the other. With a casual flip, Intef's decapitated head was discarded.

His rabble of farmers was nowhere in sight. He could not shout, could not speak. Moving his jaw didn't give him enough purchase to right himself, to move at all.

Amun-Ra abandoned the sky. In the dark of night, the wind buried Intef's still-conscious head under a tall, silent dune.

A POOR SINNER'S HANDS

Eli was weeding his corn when he saw the preacher kicking up yellow plumes of dust on the road. A colored preacher must have been some kind of lost to have come near to Eli's farm.

"Greetings, brother!" The preacher's wave was cheery, despite the hot Louisiana sun. He wore a black jacket, and a grey vest over a white shirt. Steel pince-nez perched on his nose, and his bowler had seen a lot of travel. Cradled under one arm was a thick, leather bound book.

Eli was inclined to let the man pass by. But the familiar itching in his palms told him it wouldn't happen. Maybe if the preacher turned out to be a decent person, nothing bad would happen.

"You must have been walking for some time." Eli leaned on his hoe. The heat had a raw smell of dirt and dry, layered with the ever-present reek of pigs and wandering chickens.

"I bring words of hope and comfort, brother. Glad tidings and wondrous revelations for you to hear." The preacher wore his best smile, which didn't give Eli much hope. Just another wandering sermonizer looking to unload his enormous words. Still, the sun was hot, and Eli wouldn't mind wasting some talking time in the shade.

"I am Brother Pomfret." They shook. Pomfret's hand was nut-brown, and soft. Eli's was black as charcoal from years of farm work in the pitiless sun, rough as tree bark.

"Eli Taff. Would you like some sweet tea, brother?"

They retired to Eli's porch. The ancient one-room farmhouse was more a shack than anything else. Eli's tools hung on the porch wall, protected from the rain. With no neighbors within half an hour's walk, Eli did not fear thieves. They sat on rickety chairs at the wobbly table, each with a chipped glass, a pitcher of sweet tea between them.

"How are your crops?" Pomfret was more than willing to fill the silence.

"Slow since we haven't had much rain. Where are you from?"

Pomfret smiled.

"I have come from New Orleans with some good news that could not only help you, but alter your life forever." Brother Pomfret placed his weighty book on the table, and touched it as he spoke. "It is not difficult to discern than you are not a church-going man, brother Eli. And I do not blame you. Many men see the Baptists and Pentecostals as extensions of the unfair way of things, keeping the poor man down, letting the rich man feel virtuous as he gives out scraps of charity."

Well, the man talked a good game. Eli nodded. The letters on the book's thick spine spelled out *Cthaat Aquadingen*. He expected the itinerant preacher would be carrying a Bible, but Eli didn't let his surprise show. Not long ago, a colored man could have an unpleasant encounter with the night riders if he let on that he could read. Old habits died hard.

"The pious wait for their reward in the next life." Brother Pomfret put on his preaching voice. "But there are those who hunger for justice in this one."

Eli snorted. "Ain't no justice."

"What if there could be? Forces exist beyond those we see every day. Power beyond what small-minded white men think they have."

Eli sat back in his chair. This was dangerous talk, even between two colored men in the middle of nowhere. He rubbed his hands together, hoping to relieve their tension.

"Ten years ago," Eli said. "I was fighting the Nips on Okinawa while that cracker James Pray sat on his ass because of his flat feet. Jackie Robinson and Newk helped the Dodgers trounce the Yankees in last year's World Series, and I still get called 'boy' when I go into town. I suspect you get the same treatment, so why don't you stop pussy-footing around and tell me what you are about. You talk around your meaning long enough; my hogs'll get hungry."

"A revolution is coming," Brother Pomfret said in a conspiratorial whisper. "Those who have power will be crushed, and those who have helped will reap rich rewards."

"I've heard this before. What are you, a Wobblie come to build us a union? You always come with big promises, but when you leave, your fellow men are out a glass of sweet tea and whatever else we gave you. You prey on hope, take what you can, and move on. If I talk to the right person, you'll dangle under a tree before nightfall."

Pomfret removed his steel-rimmed pince-nez and cleaned them on his jacket sleeve.

"I'm not talking about anything as small or impermanent as a union, brother Eli. I'm speaking of a universal brotherhood of man, of ancient ways that are greater and more terrifying than anything else on this earth."

"So, you're a Voodoo doctor, come to tell me about Legba and Erzulie? I may not be a good Baptist, but I don't put a broom across my door at night, either."

Pomfret put the tips of his fingers together.

"The soul of man is older than this country, more ancient even than Africa. Some dreams are so deep and powerful than we will never understand them. Only some have the courage to reach out to what is greater than us all, to find the strength to free ourselves. Only some can be free of the hypocritical morality that the powerful use to keep the rest of us down."

Eli refilled his tea. "But how? You could worship head lice for all I care, but what do you do? Charity, good works, and lemonade? Dynamite and bloody murder? What kind of revolution you talking about?"

Pomfret's hands trembled as passion overcame him.

"There shall come a time, brother Eli, when the earth shall shake, the sea boil, the sky turn strange when the stars become—"

"The last shall be first and the first last and the meek shall receive the Earth?" Eli stood as he spit the platitudes, but the preacher would not be put off.

"Nothing so simple. All shall be overthrown. The world we know shall be ruined, and only those who have prepared, those who have given proper worship to the Great Old Ones shall receive their favor." Eli walked behind Pomfret, but the preacher stared glassy-eyed at something Eli couldn't see. "All shall fall before them, whether strong, meek, black or white. Antiquated morality shall fail. Sinners and saints will share the same fate, all who are unprepared will be meat for the grinder."

Eli took a hammer from the wall. He stood over Pomfret, who was bug-eyed, staring at a private vision.

"Saints and sinners will share the same fate? That's a relief, *brother*." He smashed the hammer down.

The preacher's skull splintered from the force of the blow, making a dent the size of a teacup. Pomfret's hands flew up as his legs kicked at the table. A wordless gabble poured out of his mouth as his limbs spasmed. Eli brought the hammer up, but the body went limp. Eli caught the corpse's collar before it could slump forward and bleed on the table.

Shouldering the body, Eli brought it to the barn. There, he hung it by the ankles with the chains he used when slaughtering hogs. With the sharp butchering knife, he cut the clothes off, piling them under Pomfret's head so they would soak up the blood. With practiced motions, he hacked through the shoulders, severing the arms. The hip joints required some back and forth with the blade, but the weight of the torso pulled on the sinews, making them easier to cut.

In less than twenty minutes, Eli had stacked the arms and legs, and laid the torso a little to the side. He looked at the head, eyes rolled up and already attracting flies, the skin ashen grey, before gathering it all up and dumping it in the pigpen. He would come back for the larger bones in the morning.

The clothes he burned; the blood made reeking clouds of smoke as it sizzled, but it was better than leaving anything a bloodhound could track. Eli looked at his shaking, evil hands. Why did they make him do such things?

He clenched them into fists, and surveyed his clean-up. All seemed right, until he walked back to the house and saw the thick, leather-bound book still sitting on his table. He wouldn't be able to sell it. A book this size would attract attention. He had to get rid of it. If anyone found it, they would know he had killed the wandering preacher.

Still, he couldn't bring himself to burn it. Books were rare in his world, and precious. He would have to keep it out of sight.

He ran a hand over the old leather binding, savoring the smooth, comfortable feel. It felt worn, but cared-for. *Cthaat Aquadingen.* He muttered the name to feel it in his mouth. It tasted of dry stones, the dust of ages, and rotten fruit.

Curiosity pushed his hand to open the front cover, forced him to leaf through the book. The pages were old and rough against his fingers, uneven at the edges. What kind of book was this? It looked older on the inside than the cover suggested. The letters were strange, deformed. Had they all been hand written?

Fascinated now, he turned the pages with reverent care. Long lines of words marched across the page's white expanse, the musty smell of old books reminded him of long-ago school, and a glimmer of fondness followed.

He laid a finger on a line of text, and began to read.

For mankind is but a blink in the eye of the Great Old Ones, now growing, now waning, irrelevant and changeable as the winds. They wait, for while Their time is not now, it shall be. When the stars align and all things are right, They shall be as gods again, powerful, eternal, the new pole around which the universe shall turn.

Eli's lips formed silent words as his finger slid under them. He wasn't sure he understood the passage. It didn't sound like the Bible to him. He closed the book, that was enough distraction for one day. The sun was a blazing red ball on a black horizon, and he hadn't gotten all his corn weeded. More work tomorrow.

Assuming the preacher didn't have friends who would try to find him. A shiver ran through Eli's frame. Why did his hands need to kill?

Before he went to sleep, he knelt next to his bed, clasped his evildoer's hands together in supplication.

"Forgive a poor sinner, Lord. My hands are covered in the blood of many, and I have again sinned against You. Help make me Your tool, Lord. Help Your wayward son find a way to serve You."

Eli was a long time falling asleep.

The week went by slowly, and Eli couldn't get the book out of his mind. What were the Great Old Ones Pomfret had talked about? What was *Cthaat Aquadingen* supposed to mean? Maybe he should have listened to the preacher a little longer. The things he'd said about the coming revolution, of saints and sinners sharing the same fate, they stuck in Eli's head.

He unpiled some of the stove wood and pulled out the box he'd hidden the book in. He looked at it, then put his hand on the smooth leather cover. It reminded him of a well-worn saddle, something rubbed constantly, dark with age.

He closed the box. He should get rid of it. Burn it in his stove, and he'd at least get a hot meal out of it. But then he wouldn't have any answers.

Eli was a sinner. What if he could share the same fate as someone good, someone virtuous, someone who didn't murder? Someone whose palms didn't itch? What sort of religion taught that?

A nonsense one. Eli lay down and tried to sleep.

An hour later, he was at the wood pile, tearing it down until he had again uncovered the box. He brought it back to his shack, and lit a candle. *Cthaat Aquadingen's* weight threatened to collapse his table. Despite this, he opened the book, and began to read.

Eli walked to town that Saturday. He passed by the lunch counter and its "We only cater to white patrons" sign. Further down the road was the nameless general store. Eli took off his hat to show proper deference to Old Simon, who sat in a rocking chair on the verandah.

Inside, paddle fans turned slow circles in the listless air. James Pray sat behind the counter, fanning himself, twin half-moons of perspiration above his belt-restrained belly. He looked up when Eli came in, but didn't bother to get to his feet.

Ten minutes later, Eli placed a small handful of candles and a dictionary next to the cash register.

"Dictionary?" Pray's surprise would not be contained. "What d'you want a dictionary for, boy?"

Eli's palms itched. The image of Pray in a spreading pool of his own blood flashed through his mind. He forced the thought aside. He didn't want to end up dangling from a tree. Anyway, the thought of dragging Pray's fat carcass all the way back to his farm was tiring.

"I've been reading my Bible, Mr. Pray. But some words I don't know. Like 'asunder.'"

The fat man relaxed. A doughy hand pressed the keys on his cash register.

"Well, the dictionary says three dollars and ninety-five cents, so I'm going to have to charge you five. Another dollar for the candles makes six." Colored customers always paid more at Pray's.

Eli counted out six dollars, and laid them on the counter. Pray put the money in the register, then placed Eli's purchases in a paper sack.

Eli had never been much of a reader. Even with the dictionary open next to *Cthaat Aquadingen,* his progress was slow. Only when he was reading the book, one finger beneath each word, did his mind and his hands work in unison. During the day, he hoed the weeds out of his corn, fed his pigs, killed his chickens. His hands did the work as his mind turned over the strange phrases he had read. As the days passed, the words grew in his mind like weeds, choking out other thoughts.

Unable to sleep in the dark hours before dawn, he would return to the book. He no longer bothered to hide it. It lay open, on his rickety table, next to the dictionary. His mornings began with reading a few pages as he delayed work. The book waited while the chores got done, he studied into the lonely night.

His need to finish the book grew, his thirst for knowledge concerning the Great Old Ones. They were described as mighty, beyond the understanding of mortals. Godlike entities who insinuated themselves into the affairs of men. Their power sapped the life from humanity. Right now, they were imprisoned, constrained. But the Great Old Ones would rise in power to destroy all who opposed them.

The book's allure was powerful. Entities with strange names such as Mordiggian, Zhar, and Dagon promised their followers a liberation from constricting morality. Gangs, or cults prepared the way, on the promise of power, glory and freedom once the eldritch powers had returned. Eli imagined what life would be like under those victors, the pettiness, the viciousness of humanity unfettered.

Once these inhuman *things* were free to raven and destroy, would they feel gratitude? Eli had heard a lot of promises in his life. When people got what they wanted, they often forgot those promises. He'd made and broken a few himself. If he helped to free them, Eli would be free to kill with impunity, even authority. The thought rocked him. He could be the one with power. His killing hammer would never stop, rising and falling, smashing the skulls of men, women, even children, and face no reprisals. To spatter the whole world with blood, to swim, to drown in a bloody ocean that he shed. This, the Great Old Ones swore would happen.

He looked at his hands. He knew what they wanted. They'd killed six men and two women since he had returned from the war. Eli remembered the slaughter on Okinawa, the men who had been butchered, the ground littered with the mutilated and dying. He remembered the mad rush of Jap soldiers who died screaming on Eli's bayonet. The relief that had rushed through him when it was over, that he was alive when so many around him were not.

Eli shoved the book away, breathing fast. He shook his head to get rid of the images of gore and splintered skulls. He longed for the satisfaction, the release, of indiscriminate murder.

His sins, he knew, were too great to be dismissed. God judged him, but the Great Old Ones would not. He longed for the peace that would bring, to no longer be torn apart by the acts he could not control. To take cover from the wrathful eye of the forbidding Lord who would punish his actions with anger and suffering. More than anything, he longed to be whole again.

October had eased the summer's heat when Eli came to the last page of *Cthaat Aquadingen*. When he looked at himself in his wash basin, the face reflected was hard to recognize. The man in the mirror was gaunt, his skin ashen grey, eyes rheumy from late nights and early wakefulness.

He was not certain of everything that *Cthaat Aquadingen* said. He did not understand how the Great Old Ones could be so powerful, and yet need humans to bring about their return. Nor did he truly understand what they were, or what the book described as 'their extra terrene matter with lapses of materiality. But he knew they desired their freedom. And the book was clear that only human worship would bring about their return.

A few days later, he was again leaning on the thick pine counter top of James Pray's store.

"I've sold my farm, Mr. Pray. I'm headed out."

"You headed up North?" Pray said it with the pinched distaste he had for anyone who left his tiny domain.

"New Orleans."

"Whatever for?"

Eli hefted his new two-pound hammer. One last time, he imagined the feel of Pray's splintered skull, the sight of the fat man's blood and brains spattered across the floor.

"I met a man named Brother Pomfret who said he came from New Orleans. I aim to meet the people he worked with, and show them the ways of the Lord."

THE DARK HORSE

The dry, yellow wind off the Dominion of Manhattan brought a bitter scent to Laura's nose. The building's broken windows and splintered doors moaned in the acrid wind. She'd holed up in this apartment because the door was still on its hinges. Something skittered behind her. Laura whirled, spear at the ready. A filthy raccoon with one pus-filmed eye twice the size of the other glared at her from the doorway. She tensed, ready to pin it to the floor. The coon crouched. They considered each other, the wind's low dirge the only sound for long moments.

Laura reached behind her with one hand, and found a crinkly wrapper by feel. She tore it open with her teeth, and flung it at the coon. She didn't like to waste food, especially something as good as a Twinkie, but she didn't want trouble from the coon, either. With that eye, it wouldn't be good to eat.

The coon sniffed her offering, then tore big bites out of the golden cake. She watched it gulp the yellow thing down, then lick the plastic wrapper clean, manipulating its treasure with humanlike front paws. It glared at her with its good eye, then limped out the doorway.

She ought to follow it, find out if it knew where any food was. But she'd eaten well for days, and wasn't feeling hard up. She could afford a little generosity. The apartment building had been good to her; a safe place to sleep, good forage, and no one else around. Eating from old cans was a lot easier than scrambling after rats and roaches.

Laura threw some wood and paper on the coals of her small fire, and soon the flames leapt high. The night was cold, and the fire would be dead by the time she woke. She should have closed the door to keep the coons, cats, and dogs out. With the fire warming the concrete floor, she threw an old rug over herself and curled into a ball. She hoped she wouldn't dream.

She woke with a start to see a man squatting before her fire. Before she was fully awake, she had rolled into a defensive crouch, spear in hand, ready to kill. He just raised his hands, showing her that he had no weapons.

"I just want a can of your food, some time by your fire, and a little talking."

"I got the clap and aid." Her voice was gravelly and rough. She hadn't spoken to anyone for more than a month. "Do me and your cock'll rot."

His eyes were sad.

"I don't want that."

She'd heard that before. Looking him up and down, he didn't look like the men from the Dominion. She noted the big knife in a belt sheath, and the way he kept his hands away from it. An unkempt mane of white hair cascaded down his shoulders. A long-healed scar ran across his temple, just below the hair line. His skin was dark and weather-beaten, a flowing white beard covered much of his face. The long leather coat was only just more travel-stained than he. A heavy carry-bag was slung across one shoulder.

"What's your name?"

The rumbling undertones in his voice reminded her of her father, kind and strong. But that was no reason to trust him. She adjusted her grip on her spear.

"What kind of food do you want?"

"A can of whatever you're willing to spare." He was still on his haunches, warming his hands over her little fire.

"We'll see. What did you want to talk about?"

"Can I at least know your name? Mine is Travis Dornier, and I've come a long way to see you."

"What do you mean?"

"I want to know your name, so I can be sure you're the right person."

She eyed him warily.

"Sheila."

"That's not it and you know it."

"Mary."

"I'm not going away until I learn your name. It's important."

He didn't seem like a sorcerer. They had people to do things for them. They didn't go wandering around alone. She might not understand magic, she'd never heard anyone needed your name to cast a spell on you.

That wasn't enough reason to trust him, though. They were playing this stupid game about her name, and she could feel him trying to make her like him. She looked him over again. He was lean, probably stronger than her, but she could outrun him no problem. She didn't want to talk with him, but the need for company welled up in her.

"Laura," she conceded.

"I wondered if it was."

He reached for his bag, and her spear was at the alert again. With one hand, he made a placating gesture.

"I'm not going to hurt you. I would never hurt you."

He took a blue box from his bag. It was glossy and shiny, with a picture of a girl. Laura held her breath. She was beautiful, the way only people from Before could be. She had long yellow hair and fine, pale skin that hadn't seen a lot of sun. And yet, there was something sad and perhaps lonely about her. Inside the box were the mirrored disks that told stories of the Before time.

"What's this?"

"Laura, I've waited more than ten years, and come more than three thousand miles to meet you. I'm so relieved to finally be in your presence."

"Me? You've come to see me?" She tightened her grip on her spear. "What's this about?"

"Do you see the girl on this box? She was the chosen one who would stand against the Masters—"

"Liar. No one knew about the Masters in the Before Time."

He looked down at the fire before he spoke again.

"Some of us did. Some even tried to warn everyone before the Corpse City rose, and the world went mad and the dead were piled as high as buildings."

Laura shuddered. Though years gone, she remembered the nauseous, omnipresent stench of the corpse-piles, some half the size of city blocks. For a moment, there was no sound but the low dirge of the wind.

"Maybe if we'd tried harder ... ." He didn't finish the thought. "We failed. And a lot of people died. But now I have found you, the new chosen one. And you can put this right."

There was a lump in the pit of her stomach.

"Me?"

"You, Laura. If you cannot drive the Masters back under the ocean, no one can."

"What can I do? I'm just me."

"You are more than you know, Laura. The girl on the box, her name was Laura, too. If I could, I would tell you all the stories on these disks. Stories of her bravery, how she did not give up when everyone around her had."

Laura vaguely remembered the big windows that told the stories on the disks. She hadn't thought about them for a long time. She glanced at the broad, dark window in the apartment, but it was just so much junk, like most Before stuff.

"And you are like her, Laura. You are chosen, the one that can, that *will*, defeat the Masters, drive them back to where they came from, and make the world like it was."

Laura's goals were simple: find untainted food, locate shelter, stay away from the Dominion of Manhattan. Now, there was an unfamiliar feeling inside her, almost a hunger of the soul. She pondered her two-fingered right hand, maimed long ago when some dogs had chased her down. She had other scars, too. A large pucker where a cat had torn a chunk out of her shoulder, three thick lines across her breast where a dog had scratched her. She had a short line across her belly, and two on her left forearm from men with knives.

"It won't be as it was, not for a long time. But if you listen to me, and do as I say, you can kill the Masters, kill them all. And then, peace."

"The Dominion's tower for women?"

"No more tower."

"The Lord of Manhattan?"

"Destroyed utterly."

"Impossible. The Masters are as big as buildings. What can I possibly do against them?"

"Do you know any magic, Laura?" He said it slow and long. She shook her head, resisting his enticing tone.

"Magic is only for the Masters and the people they favor."

"There is more than that. I have a spell that I want to teach you."

The thought thrilled through her. To have that power, to be a sorcerer, like the Lord of Manhattan.

The noises he made were an unintelligible jumble of mixed sounds.

"Repeat it."

She did her best.

"No. Say it again."

She did.

"No. Do it again."

"How will I know?"

"You will know. Say the words again."

She did.

"Did I get it right?"

His sour look did not indicate success. He repeated the words, and then she did. She tried to hear the difference between what they were saying, but she ended up randomly emphasizing this word or that. And then, after ten minutes, a hot spark flew from her mouth, and she tasted tin. Her hands flew to her mouth. Her teeth were hot, her breath scorching. And she saw the triumph in his eyes.

"Now, say the words again."

She did, and got it wrong.

"Again."

The taste of tin returned. Her mouth dried out with the heat of it.

"Once more."

She got it right instantly. Her tongue felt like it had been left in the sun for days.

"You must say it to yourself every morning, and every night before you go to sleep."

"Will it kill the Masters if I say it to them?"

"It's not that kind of spell. But if enough people say it, chanting it at the same time, it will kill all the Masters."

An awe mixed with fear welled up in her.

"How many?"

"It has to be at the right time, said by thousands of people. As many as you can teach. And when the time is right, we will destroy them all." A fire lit in his eyes as he said it.

"How long will I have?" She was disappointed that she wouldn't be able to simply point her finger and destroy the Masters or their servants. In the wake of the ruined fantasy, hope remained.

"Laura, tell nobody that you are the chosen one. If the Masters or their slaves catch wind of it, they will stop at nothing to kill you. For your own safety, say nothing to anyone."

"I won't."

His hand shot out, and he grasped her with painful strength.

"You must promise me. Promise you won't tell anyone." She tried to yank her hand away, but his grip was hard, and his fingers sank into her flesh.

"All right, I promise."

He let her go.

"I didn't want to hurt you. But you have to understand how important it is that no one else knows."

It didn't feel right, but he'd given her the key to the world, shown her who she truly was. He looked away from her, his mouth set in a deep frown, eyes down as if searching for something on the floor. She wanted to say something so he wouldn't feel bad.

"When will the time be right?"

"Not for a while."

"But you'll tell me."

He shook his head.

"I won't be here." She felt a stab of fear. "I have a lot of research and preparation to do."

"You'll be staying at least a little while?" She felt lost. How would she know what to do as the chosen one if he didn't guide her? A part of her wondered how she'd come to need him so much. She regarded him again. Only her small fire held back the darkness. He looked strange and sinister with flickering shadows thrown against his face.

"I cannot. I have spent years finding you, Laura, perhaps too many. If it isn't too late, I can proceed with the next stage of my plan."

"But what do I do?" She sounded desperate in her own ears.

"Teach. Travel, find other people who have escaped the Masters. Teach them that peace is coming, and that if we all act together, Cthulhu and his spawn will be destroyed."

She shuddered at the dread name.

"When?"

"If I am not with you, I will send green lights into the sky that you will not be able to miss, no matter where you are."

"You can do that?"

For the first time, he smiled. It made his face warm, and she felt herself liking him even more.

"I can do many things. And this … this is important. Do me proud, Laura. Say the words every morning after you get up and every night before you sleep. Teach those who are willing. You are the chosen one. If you cannot destroy Masters, no one can."

He reached out and she thought he was going to caress her cheek, but instead he claimed a can of food, which he stowed in his pouch. She sat, silently amazed, as he walked into the darkness. After several minutes of listening to his footsteps recede, she closed the door.

Laura's mind whirled for the rest of the night, thinking about what Dornier had said. It kept echoing through her head; that she was the one person who could eliminate the Masters, possibly even sink the Corpse City back into the ocean.

She did not forget herself so much that she didn't keep an ear out. She woke from sleep to hear a pack of dogs on the ground below, but they passed by without stopping.

In the Before time, dogs had been pets, and people slept safe at night. In the Before time, Mom and Dad had watched over her. Before Mom had been torn apart and eaten. Dad has lasted three more years, until an infected bite had gotten him.

She remembered staring in terror at his still form, unable to believe that he would never move again. She stood vigil for two days, not eating, not drinking, waiting for him to get back up. Watching his skin sink and turn grey. She tried to keep the insects away, but there had been too many. Dogs had ended her vigil, chasing her away and reducing her father's carrion to scraps and bone. Laura hadn't remembered that for a long time.

So many people lost, until now she was alone. She remembered friendly people, and smiling faces. She couldn't bring them back. The world hadn't always been this way. Dornier had given her the means to make it better, to make it free from danger. As she thought about it, there was nothing she wouldn't do to get that sense of safety back.

Her fire had faded to embers, and she shivered in the chill darkness. She whispered the words to herself, and felt the hot spark fly out of her. This was how she would set things right.

At first, Laura skulked around the fringes of the Dominion of Manhattan. She didn't even try to talk to the men. They were all crazy because their women were locked up in the tower. They feared the Lord of Manhattan more than death. Boys were interested enough to talk with her, and she could outfight or outrun them easily.

None of them remembered the time Before, but she found that if she made promises about the destruction of the Masters, they cooperated. She taught them the spell, and told them when it was for, and they promised to repeat it when they were alone. She seldom saw any of them again. She wondered how many of them would practice like she told them, before going to sleep at night and first thing on waking.

Winter was difficult, as it always was. Laura knew how not to leave tracks for a hunting party to stumble across. If someone armed with a gun found her, that would be the end, chosen one or not. She watched the night sky for any hint of green, but the remote stars were all that stood in the unending black. Would Dornier would meet her again? She had so many questions.

When summer came, with the hot, humid weather the

fish-men didn't like, she decided to take a greater risk than just talking to boys. All the women in Manhattan were kept in an old tower made of ornate stone, about five miles from the Lord of Manhattan's court. It was old, but solid. A fence surrounded it, and above the second floor, the windows were covered with chain-link fencing. Inside this perimeter fish-men patrolled, rifles in their large, web-fingered hands, their unblinking eyes ever watchful.

Laura found another building like it, several abandoned blocks away, and learned how to climb the outside. At first, her efforts were clumsy and loud, dislodging fragments of stone, dropping them noisily into the street below. Every time she slipped, or raked her fingers bloody on the unforgiving walls, she reminded herself that she was the chosen one. She could do it. At night, when her fingers wouldn't stop throbbing and her muscles ached, the knowledge gave her comfort. After some weeks, she learned to wedge herself quietly into windows, and grip the cracks between stones. She would teach the women in the tower the spell. No one would want to destroy the Masters more.

After a month, she began to climb in the dark. She learned a slow, stealthy pace that didn't disturb the roosting pigeons until she reached up and grabbed them. She ate well. All that was left was to wait for a sweltering day followed by a hot, airless night.

The cruel Manhattan weather did not make her wait long. The sun dragged across a sky of molten metal, and the air was heavy with the reek of asphalt. Laura spent the day in the shade, her breathing shallow, mind racing at the prospect of the hot night ahead. She was slick with perspiration, and the death of the sun brought no relief. It was time.

She threaded her way through the piles of discarded and rusting cars, keeping eyes and ears open for fish-men. She hid behind a burned-out hulk of a car, watching the fenced perimeter that surrounded the tower. Enormous hybrids in ill-fitting clothes patrolled the inside of the fence with listless motion, rifles slung across their backs. Laura nearly gave up and sneaked off at the sight of their glassy and unblinking eyes, but she thought of Dornier, and being able to make everything right.

When a patrolling sea-devil had shuffled into the omnipresent dark, she ran to the fence, vaulted up with a clatter of metal on metal, sprinted to the building and started to climb.

She was nearly at the second floor before the fish-man came back to the fence, rifle at the ready. Laura froze, barely daring to breathe, and tried to press herself closer to the building's hot stones. How good was their hearing? She was sweating freely; would they be able to smell her with their flat nostrils like cut holes in their faces? Her heart hammered, and she felt her grip slipping, and perspiration seeped into her eyes, stinging like ants. Below her, the fish-man grunted, and was joined by a second one. Their movements were sluggish in the simmering heat. Laura's arms burned as she clung to the side of the building, still as a stone. How good was their hearing? Would they hear if she shifted her hand? They would see her if only they looked up. They were so close. She could have landed on them, but she would never be able to overpower their hideous strength.

Eventually, they moved on, croaking guttural imprecations. Laura didn't know if sweat or tears ran down her face. Her arms were cramped from being locked in one position, but she forced them to work, feeling for grip points and toeholds, hauling herself up.

The third-floor windows were covered with chain-link fence. Laura thanked the Masters for their consideration. With very little room, she gripped the window ledge with her toes, and clung to the fence. She couldn't reach the window, and just as she was wondering how to contact anyone inside when a gaunt face appeared in the window.

They stared at each other. Laura hadn't expected the women in the tower to be pretty, but she hadn't anticipated anyone this haggard. The face that looked at her was so worn that Laura couldn't begin to guess her age. She was frail, with colorless hair surrounding her head like a gossamer halo. Tattered rags barely covered her swollen belly. Seeing Laura, she pressed one fist to her mouth, reached out with the other. The window opened only a little, just enough for the stranger to get her hand under the sash and toward the wire fence. Her fist smothered a sob when Laura touched her stick-like fingers. At first, she didn't know what to say, clinging to the side of the building, staring at the weary, desperate woman who clutched at her fingers.

"What's your name?" She whispered it for want of any other question.

She moved her fist and said, "Monica." Her voice was tentative and achingly fragile, just within hearing. "You have to get us out of here."

"I don't know how."

Tears glistened in Monica's eyes. Laura looked beyond her, and saw lumped forms lying on the floor, sleeping or shifting uneasily. Cats lived better than this.

"I have something that can destroy the Masters. Get rid of them all."

Hope flared in Monica's eyes, and the realization of how young she was hammered into Laura's gut.

"Can you do it right now?"

"No. I have to teach you. And then we have to wait for the right time."

Monica gestured to her distended belly, tears of frustration streaming down her cheeks.

"I can't wait. I can already feel its claws."

Laura avoided the desperate eyes. What could she tell Monica? She was doomed. The pregnancies of the fish-men ended with screaming and blood. She didn't know when Dornier would turn the sky green. Would it be days? Weeks? Years?

"But you can teach it to the others."

Laura watched as Monica's newfound hope was snuffed out. Her worn, despairing face looked away and then back, seeking any sort of solace. They gripped each other's fingers, as tears ran down the pregnant woman's face.

"We can stop this from happening again," Laura whispered. "If we can kill them, they won't do this to anyone else, ever."

Monica opened her mouth, but nothing came out. Laura could do nothing but hold her fingers as she silently wept. After some time, Laura couldn't tell how long, Monica straightened up and wiped at her tears.

"Teach me."

Laura whispered the spell, her mouth filling with the taste

of hot tin. It took a long time for Monica to get it right, with Laura whispering encouragement from the other side of the fence, correcting her pronunciation as best she could. Her arms and legs were shaking with fatigue, but she hung on, desperate for Monica to get it right. Then Monica's frail hands flew to her mouth. Laura had her repeat it twice more, to get her used to the taste, and the exact words.

"Teach the others, but don't let the fish-men know. Whisper it to yourself before you go to sleep, and when you get up in the morning. When the sky turns green, it will be time."

"Make it soon." The pleading in Monica's eyes and voice was almost more than Laura could bear. She gripped Monica's fingers, hoping the frail, imprisoned woman could take strength, or hope, or anything from the contact. Only when her trembling limbs threatened to fail, did she let go. She stretched as best she could, and prepared her aching muscles for the descent. Her final glimpse of Monica was of the skinny, pale face nearly lost in shadows. Then Laura was on the ground, over the fence, and running into the darkness before the fish-men could respond.

She spent the next day collecting food, and set off north, across the river, and away from the Dominion of Manhattan.

At first, the country looked much the same, with ruined concrete, steel, and stone towers, but they got shorter as she walked away from Manhattan. After days of walking, the buildings became houses, and twisted, malevolent-looking trees crowded in on her. She touched one and found it wept a goo which burned like a knife cut. Other bloated and quaking plants squished underfoot.

Laura had never been outside the Dominion of Manhattan. Her hunting and escaping skills served her well in this savage green place. Often, she killed only to discover her prey had some sort of rot or grotesque growing out of it. These she abandoned. Only once was she desperate enough to eat a healthy-looking part of a deer whose putrid, blackened skin was peeling away from its ribs. The days of vomiting and chills in the middle of summer were enough to teach her that it was better to go hungry.

In the wilderness, she found small enclaves of humanity

that resisted the Masters' grip. Or at least, were too small to be noticed. Most drove her off with gunfire, but a few welcomed her. To these, she taught the spell, always pointing to the sky, waiting for it to turn green. She would stay for a few days, and always leave alone.

Seasons passed. She grew lean and hard, her skin darkened with sun and travel.

After three summers, at the hottest peak of the year, Laura saw a Master. A bloated, flabby, man-like body with a cancerous, tentacled head waded through the trees like a man in a pond. She was paralyzed with horror by the impossible size, and cringed on the ground, driving her teeth into the stubs of her missing fingers to keep from screaming. The ground shook as the colossal aberration shattered trees with its passing, and Laura wept with sick fear hours after it was gone. How could she ever stand against something so mighty? When Dornier spoke of dealing with the Masters, it had seemed like a pretty dream. Confronted with their enormous reality, despair clawed at her. She repeated the spell over and over, letting each hot spark fly up to the sky, each one a wish that the Masters would be destroyed.

The next morning, weak after a night without sleep, she decided to return to Dominion of Manhattan. She wanted to see if the children remembered, and teach them again if necessary. How large had Dornier's rebellion grown? How many people whispered the spell to themselves at night and the first thing in the morning? She didn't know how many times she had repeated it. The hot spark of success no longer surprised her, and she could taste nothing but hot tin.

The return to Manhattan was long, and every night, Laura looked to the sky, hoping for some hint of green. Monica would be dead, she knew. Even now, the thought saddened her. There would be fewer women left, but she would have to visit the tower again.

On a warm and clear morning, she saw again the familiar broken skyline of the Dominion of Manhattan across the great river. Conflicting emotions roiled in her. She was relieved to be home, even though the memory of Monica and the women in the tower lurked in the back of her mind.

The Lord of Manhattan had changed his ways in her absence, and Laura crept into a trap as she tried to sneak across the great, creaking bridge. Men and sea-devils with guns emerged from wrecked cars and chased her down. She cut three of them before being overwhelmed. They tied her tightly with straps onto a metal frame, and carried her, like a slab of meat, into the Dominion.

The Lord of the island kept his court in the tremendous Central Park, his throne at the bottom of a large depression with seats, his castle a little ways off to one side. Lowering above it all, the crumbling towers of Manhattan stood silent and stern.

The theater was full of filthy men, who pounded hands on their thighs as she was carried down the steep incline. They grunted an unintelligible monosyllable in time with their fists. When she reached the nadir she was pitched upright, face to face with the grossly fat Lord of Manhattan. Wedged into a leather, bucket-seat throne, at least three times as wide as she, blubbery fat as if he wanted to grow huge like a Master. His face was heavy and drooped like diseased fungus off a tree trunk. Four inhumanly tall fish-men flanked him, guns in their frying pan-sized claws. In front of the massive sea-devils were a pair of young, naked woman, absent-mindedly running their hands through the Lord's hair and touching his greasy skin. Their eyes were deader than those of the fish-men.

"A wild girl, I see." The Lord's deep, forced rasp sent unpleasant chills up her spine. "Let her go."

The straps were undone in a moment, and Laura was unsteadily on her feet. Above her the still sky was white with overhanging clouds. She stared into the Lord of Manhattan's pale-blue eyes, and said, very slowly, "There will be a time when you and your Masters will die."

He laughed, a heartless, fleshy earthquake that left him coughing and wheezing.

"You're one of Dornier's little followers, aren't you?" He moved his face close to hers. Laura turned away from his reeking breath, but someone grabbed a fistful of hair and forced her head back to him.

"Let me guess, he told you that you are the chosen one."

"The what?" She tried to bluff, but her heart quailed. His laugh was cruel.

"Release her." And she could move her head again. "Dornier is just like us; the only difference is that he was stupid and backed the wrong horse. We came to power, and now he's just a beggar, seeking after the scraps left by of our lord. He finds gullible children and tells them they're the chosen one, like a fable off TV. He teaches them a useless spell so they think they're something special, then runs off to find another one. We've killed six of his chosen ones this year. I don't know what he thinks he's doing, but he can't stand against the might of Great Cthulhu."

The crowd shuddered at that awful name.

"You see that?" He regarded the cringing throng with open contempt. "That's power. *Fear* is power. You want to get anywhere, people have to fear you. I've got the power of life and death over everyone here, and your Dornier lives like some sort of shit-eating scavenger. Nobody tells me what to do." He glared at the mob.

"You!" The man he pointed to was pale and wasted-looking, with few teeth left in his head. The crowd backed away, as he fell to his knees, too paralyzed to beg for mercy.

"Tear him apart and feed him to the crowd."

Two of the sea-devils were on the man instantly, his inarticulate screams replaced with wet tearing and the spatter of liquid on concrete. Laura didn't even bother turning away. After they'd ripped the terrified man into raw chunks, they jammed handfuls of human meat and offal into the terrified faces of the crowd. They ate, the blood coursing down their chins. They hated it, and glared in the direction of their Lord, but they ate.

"That's power, little girl. They hate me. They'd kill me if they could. But I've got power, and your precious Dornier doesn't. All he can do is seduce the young and send them out to learn one of Azathoth's idiotic spells."

Azathoth. One of the words of the chant. Laura tried not to show recognition, but the Lord of Manhattan smirked.

"Azathoth. Goddamn blind demiurge, the size of a star. The awesome daemon-sultan that sits and does fuck-all at the center of the universe. Destroys everything he touches, doesn't even know what power is all about. What the hell is your idiot god going to grant anyone? The power to drool and shit themselves? Dornier backed a second-rate loser. Not even a contender. Your spell doesn't do anything, you stupid bitch."

Laura concealed a relit spark of hope. The chant did something, even if she didn't know what. And if the Lord of Manhattan didn't know what the spell was, it would take him by surprise. She looked at the sky.

Two fish-men grabbed her and took her away. It didn't do any good to struggle—they had hands like steel. They wrestled her into a cell at the Lord's castle. The door was too strong for her, the walls unforgiving stone.

Now she knew the despair that Monica felt. Tomorrow she would go to the tower, and sometime later, a fish-man baby that would tear its way out of her. If she survived the first one, there would certainly be another, and then another until whatever luck or strength had sustained her gave out. Would the spell work if she was dead? She thought about the Lord's jibe about Dornier and the chosen one. He was a liar.

She watched as the clouds slowly broke up, revealing a fine red sunset. Daylight turned to darkness, and no one bothered her, not even to feed her. She paced in the nearly-blind dark, the stars remote and uncaring. Did she have it in her to escape from the fish-men?

She curled into a ball for what might have been hours in the timeless, trackless cell, sick with fear and failure. Almost imperceptibly, darkness gave way to a faint green luminescence. She looked up. Beyond her tiny cell window, the sky was a roiling, inverted pot of boiling green water. She marveled, dumbfounded, before realizing what it meant. The time had come. Dornier was calling for her and everyone who knew the spell. She chanted. Somehow, she had imagined doing so surrounded by many people, the women and children she had taught, their voices joining up into a triumphant, ascending chorus. Instead, she pressed her face against her cell's filthy bars, chanting alone, her words echoing off stone walls. Nothing happened. The hot spark flew up, but that was all. Was that it? She started again.

And then she heard a reply, off from the distance. First one voice, then many. Women's voices, and then more, men now, men angry with the Lord of Manhattan. Laura sang it, stronger now, exulting in the sound of the people around her, all chanting the same spell. After two inconclusive tries, they were suddenly all saying the same words at the same time, clamped together by some force greater than all of them. When the last syllable was said, an invisible hand pulled her tongue out by the root.

Laura collapsed, hands at her mouth. When she moved them, there was no blood. Her tongue was numb, her teeth scorched and blasted. Somewhere deep inside her was a dull ache. The green churning had vanished from the sky, leaving once again the moon, and remote stars. Nothing had changed. She measured time by the painful throb of her body. Laura wept. She hadn't been good enough, or strong enough. Not enough people had chanted, and their single opportunity had been wasted. They were defeated, the Masters had won.

When she glanced up, a strange new light was filtering into her cell. Hope surged, and she pressed herself against the bars of the window. The sky had turned a tainted red. A tremendous new object dominated the horizon, nearly touching the zenith directly overhead, somehow behind the moon.

Laura stared, her mind numb with fear at the sight of the impossible, seething monstrosity of chaos. She saw its inconceivably alive, churning surface, and the thick tentacles like the snouts of blind worms, questing with slow, terrible majesty. She quailed before Azathoth's horrifying size and awful splendor, its utterly alien nature.

Uncountable tentacles groped out blindly. One touched the moon, and then a storm of tentacles swarmed over the surface. Laura watched in sick horror as the thick worms rent the moon asunder with slow grace. In fifteen minutes, all that was left was a coating of light dust on the reddish tentacles. Done with that, they reached out again, inexorable, blindly seeking something new.

Laura scrabbled at a corner of her cell until her fingers were bloody, desperately trying to find something—anything—to put between her and the slow, monstrous tentacles that grew ever larger.

Then, crushing what he chanced to mould in play,
The idiot Chaos blew Earth's dust away.
HP Lovecraft, *The Fungi From Yuggoth*

PAIN WEARS NO MASK

"Excellent port," the Marquess of Queensberry commented, his words colored by a Scottish Brogue. Wrinkled and shrunken with age, his evening dress hung on him like a shroud. To Ernst Udet, sitting opposite him, he seemed jaundiced, his skin's pallor unhealthy. Udet remembered that the noble had once been a great boxing enthusiast, and wondered where that young powerhouse had gone. "You young gentlemen know how to treat the peerage, even if your Frenchmen are guillotining me with their eyes."

"France still has scars from the depredations of Henry the Fifth and other British tyrants," Georges Guynemer said with a Gallic shrug. His rich blue velvet dinner jacket matched his eyes. The youthful George never wanted for pleasurable company.

"The aristocracy was made for the guillotine, not the other way around." Charles Nungesser twisted his face into a sardonic smile. He sat behind a palisade of bottles, mainly wine, but also brandies, ports and an absinthe. "Else the world would not have followed the example of *La Révolution* so closely. It is 1925, and there hasn't been a king anywhere in the world for a decade." Ernst suppressed a chuckle. Drunk, Nungesser was more impressively mordant than he was sober.

"Men are happier with kings to rule them," the Marquess remained defiant in the face of the Frenchmen's anti-monarchist sentiments. "Freedom is seductive, but without their betters to govern them, the common man will fritter away his limited industry away on frivol and dissipation. Do you think an establishment like the Gundel could possibly have been built under a republic?" His encompassing gesture took in the cream-colored walls of the room, its fine crystal chandeliers, gilt tracery, and the elegant portraits of Andrea Ilona Lang.

"It wasn't built by the aristocracy, though." Eugene Bullard's face was impassive as a mahogany idol in a smoking jacket. "Why do I doubt the men who built it were paid a fair wage?" Udet knew Bullard's father had been a slave in the American Confederacy, and considered that the Marquess was unlikely to win this argument.

"You promised us information, not banter," Bill Wellman, captain of the *Black Cross* and self-styled pirate of the airways, shifted uncomfortably, as if his American tuxedo chafed. Handsome enough to be described as dashing, Wellman's tall forehead and pencil thin moustache marked him as an American, even when he kept his mouth shut.

"Americans, relentlessly to the point," Queensberry's mutter was dark and resentful. Udet pursed his lips.

Cigar smoke formed strange, drifting coils around the crystal chandelier.

"There is nothing to say. I don't know a thing about this so-called marriage of the former Queen," their guest muttered into a glass of brandy.

There was a general exhalation of frustration around the table.

Udet stood, pulling himself to his less-than impressive 5'2". But the former Marquess was sitting, so Udet loomed over him like a frowning thunderhead.

"John Douglas, I have seen the shabby hotel you live in, and I would have been ashamed of it in my student days. What we offer will keep you well fed until the end of your days. Spent wisely, it will allow you to keep the shreds of your former dignity in a more spacious and better-heated location. If you tell us nothing, you will return to your chilly rooms with a full belly today, and only the pale shadow of that memory in a week's time."

Queensberry stared up at the German, his jaw clenching. The rest of the table didn't breathe. And then something broke inside the Marquess.

"It was disgusting from the start. I knew the prancing white-feather playwright from before, but he began to pay court to

Her Serene Majesty, more than twice his age. He, a commoner, like that Brown, and a sodomite to top it all off. Revolting."

The table was silent, all eyes on the Marquess. He glared back at them.

"Only a few, mostly public atheists, and only those with titles, attended. I doubt any members of Parliament were invited, certainly none were there. Republicanism was on its triumphant upswing, and the Queen's ministers probably feared that the wedding might lead to an insurrection." He grunted. "If only we had known.

"Of course, this didn't happen in a church. They chose the lawns of hideous Gothic house in the country, Borley Rectory or some such ridiculousness. Rumored to be haunted by the ghosts of indiscreet monks and nuns and other flights of fancy. The *playwright*." he spat the word, "said it was somehow appropriate.

"I suspect only atheists were invited because only we would have stood for it. That prig the Archbishop of Canterbury would have died of apoplexy."

The smoke formed weird swirls in the yellow light that caught Udet's eye. The rest of the table were rapt, intent on the Marquess's story.

"They put up a pagan altar in the middle of the grounds. To the left and right were staked painted draperies, supposedly the work of the groom, entirely of decadence and corruption and I won't begin to describe them here.

"The less said about the groom, the better, but the bride... Victoria was clearly besotted. She wore flowers in her hair, as if she were some blushing Irish virgin rather than a grandmother more than thirty times over. The music was... I can only assume of the groom's own composition. Grotesque would be the best way to describe it. It hung in the ear like a sickness, insinuating itself where it was not wanted." The Marquess slammed down another gulp of expensive port.

"They processed between ranks of lit torches and exchanged some ridiculous set of vows before a pallid worm in yellow silk vestments. I was not close enough to hear them. They exchanged as, as *private* a kiss as ever man bestowed on woman in the confines of their bedroom.

"I think they only invited me so the Irishman could cement his triumph over me."

With a hiss and a clump, a mechanical waiter opened the door to their private dining room. All eyes were on it as it stepped, with frequent halts, up to the table. Udet didn't like the permanently smiling face, as inexpressive as a dead man's.

"Is sere anysing elese the cus'omers hwisshh?" It fluted through metallic lips that flapped in a regular pattern that did not form words. Tiny tubes in its mouth, like a miniature organ, were more suited to fluid, vowel-rich Magyar than to the harsh fricatives of English. The sleek, clockwork waiter was supposed to ensure a measure of privacy, but the pirates did not trust that there were no listening devices secreted on it.

"We are fine, thank you." Wellman said it with careful enunciation that would not confuse the automaton.

"Ssank you," the mechanical waiter turned in fits and starts, and headed back across the floor.

When the door had closed, Wellman brought out a small briefcase, stuffed with Hungarian *libertás* bills, and extended it over the table. The Marquess reached for it, but Udet's hand came down, blocking the old man.

"You haven't told us all you know," the German said.

"I am an old man, older than I ever thought to be. I have lived long past my time." The Marquess shrank back, looking more frail than he had. Exactly how old was he?

"What was the groom's name?" Udet ground out the pitiless question. "Where can we find him?"

With a glare of pure hate, the former Marquess upended the table, raining the dishes and tablecloth onto Wellman. The withered hands turned to claws, the jaws foamed as he raved. "He has my heart! Don't you understand, he has my heart!" With uncanny speed, those clawed hands reached for Ernst's throat, but Bullard's fist crashed into the Marquess's face, sending him sprawling. Ernst, recovering himself, remembered that Bullard was reputed to have the most fearsome left hook in all of Paris.

"What's that damned idiot doing?" Wellman struggled from under the tablecloth, shards of broken china raining onto the tile floor. "What the god-damned hell is that son of a bitch doing?"

Georges approached the downed nobleman, and Ernst came up on his other side. The fight seemed to have gone out of him.

"Tell me the name, old man. Who did Victoria marry?"

Queensberry's face contorted with fury

"Wilde," he shrieked. "That disgusting reprobate Oscar Wilde."

The pilots looked at each other in silence. Georges motioned for the briefcase. Wellman, now disentangled, passed it to him.

"Where?" Georges placed the suitcase on the floor, keeping himself between their guest and the money.

"Kuala Lumpur." Queensberry's tone was of defeated resignation.

Guynemer helped the Marquess up, and handed him the briefcase. Those shrunken hands clutched to his chest, like a drowning man holding a life ring.

"You're mad to seek him," was all the Marquess would say before turning and shuffling out the door.

The pilots were quiet for a moment, each thinking their own thoughts as they righted the table and assembled the shards of smashed china.

"Is he telling the truth, or is he just a demented old codger who walked away with our money for a fairy story?" Wellman asked.

"Might be both," Georges responded. "Still, we've got a name."

"It's too fantastic, though." Bullard was hard-headed and practical, and Udet liked that. "Wilde? The playwright?"

"And what did you make of that heart business?" Of all the strangeness in the man's story, that had disquieted Udet the most.

"Have you read Wilde's last work?" Charles Nungesser's question was quiet, but cut through the conversation.

"I seem to remember something after *The Importance of Being Earnest*," Georges was vague on the point.

"It was called the *King in Yellow*." Nungesser held a glass of absinthe, staring at a portrait of Andrea Lang which regarded him with pity. "It had two performances, and during the second, the audience rioted, ending with the theater in flames."

"Poor critical reception." Ernst said with a small smile.

"It's no laughing matter," Charles said in that same quiet voice. "Dozens were killed, and none who attended those performances were ever right again."

"What do you mean, were never right again?" Bullard leaned closer.

"My uncle was one of those who managed a ticket to the second show."

"And?" Wellman's drink sat neglected by his elbow.

Nungesser looked at the china that littered the floor.

"And he was never the same. It is partially for him that I painted that sigil on my plane."

"Let's see, a skull and crossbones surmounted by a coffin, candles left and right all in a black heart." Wellman recited from memory. "You don't seem that morbid."

"I was inspired by my uncle's drawings. After seeing *The King in Yellow*, he continually drew strange and fantastical pictures, images of death and dying, as if he were possessed by the spirit of Hieronymous Bosch. It broke my aunt's heart. He died a few years later. He never spoke about the performance, but I remember my mother saying that similar things had happened to other attendees. One never spoke, only hummed the same tune over and over. Another locked herself away and wrote, on paper when she could, on the walls of her house when she couldn't. My aunt still thanks God that my uncle hadn't found a pair of tickets. She'd loved *The Importance of Being Earnest*."

"We're looking to score the British Crown Jewels, and you're telling us ghost stories?" Bullard's expression was one of disbelief.

"The old world protects itself with stories and superstitions," Georges said. "You Americans don't understand, your country is too young. With more than three thousand years of history behind her, Europe has had time to wrap her secrets in myth. They may be metaphors, distortions, or even the remnants of lies a hundred years dead, but it never does to ignore something like this, Eugene."

The pilots eyed each other quietly. Udet wondered if Georges believed in this hocus-pocus. Or Bullard.

"I fancy a crown," Bullard adjusted an imaginary coronet on his head. The rest of the table nodded in consensus.

"Gentlemen, the *Black Cross* will be ready to depart for Kuala Lumpur in five days," Wellman's tone was slow and deliberate. "I don't think I need to remind you that it's best to keep our destination and everything discussed here a secret. If you have concerns, bring them to me before we lift."

Udet stood in the internal hangar of the *Black Cross*, looking at the planes. Four Sopwith Snapdragons were racked there, were racked there, vibrating almost imperceptibly in sympathy with the airship's steam engines. Each aircraft was each less than a year old, all trusted and reliable. His eyes lingered on the strange symbol on Charles Nungesser's plane, the morbid coffin, skull, and black heart. But they all had done something unique with their planes. Udet's own plane had "Do Doch Nicht" written on the tail, "Certainly not you." Bullard had the silhouette of a bird on his.

"The Black Swallow of Death," said Bullard as he entered the hanger behind Udet.

"Was this how you felt when you came to Europe?" Ernst asked Bullard. Below them the verdant green of the Indian subcontinent crawled past. The *Black Cross's* propellers whispered in the twilight. Below, everything was silent.

"There was more work to do on the steamer. I was shoveling coal once they found out I was on board. Didn't leave a lot of time to think about where I was going." But there was something else working behind Bullard's face. Udet knew enough to let it work its way to the surface.

"But this feels strange," he finally said. "Not just distant, but like we're intruding. Like we don't belong."

"A fair number of the people we're flying over would agree. It's frightening to think that we could land and not be able to find anyone who speaks a language we understand."

"Alien, is what we are. Strangers intruding into places where we don't know what's going on," Bullard had been quiet since leaving Budapest. Udet could not disagree.

"I don't like the way they stare at us," Udet said. "And the further we get into Hindustani territory, the more they stare."

Bullard sighed.

"This isn't about the stares. This is about Wellman keeping us on the *Cross*. If you're not flying, you're not happy." Bullard placed a comforting hand on Udet's shoulder. "Not much more than a week, he says. Then we'll be at Kuala Lumpur."

"Can't be soon enough," Udet said.

After an interminable six days over the Bay of Bengal, land was finally sighted, and Wellmen set the pilots loose to scout.

The great armature lowered Udet's plane out of the *Black Cross's* belly. His stomach leapt into his mouth as the plane dropped like a stone toward the green carpet that spread out below him. Fleecy clouds raced past him as the propeller caught, stuttered for a moment, then hissed into full throttle. An invisible cow sat in Udet's lap has he pulled the Sopwith biplane out of its dive, and then the exhilaration of too-long denied flight was on him. The land was a brilliant emerald patchwork below him; fields and swathes of trees.

He flew for long, pleasant minutes, enjoying the warmth of the air, even two miles up. He rolled and looped, happy to be aloft. He shared the sky with no one; Udet was lord of all he saw.

Below him, a trickle of ants moved along a ribbon of roadway. A busy street had something at both ends, and Udet decided to follow the road as far as he could.

Through the patchy clouds, he could see that he was approaching a city. They couldn't have been so far off course that this was anything but Kuala Lumpur.

A tricky cloud shifted, revealing a fantastically huge airship, larger even than the *Black Cross*, squatting over the city like an obscene toad. The canvas was patched with age, overall a filthy yellow color that filled Udet with loathing. When an airship was that old, that mildewed, it was slick and disgusting. What was it still doing in the air? How long had it been here?

Making for the enormous zeppelin, he read the name

Carcossa on her nose. Roman letters, but the name meant nothing to him. Could this be their prize?

The hiss and smack of bullets striking his plane made him turn and dive. Two planes dove past him, from out of the sun. Udet twisted his Snapdragon away, keeping an eye on both fighters. Fokkers, from their thick wings and extended flaps, but he could not place the model. He pulled the protesting Snapdragon up into a half-loop and then a roll. The Fokkers spun away in different directions. He followed to the left. Evidently, they didn't know the Boelcke turn. His enemy twisted and spun, but Udet was on him. His thumb pressed the Winans trigger just as his prey nosed up.

With a *whump*, the boiler in the Fokker's nose ruptured, scattering shrapnel and a cloud of superhot steam. Udet swerved and held his breath. The pilot would have been boiled and flensed to the bone in an instant. Even as Udet flew on, he couldn't avoid the reek of boiled meat.

He pulled the Sopwith's nose up, the engine clawing at the air. Somewhere was the second fighter, but after excruciating minutes of searching, he could not find it. Weaving around the patchy clouds, he found nothing. Perhaps it had returned to the *Carcossa*, or zoomed away with the death of its wingman.

He circled the enormous airship once, taking in what details he could of the broad and elaborate gondola slung below the gas bag itself. All the while, he kept an eye out for more Fokkers. But there, on the side of the gondola, the baroque lion and unicorn of the House of Hanover coat of arms.

He dove away, excitement squirming in his guts.

"It doesn't prove the crown jewels are aboard." Wellman tried to remain cool in the face of Udet's excited report. The scent of the quarry had the rest of the pilots humming with eagerness.

"An airship with the Hanover crest? We certainly know where we're going to look next," Guynemer said.

"All four of you will go out, assuming the *Carcossa* hasn't fled. They attacked without warning, and now they know there's someone else in the area."

"They seem inexperienced. Despite their Fokkers, they were

surprised by Boelcke's Turn."

Wellman nodded.

"Did you draw any fire from *Carcossa*?"

"No."

"Did you see any gun emplacements?"

Ude thought for a moment. "Again, no."

"Well that makes everything easier. Bullard, you'll be flying Udet. Charles fly George. It doesn't look like we'll have to bring the *Black Cross* in for support, but we'll stand ready just in case. You boys have any trouble, zip back here and we'll work a different deployment. Now, let's be ready in ten minutes, there's treasure to be won."

Udet constantly scanned the skies from the rear of the lumbering two-seater. Bullard concentrated on flying. As they approached *Carcossa*, they saw no other planes in the air. Surely the loss of only one couldn't have crippled the airship's contingent, and it wasn't as if they were actually able to creep up on the airborne leviathan.

Nungesser approached the airship to the rear, slowing until he was close to stalling. Udet now had to watch both the surrounding sky and keep a nervous eye on his fellow pirate. Guynemer easily hooked his grapnel on the rear-facing balcony. He pulled the line and was abruptly left swinging in space, nothing below him but two miles of air until the forest canopy. He pulled himself up, hand over hand, wrapping the slender cord around his leg.

Udet didn't see how it happened, but he glanced at the hanging cord and saw that Georges was no longer there. He leaned over the side of the cockpit, and saw his fellow pirate falling with a slow, vertiginous horror. In a moment, Guynemer's falling body was out of sight.

Cursing, Udet fired his own grapnel, and hauled himself up the slender rope. Clambering over the balcony's railing, he had his pistol out in an instant. Without Guynemer, he was alone. Bullard and Nugesser would have to fly back to the *Black Cross*, and refill the plane's boiler before returning. He could wait for them, or he could attempt to take the ship by himself.

Above him, the gasbag of the *Carcossa* loomed, rivulets of green crawling down the aged, parchment-colored canvas. The blades of the propellers stroked the air gently, guiding more than pushing. He didn't like the quiet, or the fact that no one had come to challenge him. What kind of ghost ship was this? Surely they didn't think that just being an airship was protection enough.

He moved his way forward, tried the first door he came to. The wood was mahogany, elegant and heavy, the knob verdigrised brass. No one had taken care of the *Carcossa* for a long time.

With a shove, he opened the door. A man in a slovenly uniform, once a dark blue but now patched and faded, looked up in alarm. Udet extended his pistol.

"English? Deutsche? Francais?"

The man's flesh was pallid and damp, as if he were a fungi grown in an oozing, lightless cavern. He did not speak, instead covering his head with both arms and fleeing out the other end of the corridor. Sick with the loss of Georges, Udet didn't have the heart to shoot at the retreating form.

Two doors stood in the middle of the corridor. Udet chose the more elaborately decorated one.

The room was massive, almost a ballroom, had the ceiling been higher. Some thirty yards away, a shrunken and pallid Wilde sat on a mighty throne, clad in yellow silken robes. Dozens of flexible tubes thrust out from the hem. Men and women, the dimness making their skin tone indistinguishable despite their nakedness, lounged on pillows of rotten silk in a scene from a sultan's seraglio. Hot air and hazy smoke made Udet's head swim.

They looked up with languid motions, elaborate masks covering their faces. One odalisque's face covering sprouted a multitude of goat and ram horns in unnatural profusion. Another's mane of long feathers emphasized her hesitant, trembling movements.

Wilde wore no mask, but a magnificent crown rested on his head. Hundreds, if not thousands, of diamonds flickered in the dim light, forming crosses and thistles, which must have pleased Wilde's Irish heart.

The man himself—the King of Britain—looked with indolent languor from Udet's face, to the pistol he carried, and back.

"An assassin? Come to kill the last king?" His voice was deep, resounding.

Udet found he did not hate this man. His mouth quirked into a grim smile.

"I'm sorry, your grace. I am only a thief."

Wilde swept a withered hand up and touched his chest with sticklike fingers.

"The proper form of address for a king is 'your majesty.'"

"You are the only royalty I have ever met, your majesty. Please pardon my lack of social propriety."

One of the drugged figures fished around under a cushion, and Udet's pistol was instantly covering her. Oblivious to the threat, she pulled a small instrument out and began to blow a low, mournful tune, never acknowledging Udet at all.

"Cassilda is no threat to you," Wilde said with a sigh. "You seem typical of the modern, low class of criminal. Not even a proper sense of deference."

Udet felt his mouth quirk again. With a great hiss of released steam, the great man glided off his throne. He did not appear to have legs; the tubes carried his weight. Udet wondered how far up that mass of tubes went, how much of Wilde was left under the yellow silk robe.

Wilde drifted across the room, skirting piles of listless bodies and heaps of stained cushions. Udet raised his pistol.

"Stop there, Mr. Wilde."

Up close, Udet could hear the churning of fluids and the hiss of gases that washed through the pipework that kept the King off the ground.

"I only want what we all want: an appreciative audience." Wilde looked around him, fragile hands brushing at his concealing robe.

"I am here to rob you, Mr. Wilde. Not hear your art."

"I stood in symbolic relations to the art and culture of my age," Wilde went on as if he hadn't heard. "I was a lord of language. But what good is art, or culture, no matter how masterful, without an audience? Creation is not made to echo alone in the abyss. It can only exist with the cooperation of an audience. And therein lies its limitation."

Wilde's wrinkled face looked down on Udet, the perfect picture of the man of sorrow.

"There are so few receptive minds, and living in this wretched exile, I have been so very alone. These," a negligent wave of his hand encompassed the room, "are little more than extensions of myself. I cannot bear to part with them." He paused.

"Politics are pervasive, inescapable. It does not require one's consent to be ruled. Thus, should be art. That which sheds light on human truths should be just as inescapable. Far too many turn their backs on difficult truth or unaccustomed beauty. *Ars longa*, it is said, but how can we make it last? We live in an era where books are forgotten in a year, and few but the most ardent spirits bother to read anything of true meaning."

The air was becoming thicker, more difficult to breathe. The damnable, repetitive tune swirled, and Udet shook his head. He should shoot the musician, the one with the horns on her mask. His pistol wavered, unsure, and he blinked to clear his vision. Was something happening? The floor was gone, and he was in darkness, the air rushing past him at a furious rate, a monstrous presence he knew he must not look at looming hatefully above him. Something whispered, like a giant's rumble a thousand miles away; *Have you heard the yellow sign?*

"I wanted to find a new art, a perfect art. Art that does not merely affect the observer, but makes them a conduit, infests them, so they cannot but help transmit it to others."

"*The King in Yellow.*" Udet heard his own voice say, even as he thought back to the strange behavior of Nungesser's uncle.

"I searched far and wide for the means to make my words, my thoughts, contagious. I was near to despair when someone, something found me. The spirit of truth that is Unspeakable."

Udet's brain was buzzing like a balloon full of bees. He was being crushed into insignificance by hands somehow larger than the airship.

"I did not understand fully when I wrote *The King in*

Yellow." Wilde's voice was sinuous, everywhere. Udet, tumbling through nothingness, clapped hands to ears in an attempt to block out the noise. He had a pistol. He could put it in his mouth and make everything stop.

"It was too crude, the participation of others diluting my intent. The results, unsatisfactory. Pain, true pain, perfectly expressed, can wear no mask. Naked expression cannot be hidden behind interpretation. I wanted my rage to infect, to violently tear minds open and expose them to unspeakable truths." The Last King was silent.

Udet gasped, snapping back to the present. All that surrounded him were the strange skirling notes of the mournful song the woman played. Wilde towered over him, close enough to touch. Udet extended the pistol, finger stiffening on the trigger, but he eased off when he saw the crown in the king's hands.

"I'm being a poor host, nattering on about myself. This is what you came for, isn't it?" Wilde extended the glittering crown. "My baubles. Rob me. I have nothing precious to live for, and these nothings lost their luster long ago."

Still in a daze, Udet extended his left hand, and the Last King put the crown in it. It was cool to the touch. He gazed down on four crosses, and four diamond-encrusted clusters of rose, thistle, and shamrock.

"It must have been very heavy," Udet mumbled, in awe at the hundreds of diamonds mounted in the crown. Somehow the woe-filled dirge floating in the air described the double band of pearls than encircled the base.

"The years have been heavier," Wilde looked down at Udet, his face an ocean of despair, but there was something furtive and hungry in the Irish poet's countenance. In a rush, Udet remembered the Marquess of Queensberry's frenzy, and the old man screaming that Wilde had his heart. In the close confines of the Last King's court, his head buzzing, did he truly want to know?

He didn't.

"Do you still have the Koh-in-Nor?"

"Victoria's broach? In the treasury. I'm sure you will find

everything you are looking for there, the diadems, and scepters. All heavy gold and jewels that no longer sparkle under layers of dust and spider webs." Wilde's gaze was worn. "I had feared men like you for so long, and now that you are here, I cannot care. Do as you will, thief."

Carrying the crown in his left hand, pistol in his right, Udet exited. In the fifteen minutes it took to find the treasure, every crew member shambled out of sight.

The treasure itself was more than he expected, a dozen crates embossed with the House of Hanover seal, sat moldy and decaying, undisturbed for decades. The smell of mold and rot teased his nose. He made quick work of shoving three of the heavy crates to the edge of the observation deck. He attached all three to a parachute and shoved them off, before stepping into the void himself.

Despite his misgivings, his own chute opened, and he drifted down into the jungle canopy.

And yet, he couldn't get Wilde's strange words out of his head, the idea of the artist as the spreader of contagion, with infectious words.

In the buzzing, singing jungle, it took less than an hour to find the crates. As he looked up, he saw a third parachute. Hoping against hope, he rushed to where Guynemer had impacted the ground. He knew even as he approached the site, that Georges was dead. Swarms of insects hummed around his body.

It only took a moment for Udet to realize that they were buzzing in the same maddening tune Cassilda had played on board *Carcossa*. He was infected now, a carrier of the music of the Unspeakable.

ABOUT THE AUTHOR

John Goodrich lives and writes in the haunted Green Mountains of Vermont. Two of his books, Hag and I Do Terrible Things, were published in limited editions by Thunderstorm books, and are now coming to paperback thanks to Crossroad Press.

Curious about other Crossroad Press books?
Stop by our site:
http://store.crossroadpress.com
We offer quality writing
in digital, audio, and print formats.

Enter the code FIRSTBOOK
to get 20% off your first order from our store!
Stop by today!

Made in the USA
Middletown, DE
20 October 2021